That Week in June

Robert Underhill

Also by the author:

Strawberry Moon
Cathead Bay
Providence Times Three
Death Of The Mystery Novel
Once Dead Long Dead
Suttons Bay
A Desperate Ruse

That Week in June

Robert Underhill

delicti press

Delicti Press
6593 Omigisi Beach Rd.
Northport, MI 49670

That Week in June / Robert Underhill - 1st. ed.
 p.cm
ISBN 13: 978-9798526-8-8
  1. Coming of Age - fiction 2. D-Day 3. Crime - fiction
4. Hendersonville, N.C. - fiction

Printed in the United States

For Trudy

Hendersonville, North Carolina
Thursday, June 1, 1944

"Going to Schauger's - see ya later," Ben called out from the front door.

"I'm going to town in a few minutes - want a ride?" his father yelled back from the kitchen.

"Thanks, I'll walk."

He'd said, "in a few minutes," but his father always took so much time to get started, looking for one thing or another, stopping to put something away, remembering a task that couldn't wait. His father's delays could drive a guy off his rocker, and tonight Ben had no reserve of patience. He was anxious to get on his way to the drugstore where the whole gang would be. Today had been the last day of school. Tomorrow was the graduation assembly—attendance mandatory—but then followed a whole summer's worth of freedom.

Stepping onto the porch, the instant flash of a passing white car snatched his attention. He ran down the front steps and out onto the sidewalk to get an unobstructed view. Yes, as he'd hoped, it was Congressman Sinclair's Lincoln Continental—back in town and *she* was driving, her jet-black hair freely floating in the wind of the open car. Valery Sinclair. Ben had only had a few glimpses of her last summer driving the same car. She went to a private school in Charleston and none of his friends knew her. She belonged to a world foreign to them—far away in many ways. But, from those glimpses he'd had, he'd concluded she was the most beautiful real-life girl he'd ever seen and so she'd become the ideal girl of his freshly emerging romantic fantasies, and, since she was out of reach, a safe object for these hormonally saturated yearnings.

And then, the car itself nearly rivaled the girl in Ben's interest. He thought the Continental was the sexiest car on the road. The placement of the spare tire on the rear bumper was a stroke of designing brilliance. Congressman Sinclair had a '42 model, and the story was that only four hundred were built before the war shut down production. He thought it must have been through the clout that all Hendersonville believed Sinclair had in Washington that he'd snared one.

Ben covered the five blocks along 5th. Avenue into the city at a near jog so eager was he to get together with his buddies. Tomorrow was the last day as a freshman. Back in September he'd been elated to be in high school, but had soon found out that he and his classmates were regarded as something on the order of unwanted younger siblings to the upper classes. Barely visible. One more day and that would change. One more day and—although he would laugh at the hypocrisy if it were pointed out to him—he would become the older brother, so much wiser and more worldly than the wide-eyed and naive freshmen.

Also, in the back of his mind was the idea that something significant was going to happen this summer vacation. Of course, last summer there had been the same expectation, which soon gave way to routine, which finally merged with boredom around the middle of August. But this summer would be different. Now he was fifteen and although he'd had a licence for a year, he was finally getting to use the car alone. The big difference, however, although he couldn't have stated it as such, was girls. Last summer he and his friends still occupied themselves building and flying model airplanes. That was over. How had that interest evaporated? Who knew? Mysteriously, girls had newly materialized in his and his friends' worlds, as if they'd not existed before. Well known were the basic facts of sex, but how those facts and his real world could intersect was shrouded in mist. It was like having memorized a detailed map of a foreign city without any plan of actually traveling there.

At the intersection of 5th. Ave and Church Street he was about to hurry across against the light, there being no traffic at all, when his peripheral vision registered his family's 1941 Plymouth sedan pulling up to the red light. He immediately put on his own brakes. It was imperative that he gave his father no evidence of being a scofflaw, as his use of the car was a fragile privilege resting on the myth that he was dedicated to being a well-behaved, live-by-the-rules, totally responsible person. His father tapped on the horn and waved. He waved back and watched him slowly drive away when the light changed. Ben followed, shifting up through his mental gears to arrive on the opposite sidewalk back up to his original emotional speed. He looked down the long slope of Church Street toward the corner where Schauger's Drugstore stood. Beyond this, a half-moon rose above the courthouse into a clear sky deepening into evening.

Ben noticed activity on the sidewalk outside the store. Several people going in and a girl coming out and opening the door of a car parked at the curb. It was *the* car! The white Continental. It brought him to a stop. He started off again at a quickened pace. Here was a chance to see them both up close, Valery Sinclair and the car. As he got closer he saw that the girl who had come out of the drugstore and was now in the passenger seat was Connie Walker, a classmate, but not one of his friends. Valery was bending forward apparently adjusting the radio. She looked up right at him! Every cell in his body vibrated. People said she was a ringer for Hedy Lamarr, and by God they were right! He had seen *The Heavenly Body* a few weeks ago at the Carolina—same halo of black hair, same eyes, same perfect features.

3

Valery leaned toward Connie and said something and Connie seemed to protest, but Valery spoke again and Connie turned toward Ben and said, "Hi Ben, wanna go for a ride?"

He was shocked—totally surprised. The possibility of being in the same car as Valery Sinclair was as likely as being asked to dinner at the White House. More puzzling; it was evident that it was her idea. To start with, he had never met her and in his world it was strange—unheard of—for a girl to ask a guy she'd never met to go for a ride. Plus she was of another caste: private school, country club and from an aristocratic family, for Congressman Sinclair was as close to royalty as it got in Henderson County. Why had she asked him? That question had to wait, since there was no more time to ponder it than a paratrooper had standing in the plane's doorway to question the validity of war before stepping out. Both girls were looking at him, waiting for his answer.

"Ah . . . sure, where're you going?"

"Just 'round," Valery answered.

Connie opened the door and Ben squeezed through the narrow space between the back of the passenger seat and the car's body. The radio was playing a new Ellington recording. He settled into the soft leather of the back seat, the only leather car seat he'd ever sat on, the first convertible he'd ever been in. Valery gunned the engine and shifting smoothly, accelerated up Church Street while leaning forward to turn up the radio volume. Ella sang, "I never cared much for moonlit skies, I never wink back at fireflies." Damn! Was this really happening? Yes, it seemed to be happening. He had just stepped out of his routine life and into a Hollywood scene like Alice falling down that rabbit hole. He wished his friends could see him.

Sitting behind Connie, he had a view of the side of Valery's face, a first chance to see her up close and study her. She was beautiful in a way like none of the other girls he knew. Not just good looking, but really beautiful. There was also a confidence and fire that others lacked. He didn't know how old she was. He'd heard she was in high school. She seemed older.

She glanced over her shoulder toward him. "I'm Val. You're Ben, right?"

"That's right, Ben Roberts."

She hadn't supplied her last name Ben noticed. Did she assume everyone knew who she was? And why not, everyone did. Was she establishing rank? Well, that was already established, but was she underlining the fact? In his mind, he heard the voice of his best friend, Eddie, "Don't pull things apart all the goddamn time, Roberts—just enjoy it!" He relaxed, laid his arm along the back of the seat and smiled. There was no better place in the whole world to be at this moment. None. He didn't know what was going on here, what this rich, beautiful girl was up to but he was captured.

Valery made a couple of right turns and slowed to a crawl along the four blocks of Main Street. The streetlights were now on and the sidewalks were busy. Ben scanned those standing in line at the Carolina to see *Buffalo Bill*. He saw N.C. Foster and Johnny Farmer and gave them a casual wave as if it was the most natural thing in the world to be chauffeured around town by Val Sinclair.

She stopped at the last light on Main and Connie lit a cigarette. Ella ended the number with, "Now that your lips are burning mine, I'm beginning to see the light." Ben sensed it was now time for him to say something. He could think of nothing except, "Nice car," which was dumb, so he said nothing. Connie turned in her seat and offered the pack of Lucky Strikes. Ben shook his head saying no thanks. He didn't smoke as did none of his friends. He hated smoking. Both of his parents were heavy smokers and he hated the smoke-filled car, the dirty ashtrays. Their mantra to him was, "Don't start! Don't start!" And then there were sports. He played football and dreamed of playing in college and it was said that smoking hurt your wind. Connie raised her eyebrows as if his refusal earned him a demerit.

"The school you go to must have let out early," he said toward Valery. To hell with Connie.

"Yes, last week. The Fairchild School in Charleston. Heard of it?"

"Yes."

And he had. He'd seen an ad for it in the back of *Redbook* magazine and noted it, because he'd heard she went there. The ad showed a white building with pillars across the front like an old plantation mansion. Underneath the picture was the slogan, "Where nice young girls become fine ladies." When he'd read this, he'd thought it to be old fashioned and snobbish, but in truth he still felt envy of a world from which he felt barred.

"Like it there?" he asked.

The light changed and the car eased away. She looked back at him for an instant considering how to answer.

"Yes," she said and then looked back again. "But I'm anxious to finish—two more years."

That made her a year older than he was. He took a chance. "And will you then be a 'fine young lady?'"

She screamed a laugh and flashed a smile at him. "So you know about that. Never! That will never happen."

She stepped on the gas and the big car rushed into the countryside southeast of the city. Ben felt that the dynamics of the scene had shifted from two girls picking up a guy to that of a guy and a girl and an extra girl. Maybe that was only a wish. What was on her mind, this girl from another world? Her father was an institution, having been in office for many years and likely to remain there as long as he wished.

He was a Democrat and there were no Republicans in sight here in western North Carolina in 1944. The size of his wealth—a popular calculation for the local citizenry—was based on what people could see: a mansion in town, several farms, several servants and multiple vehicles.

Valery reached forward and turned up the volume of the radio as the wind noise increased. Bing's plea of, "I hope you do believe me," flew past Ben into the night. He could see by the glow of the instrument panel that she was smiling and repeating the words. They had driven miles along a dark stretch of road leading toward Spartanburg when Valery slowed to enter the small town of Saluda. The few people on the street turned to look at the Continental and Ben felt a flush of importance. After Saluda, the road grew dark again for several miles before Ben became aware of a red glow up ahead in the sky above the roadside trees, then the neon sign—Elite Tavern.

Valery braked and swung the car off the pavement and onto the gravel parking area at the side of the low frame building. Ben had a sudden insight. He'd heard some seniors on the team talk about a notorious tavern miles out of town on the Spartanburg road called the "E-lite Tavern", an odd name he'd thought.

"I'll be damned, so this is the E-lite Tavern," he said into the silence following Val's switching off the engine.

She laughed, "Yes, that's how the locals pronounce it. My brother owns it and he jokes and calls it the E-lite too. Let's get something to eat."

Val opened the car door, stepped out and stood holding the door for him, looking into his eyes, smiling. For sure this was now about the two of them. His excitement swelled. She stood close as he stepped down to the ground assuring that he'd have to brush against her. His glance took in the whole of her. Only a brief glimpse was possible, since he couldn't allow himself to stare, but he saw that she was tall and slim yet pleasantly curved. She wore a short, tight, yellow summer sweater and linen slacks that fit tight around the waist and buttocks. Lust joined excitement.

Ben took a couple of hurried steps to take the lead as they rounded the corner of the building so he'd be in position to open the tavern door for Valery. A motorcycle sat smack in front of the entrance. The light above the door lit up the bike's unique swooping fenders—an Indian Chief—shiny red. Two older guys, maybe thirty, stood next to the entrance door. One leaned against the wall, leg bent so his shoe bottom rested on the siding, a pack of cigarettes held in the upturned sleeve of his white T-shirt. He interrupted his conversation and held up a hand toward Ben as if to say, "Whoa there." This dampened Ben's expanding confidence like the sudden appearance of flashing lights in one's rear view mirror will do. A second later the guy saw Valery and his challenging smirk instantly changed to the gracious smile of an employee who enjoyed or wanted to enjoy a favored status with his boss. The warning hand dropped. The foot came off the wall. He reached for the door handle before Ben could and opened the door for her.

"Evenin' Miss Sinclair," he said emphasizing "Miss."

"Hi Charlie," Valery returned as she walked past him.

Ben wondered about that exchange for only a moment, because he now found himself in another unfamiliar situation. The interior was dark, very smoky, maybe a couple dozen people sitting at tables and along a bar that ran across the entire rear of the room. Those at the table nearest the door looked up at them as they entered. Ben reckoned that he and the girls were younger than anyone there by a good ten years. "This is a roadhouse," asserted itself in Ben's mind and a roadhouse is a rendezvous for drinking and flirting and sex. Except for flirting, he and the girls were legally underage. He knew it was illegal for them to be served drinks; was that true for even being here? He felt very out of place.

A pale man in his forties wearing a forced smile came toward them from the rear of the room. He motioned with his head toward a booth near a back corner and followed them there.

"So school's out Val. Did you pass?"

He was trying for a relaxed intimate delivery, but Ben sensed the man was as uncomfortable with their presence there as he was.

"They wouldn't dare flunk me, Barney. I know too many of the headmistress's secrets."

The guy gave a knowing nod. "I'd bet you do, Val."

"I brought my friends for your great burgers and some of your special coffee. Barney, these are my friends Connie Walker, Ben Roberts - Barney Youngblood."

"Is my brother here, Barney?"

"He was, but he left a while ago. Got a phone call and left without a word. I wish he'd come back soon. He made a date with a guy who wants to sell a motorcycle. Guy keeps bugging me about when Hunter's coming back."

Barney ran an appraising eye over Connie and Ben. "Pleased to meet y'all. OK. What coffee will it be white or red?"

"You can do better than that, Barney. Some of that tea-colored coffee."

"You know we don't sell anything that color, Val. Don't have it on the premises."

Ben thought the guy hoped Valery would accept that reply. If so, he was going to be disappointed, because she continued her look of determined expectation.

"I'll see what I can find," he said with resignation and left.

9

"So, this is your brother's place," Ben said.

"Yes. It's the kind of thing that gives him a kick. Something on the wild side, like stock car racing."

The association between stock car racing and illegal liquor came to Ben's mind. "I've heard that the best race drivers learned their skill running liquor."

With a smile like the cat that had swallowed the canary, she said, "I wouldn't know about that."

Her answer made Ben suspect the E-lite was a delivery point.

"Is South Carolina, where you go to school, a dry state like here? I mean beer and wine but no liquor?"

"Not dry if you're twenty-one . . . and I've got a friend who is. And the thing is, a state law requires that bars use the small sample-size bottle of whiskey or gin to make drinks so the customer doesn't get cheated on the measure. Those little bottles are very easy to smuggle into the dorm."

The jukebox had been playing all the while, but Ben only now became aware that Ernest Tubbs was once again *Walking the Floor Over You.*

Barney came to their booth with three hamburgers and three cups on a tray. Valery thanked him - but coolly.

When they'd sat down Ben noticed four women wearing dark blue Eisenhower jackets with a gold wing emblem sitting at a nearby table. Curious, he asked Barney, who was turning to leave, "Sir, those women with the blue uniforms; are they in the Air Force?"

"No, they're a separate group, the Women's Air something or other. They ferry military planes across the country from the factories out west to the Atlantic coast where ships take them to England. Those four fly B-25 bombers. They use the new airfield the Air Force built near Fletcher.

Ben hadn't heard of a new airfield and his face showed it.

"Yeah, not many people know about it." Laughing, Barney held his finger to his lips. "Maybe it's a secret."

When Barney had gone, Connie tasted the whiskey and said, "This is good stuff."

Ben wondered if she'd tasted whiskey before. He was pretty sure she hadn't tasted enough to be a judge of quality. He'd tasted it once. Eddie's father had a bottle of Four Roses hidden on a shelf in the bedroom closet. Both boys had decided it was an acquired taste. At least he knew now what to expect and could take a swallow without showing initial shock. He could, in fact, experience the burning in his throat with a degree of appraisal—still nothing he'd pay good money for. He "washed" it down with a swallow of burger.

The three began to observe and comment on the other patrons of the tavern, who, they noticed, had been sizing them up as well. Ben continued to feel they didn't belong there. He thought Connie did too. Valery, on the other hand, presented a convincing air of sophistication. He glanced several times at the group at the nearest table: three men and one woman. Ben couldn't hear the words, but he was sure the one guy was saying something sexually suggestive and teasing. The woman wasn't discouraging him while the other two men, although silent, were eager participants. The reality of what was going to happen after they left the tavern aroused Ben. This wasn't adolescent fantasy; this was the real thing. The tenor of the glances the woman threw in their direction said she didn't appreciate her teenage audience.

Connie brought out her cigarettes and held out the pack to Valery, who took one. Connie then turned toward Ben as she took one from the pack. She didn't offer him one, remembering his earlier refusal, but seemed to be waiting for some response from him. With an expression of exasperation, she took a lighter out of her pocket and handed it to him. He was confused for a moment and this increased her disdain. Then he realized she was waiting for him to light her cigarette. Embarrassed, as if he had committed a social faux pas, he took the lighter from her. He'd never lit anyone's cigarette before, but had seen it done so many times in the movies that his hand seemed to have memorized the action—hold the flame near enough and let her lean forward. Valery held his hand when he lit hers and he felt reassured. Then he began to feel stupid for being reassured. How could Connie expect him, a non-smoker, to carry a lighter to light her damned cigarette? That was nonsense! He wanted to tell her so, but he couldn't with Valery there. Still he felt stupid for going along and angry with himself for having felt inadequate. To hell with Connie!

"Want some more whiskey? Valery asked.

"You bet," Connie said with inflated enthusiasm.

"I'll pass," Ben said.

Valery looked toward the bar to get Barney's attention. He was there, but he avoided looking her way. She saw this and looked back at Ben. He had just put the last of the burger in his mouth. She had only taken a couple of bites of hers. She tapped her cigarette on the ashtray and said, "Let's leave. I think we're done here."

Connie, who was in the act of raising her half-eaten burger to her mouth, watched with surprise as Valery slid out of the booth. Connie scrambled to follow still holding her burger.

Stepping out the door was a relief from the smoky interior. Charlie and his friend were no longer by the door. Neither was the motorcycle. The guy must have gotten tired of waiting. Valery took several steps away from the entrance and its light and stood looking up at the sky. Ben followed, first taking in the sky as she was doing and then shifting his gaze to her face. She was smiling at the moon. Ben sensed that the tavern and whatever had happened there was now a page turned for her.

"Let's go," she said and led the way to the side of the building where the Continental was parked.

Charlie and the other guy were there, Charlie's hand on the driver's door. He stepped back quickly taking his hand off the door as if the metal were red hot.

Valery surmised that the two had been sitting in the car. "How does it feel behind the wheel?" she asked, voice matter of fact, presenting Charlie with a dilemma; should he admit that he'd been in the car as if they were on such a familiar footing that sitting in her car was no big deal, or should he stick to the role of the respectful employee and deny it?

"Cat got your tongue, Charlie?" she said laughing. She threw her cigarette carelessly on the ground, opened the door and motioned with a nod to Ben to climb into the back. Connie hurried around to the other side.

Leaving the parking area, she turned the car northwest back toward town.

"Where are we going now?"Connie asked with forced gaiety.

Valery delayed answering while she turned on the radio and adjusted the volume.

"I'm going to call it a night," she answered as she accelerated along the highway. The finality of her tone overrode any objection. The wind and the radio cancelled any notion of conversation.

Ben began thinking of what had just happened—what it meant.

Had the roadhouse trip just been showing off? To impress him? Connie? Both of them? The guy, Barney, hadn't given her the hearty welcome she'd been counting on. He'd communicated, intentionally or not, that she and her friends were a problem for him. Not a smart way to treat a princess, a princess who would in a few short years be

13

a queen, a queen with a memory. Ben wondered about his thinking of her as a princess. He had never thought of any other girl this way. He decided it was because she had all it took to claim the title, more so he'd bet than most who'd inherited it. She was goddamned beautiful and in command of herself and those around her. She'd made a mistake back there, the mistake any teenager makes believing adults would accept you on your own terms. But she'd discerned her mistake quickly and recovered. She'd decamped with her entourage on her own terms, and Ben could see by the way she tipped her head back to let the wind toss her hair, smiling, her lips following the words of *That Old Black Magic,* that she was once again totally in command of the evening. Fine with him. He sank back into the leather seat, looked up at the moon and listened to the music, wanting to absorb and remember it all, for he had resigned himself to this fantasy night being over very soon. For a moment back there, under the delusion that she could be romantically interested in him, he'd been competing with Connie for Valery's favor. Admitting that to himself now, he laughed out loud. Connie heard him and looked back. He gave her a big smile. Puzzled, she turned back.

Valery entered the lower end of Main Street, slowed and turned the radio down. She glanced in the mirror running her fingers through her hair putting it back into rough order. Fewer people were out now and Ben saw no one he knew. He expected that she would let him off where she'd picked him up, but she didn't turn off Main, continuing instead through town and onto the Asheville Highway. After a few blocks, she went left into the Druid Hills neighborhood. On Norwood Street, she stopped in front of a white colonial house.

She turned to Connie. "Say hello to your mother for me." - a nice way of saying, "This is where you get out."

Connie, to amend this dismissal, asked, "Are you going to Betty

Leonard's party?"

Betty Leonard was another girl who went to a private boarding school. Connie could be sure Ben hadn't been invited.

"I'm thinking about it," Valery answered while turning in her seat to look back at Ben. "C'mon up front."

Connie, now standing outside the car and still holding the door in her hand, pushed it closed causing Ben to have to reach outside for the handle in order to come into the front seat.

As Connie passed through the headlight beam on the way to her house, Ben said, "I don't think she likes me."

"Do you care?"

He thought a moment. "No."

"I didn't think so," she said smiling while pulling away from the curb. "Where do you live, Ben?"

"Fifth Avenue. Fifth Avenue and North Oak."

"That's on my way home."

"I know."

She looked at him sharply as she pulled up at a stop street. "You know where I live?"

He laughed. "Everyone knows where you live, Val."

"Ah yes, everyone knows where the congressman lives—right?"

"Does that surprise you?"

"No, no. It's just that I forget the meaning that has for other people. He's been a congressman all my life."

She then accelerated through the intersection, driving faster than Ben would have along residential streets, squealing the tires with each turn: Druid Hills Avenue then left on Hayward then right on Justice. At Fifth Avenue she stopped and looked over at Ben. He was expecting her to say goodbye. The unbelievable evening was over: meeting the illusive and beautiful daughter of the most famous man in his world, a moonlight ride in a Continental, the infamous E-lite Tavern, whiskey in a coffee cup.

He said, "Thanks for asking me to come along, Val. It was fun."

"It was mah pleasure, Ben."

He loved the easy way she spoke, the smooth caressing way she said those words, "Mah pleasure."

"Are you in a hurry to get home?" she asked.

Surprised, he said, "No, not particularly."

"It's such a great night. That moon. It would be a shame to go indoors."

He met her gaze but said nothing.

"I think we should go for a swim."

"A swim," he gasped in total surprise.

"Laurel Lake is only ten minutes away."

Reflexively he made an objection. "The beach is closed at night."

The objection revealed just how afraid he was of this girl.

"No problem," she returned. "I've swum there several times at night."

The beach belonged to the Laurel Park Inn, which stood on a hill across the road from the lake. The Inn charged admission to the fifty yards of sandy beach, and they'd built a fence to enforce that.

"It's easy to walk around the end of the fence," she added.

"You've done it alone?"

"Sure."

He pictured this. Here was a bold independence hard to imagine in any other girl he knew.

"What do you say—shall we?" she said invitingly, teasingly.

She had led him about all evening. No harm so far. "OK, sure."

What would come next? Stop at his house for his bathing suit? Change there?

She swung the great car onto Fifth Avenue and stepped on the gas. The exhaust rumbled a moment and then, silently, as if riding a zephyr, they flew along the avenue past the houses of mere mortals. She didn't slow down at his house and he glanced at it as they passed, feeling the severing of ties to the familiar as a pilot must feel thrusting into the sky and glancing back at the receding earth. Squealing the tires, she turned onto White Pines Drive causing Ben to grip the seat against the lateral force, and then she began braking, reining the beautiful white stallion down to a slow canter as she angled onto Lake Drive. Once again the night air and the moonlight filled the open car softly.

Ben realized now that there were not going to be bathing suits. He was wearing boxer shorts. No female except his mother had seen him in his underwear and he had seen no girls in theirs—only the pictures in the Sears and Roebuck catalog and the calendar pictures at Stern's Garage and the barber shop.

Ahead of them on the hill, the lighted windows of the Inn appeared. Valery slowed, looking first toward the parking area at the beach and then up at the Inn.

"We'd better park at the Inn. A lone car in the beach lot will attract attention."

She switched off the headlights and entered the Inn's drive. Now here was another bold transgression in Ben's experience—sneaking, headlights off, onto private property. Half a dozen cars were parked there. She put the Continental on the far side of the car most distant from the building. They got out and stood quietly looking at the Inn. Laughter and Big Band music came through the open windows of the main public rooms where silhouetted people walked past, oblivious of the new arrivals.

Valery began humming with the music. She took his arm and

steered him back down the drive.

"The beach is ours," she said.

Laurel shrubs met the far left end of the fence at the beach. Valery, hugging the end post, pushed past the branches and Ben followed. Immediately, he came upon and almost tripped over a tarpaulin-covered rowboat kept there for the lifeguard's use. The full length of the beach was now before him. Although only a half-moon, its light was very bright making the sand glow white. Valery, some twenty yards ahead stood out against it unfastening her slacks. Ben's heart raced, his breath held.

She took off her slacks, folded them and laid them on the sand. She began to take off her sweater and then halted before pulling it over her head to look his way.

"C'mon slowpoke."

She folded her sweater and put it on top of the slacks. She had already acquired enough tan in Charleston to make her white panties and bra stand out. As an attempt to govern his excitement Ben told himself that, after all, a bra and panties were pretty much the same as a two-piece bathing suit. But then she slipped off her bra and stepped out of her panties. Ben came to an abrupt halt. She stood facing him, shoulders back, hands on hips, smiling teasingly. Her body was as voluptuous as the calendars. His gaze stopped for a moment at the black patch between her legs and quickly returned to her teasing smile.

"Waddya think?" she said and then added, "Let's see what you've got."

No girl had ever said anything like *that* to him. His brain froze, but he mechanically began to lower his shorts while turning a little to one side.

He straightened and met her gaze. Her smile was friendly, no trace of the teasing or mockery he'd expected.

She left the beach and began wading into the water. Only then did his mind catch up with what he'd just seen, but he had no time to review it. Present action was demanded. As he waded into the lake, he heard the splash of her dive. She surfaced and with an effortless stroke, headed toward the raft that was anchored about forty yards from the beach. He swam as fast as he could and he considered himself a good swimmer, but she had mounted the raft's ladder and stood pulling her long black hair together behind her neck by the time he got there. He held onto the ladder and looked up at her. Long, perfect legs, firm and rounded buttocks, sculpted back. He noted now that her tan was complete, no bathing suit lines, and again his mind sought shelter from overload by wondering where she did her tanning—dormitory roof? Then back to the wonder of her body. Again he asked himself if this could really be happening?

Climbing the ladder he saw that she'd lain down on her back. Self-conscious of his nudity, he lay face down next to her. Immediately he saw this wasn't right. He rolled onto his side facing her and without willing it, nature took over guiding his hand to cup her breast. The sensation was unreal. His mind sparked and flashed. He leaned down to kiss her inviting lips.

A light flooded the raft!

Ben withdrew his hand as if caught doing the forbidden. Valery lifted herself onto her elbows and calmly said, "A car. Parking in the beach lot."

The headlights went off. A door closed.

"Maybe they're going swimming too," Ben said.

"Maybe, but it isn't 'they'. Only one door closed."

Some time passed as they watched and listened, wondering what, if any, alteration this would impose on their plans.

19

"I don't think," Ben began to say, when a new sound came from the beach—a loud thud like a hammer hitting wood and then a splash.

"An oar," Valery said in a low voice. "The person is rowing that boat."

They both strained to see.

"Coming this way," Valery decided. "We've got to get under the raft."

She slid toward the ladder and Ben followed, disappointed and confused. Valery led the way between the six barrels in two rows upon which the raft floated. The barrels were oriented so that the space between the rows faced the beach. Through that space and between the rungs of the ladder they watched the boat draw nearer. Soon, the moonlight being bright enough, they were able to make out the single rower, a man wearing a white shirt. He paused his rowing and looked toward the raft, and then pulling on his left oar, he altered his course to pass it by several feet. Ben lowered himself in the water, but Valery peered out between two barrels as the man went by. The raft bobbed up and down with the waves from the boat. The guy rowed on another minute before the rowing stopped and they heard the oars being shipped. Perhaps another minute passed before they heard a loud splash.

Valery's head blocked Ben's view. Over her shoulder she said, "He jumped in the water."

"Why go way out there to swim?"

"Don't know. Maybe he likes deeper water."

Ben could hear nothing except the ripple of the wavelets against the barrels.

"What's he doing?" he asked in her ear.

"I can't see. I guess he's just swimming around."

"Damn it," Ben mumbled. "What if he swims here to the raft?"

"And leave the boat out there? Wait, now I see him. He's getting back into the boat—pulling himself over the transom."

"Transom?"

"The back of the boat."

"He's rowing back, she said pushing back against Ben, pressing into his penis. His mind became totally occupied with that contact. He reached his hand around her waist and pulled her closer. She had become an object of burning desire, the greatest desire he'd felt in his life. The man and the boat forgotten.

"He's almost here again," she said, her voice urgent, hushed.

Ben could hear the sound of the splashing oars. He moved his head forward to see over her shoulder as her hand closed around his now erect penis. Everything in the world except the feel of her hand disappeared. Vaguely he heard the boat pass.

"Let's go back on top," he whispered into her ear.

"Shh. We can't yet. He's looking right this way."

"Yeah, but who cares?"

She squeezed his hard penis. "Patience."

Only the man's white shirt was still visible. Several minutes passed then they heard the sound of the oars banging against wood, as if the guy had dropped them in the boat. Valery moved out from under the raft, but remained in the water holding the ladder.

"He's paying no attention to the raft. Let's go back on top," Ben urged.

A sound came from the parking lot. Then the car door slammed and the car started. The car drove out of the lot with the headlights off.

Valery let go of the ladder and began swimming back toward the beach.

Surprised, Ben yelled, "Where are you going?"

She either didn't hear or ignored him. He had no choice but to follow.

When he was able to stand, he began the slow water-impeded ascent to the beach. Valery had already put on her panties and bra and was preparing to step into her slacks. Neither spoke. She waited until he bent to tie his shoelaces before she walked off across the sand and slipped around the fence post. Disconsolately, Ben followed her. He glared at the rowboat as if it had been at fault for the agitation he felt. He noticed that the guy had neglected to replace the tarp.

They climbed the hill to the Inn's parking lot in silence. He was angry, confused and searching for some grounds for consolation. Before starting the engine, Valery lit a cigarette. She didn't do it with the careless savoir-faire as earlier. She was tense. Ben noted that her poise had evaporated. Had her image of the carefree spirit been a bluff? Was she as inexperienced, hesitant and conventional as he? Was she now embarrassed? Then he had a thought that yanked away any comfort he'd gained by blaming her. Maybe she'd changed her mind about him, the interruption of the rowboat giving her a moment to realize she was making a mistake—that he was a mistake.

So far nothing had been said. She threw away the cigarette and looked over at him.

"I'm sorry," she said. "That interruption destroyed the mood." She reached for his leg and squeezed it softly.

Ben felt totally confused. He had no idea where he or things now stood. Did she truly mean that everything had been fine and progressing toward the ultimate, or was she smoothing things out to cover her change of mind?

Neither spoke on the way back to Ben's house. Valery drove into his driveway and shifted into neutral. Seeing his distress she pulled him toward her and kissed the corner of his mouth.

"Another time—all right?"

He managed to return, "All right" and got out.

She reversed out of the driveway and began driving home, the gorgeous white car standing out against the dark road and trees. He stood watching until it disappeared.

Friday, June 2nd.

Mr. Tennant, the science teacher, stepped out of the auditorium onto the sunlit sidewalk and observed, "Perfect day for a graduation: God did his part."

Ben didn't believe God would give a hoot about the weather for the high school graduation, but he too had already noted how the weather was in harmony with the event. The sunshine bright, the air clear and dry, causing objects and shadows to be sharply defined, a light breeze rippled the leaves. The day was like an eager puppy, "I'm ready, let's go!"

Memories of last night dominated his thoughts except for brief interruptions by the morning's ceremony such as the valedictory speech by Harriet Gowdy (Dowdy to senior boys). She said their class must now join the fight for freedom going on around the world and make Hendersonville proud. The principal had said pretty much the same thing—same words—immediately before Harriet's speech. Not good. Not fair to Harriet. He was beginning to notice such things. He probably couldn't tell you his growing awareness of form and order could be attributed to Miss Jarvis's English class, but it was there his understanding of thesis, rising tension and resolution derived. That's also where his appreciation of learning and its application had begun. Whoever had plotted the graduation program got a failing grade and Ben didn't think it was Harriet. But then he was ever ready to be critical of adults.

He stood acknowledging his friends as they passed him. Earlier in the hallway he'd encountered Connie Walker and watched her become engrossed in conversation with one of her friends when she saw him approaching. About what he'd expect. He was waiting now for Eddie White. He and Eddie had formed the kind of relationship war buddies form sensing they are moment by moment sharing unique and defining experiences for the first time in unmapped territory. He and Eddie were true friends yet they were not alike. Ben thought of his own mind as "messy," his thoughts needing to be qualified and footnoted. Eddie's thinking tracked to the mark. If that mark turned out to be faulty, a new, corrected aim was taken at the target. Ben dreamed of ideal girls, Eddie went up and asked the best-looking available girl to dance.

Eddie came through the door carrying a bulky laundry bag over his shoulder filled with the contents of his locker. He'd waited until the last moment before the janitor, hacksaw in hand to cut the padlocks, carried out the threat that had been posted for a week.

"Let's go to Schauger's," Eddie said.

"Are you going to carry that bag around?"

"I was planning that you'd carry it some of the way."

"Dream on. Why not leave it at Ann's and pick it up when you've got the car?"

Ann Taylor lived across the street from the school and her front porch was the regular after-school gathering place for the girls of Ben's social set.

"Why didn't I think of that?"

Both boys had had driver's licences for a year, possible in North Carolina at fourteen. The problem was they had no cars and no foreseeable change in that condition. It came down to the occasional loan of the family car and the stars had to be in a favorable position for that to happen.

Ed Bagwell, the football coach, came hustling through the door, noticed the boys and smiled.

"See you two in the fall. Stay in shape now. I'm depending on ya'll."

A wave of good feelings swept over them and they began to cross the street to Ann's house with a confident swagger. Recognition, the notion of being valued and the idea of being depended upon was the meaning both had taken from the coach's words, although after a few steps, Ben had begun to reconsider. They would be sophomores in the fall. They could be no significant part of the coach's plans for the team he would have to field come September. Ben's swagger wilted a bit, but he still retained the lift from having left the rank of "freshman" back in the auditorium.

Ann's home was like most on the block, medium-sized, frame, two story with a full-width veranda fronted by huge hydrangea bushes. The half-dozen girls who had been talking together on the veranda saw the boys coming toward them, grew quiet and then, leaning in to each other, spoke sotto voce. Ben wondered what on earth they had been talking about that had suddenly become secret. These six girls made up the inner circle of the clique of the "popular" girls of Ben's class. Membership was as closely guarded as Fort Knox. Ann Taylor was the acknowledged head of the membership committee. The approval of this group carried a powerful force in the social fabric of his class. Disapproval cast one into outer darkness. Ben had always accepted their authority. Now, after being with Valery, their stature had suddenly shrunken.

One of them, Beth Reynolds, whose gaze had been focused on Ben said something to her friends, who looked his way and erupted into giggles. He wasn't close enough for them to see something stuck between his teeth, so what was so damn funny, he wondered. Girls in a group were strange; they seemed to judge you in a competition you hadn't even entered.

"I think you must be sophomore girls," Eddie called out from the bottom of the porch steps. "You have that soph - isticated way about you."

That stirred up laughter and broke up the huddle.

"Ann, I wonder if I could leave this here bundle with you for a few days until I can pick it up with the car. It's heavy to haul around: a year's accumulation of books, shoes and dead teachers."

The girls screamed with laughter.

Ben chuckled to himself. The dynamics had shifted. Those who had done the judging were now a helpless audience in the master's hands.

"That's OK," Ann said. "But will this make me an accomplice—the dead teachers I mean.'

"If you don't peek in the bag, you can claim innocence, "Honest officer, I know that lump looks pot-bellied, but how was I to know it was Mr. Shaw?"

Eddie had them all laughing, even Ben.

The two resumed their walk to Schauger's, Eddie still evidencing the extra swagger generated by the coach's remark. Beneath that swagger, however, was a gait they both had adopted through a subtle identification with the older members of the football team, a slow easy stride that at the same time was to project the potential of sudden power and menace—lions ambling.

Ben was taller than his friend, on his way to six feet or more. He had dark hair and brown eyes and the girls in his class had defined him as "cute." Eddie was sturdily built, sandy haired with grey/green eyes. His face was out of alignment, his jaw being pushed slightly to one side as if he'd suffered a right hook in-utero. His nose tried to restore balance by angling a few millimeters to the other side. The girls thought he was cute too, but in a different way. His usual mood was open and friendly, but he was also open to a fight if that's what you had in mind.

"Ann's got it bad for you," Ben said.

Eddie came back with his standard line. "She only wants me for my body."

"When will a girl want Eddie White for his beautiful soul? Listen in next week," Ben said in his radio announcer imitation.

The urge was there to tell Eddie about his adventure with Valery Sinclair, but there was an equal force holding him back. Much of what had happened seemed to be private in a way he hadn't known before— the first modification of telling his friend everything.

Schauger's, the venue at which everyone in their crowd tried to make an appearance at least once a day, lay four blocks east on Church Street. The route there took them past the back lot of Mast's Texaco Service. Mast's did all of the wrecker service for the surrounding area and the back lot was the depository for seriously damaged cars. Of special interest were the remains of the cars modified to haul illegal liquor up the mountain from South Carolina, the liquor runners' cars—runners who had not quite outrun the sheriff. Morbid interest usually dictated a detour from a straight line to the drugstore to view the gory interiors. The boys halted now, spying a new wreck in the yard.

"Damn! That son-of-a-bitch rolled right down the mountain," Eddie observed uneasily. "Smashed flat."

The soft breeze that ruffled the trees suggesting promise earlier at the school, now brought the aroma of whiskey across the lot.

"No drinks at the Elk's Club tonight," quipped Ben.

Neither wanted to dampen their good mood to view evidence of violent death. They skipped the detour and resumed their walk. Stern's Garage was at the corner of 4th. Avenue. Sam Stern was in their class. His older brother, home on leave from the Army was pumping gas in his uniform.

"Is that legal do you think?" Eddie said.

"What?"

"You know, working in your Army uniform."

"Ben laughed at the question. "As long as you don't get paid I'd say it's OK, and old man Stern is sure as hell not paying. He owns the station and makes Sam buy his own gas when he uses the car."

"Do you know anyone who is overseas? I mean overseas in combat," asked Eddie.

This came down to the older brothers of his friends and the boyfriends of their older sisters. He couldn't think of anyone not in one or another base in the U. S. He had a cousin in the Air Force, who was stationed in Arizona.

"Can't think of anyone."

"Me neither. Is that strange or not?"

Ben had had a thought along these lines recently when thumbing through a copy of *Life* magazine. One article showed pictures of a troop convoy crossing the Atlantic and the next article covered a debutante ball as if there were no war. Some movies were about the war, more were not. The war movies seen at the Saturday matinees were treated to a special teenage critique. No one remembered just how this sport became established, but now matinee films, especially the

29

usually simplistically plotted war films, were the victims of a joyous demonstration of teen intelligence over adult stupidity. As the movie characters were assembled, there was a rush to loudly identify the sweet innocent private who'd be killed, the nasty guy who'd become the hero in the end and the pompous officer who'd prove to be a coward. Following these shouted prophesies came the sport of anticipating dialogue - "You can depend on me, Captain," "I'll wait for you sweetheart no matter how long this lousy war lasts." Two seniors, a girl and a boy were remarkably adept. The girl, Marge Stevens, scored three correct consecutive speeches (*Saboteur* was the flick) to the howling delight of her peers—a scream of victory over the Hollywood filmmakers who thought they could so easily hoodwink such a smart and savvy group. At any time there was more talking going on in the audience than on the screen. One effect of this cynical orgy was that any propaganda value the producers hoped for was washed away.

This cynical, malicious behavior was in contrast to their general compassion. For instance, two of the teams in their sports league were located many miles away and because of gas rationing and wartime travel restrictions, few of their supporters were able to follow the teams to games in Hendersonville. The compassionate response was an agreed upon restraint on exuberant cheering for the home team.

So why this runaway attack upon transparently manipulative war movies? None of the matinee crowd could have understood it and expressed it at the time, but the reason lay in the group's need to protect the other Hollywood films upon which they depended for so much. To be able to believe the truth as conveyed to them by the films required that "willing suspension of disbelief" that allowed one to uncritically enter the world spun by fiction. The war films were so patently hamfisted that they threatened to snatch that away. Everyone knows a magician is only using skill to fool you, but when he or she performs seamlessly you are thrilled by the "magic" you've just witnessed and applaud. You are grateful to the performer for that charmed moment. If, however, the performance is clumsy, the performer must pay. You are not a fool for wanting there to be magic, instead the dolt of a magician deserves your ridicule.

So much of Ben's and his friends' notion of the world beyond this small isolated town came through the movies: how to behave, smart talk, what made a hero, a villain, the idea of romantic love (devoid of sex, of course) was absorbed, cliches and all, fully formed twice-a-week in the familiar, secure darkness of the Carolina Theater. They unconsciously strove to be living models of what they'd seen on film and so Hollywood's evolved cliche's came to form their world view.

In the background, a war was going on, but none of Ben's friends talked seriously of being drafted; it was assumed the war would be over before they became old enough. People grumbled about gas and sugar rationing, but none of his friends talked much about actual warfare and the war had been going on for two and a half years already. Ben was more aware of the stage of the war in Europe than his close friends were, but he assumed this was because his father, who had emigrated from England, still had family there and talked about the bombing they experienced. Unlike his friends, Ben had put up maps on a cork bulletin board and marked the Allies progress with pins.

Just then an open stake-bodied truck drove past the boys along Church Street. In the back, holding onto the side railings, stood a dozen or more men wearing T-shirts. But what caught Ben's attention was the kind of khaki caps they wore. The front of the cap rose up flat and higher than the back of the cap in a distinctive manner, which Ben recognized from pictures in *Life* of German prisoners taken in North Africa.

"Look!" Ben exclaimed, pointing. "Those are German soldiers in the back of that truck!"

"What are you talking about? German soldiers? I'm worried about you, son."

"I'm serious."

"I can see that and that's what worries me."

"I recognized the hats they're wearing. You know, the front is higher than the back."

"What would German soldiers be doing here? Do you think we've been invaded?" Eddie said, continuing to walk.

"Of course not. They must be prisoners, the ones from North Africa."

"And you think we'd let German prisoners ride around loose in the back of a truck?"

Eddie paid no attention to pictures of German prisoners. To do so was a waste of time. It would be soon enough if he ever met them on the battlefield. He was repeatedly surprised by the kind of shit his friend seemed to get hung-up on.

Ben decided to drop the subject. Eddie had a point, but still there were those caps. They arrived at the drugstore and the spot where Valery had picked him up the night before. Again the urge to tell Eddie—some of it.

"I didn't meet you here last night, because I went for a ride with Valery Sinclair, the congressman's daughter."

Eddie stopped walking and looked at Ben. "Yeah, I heard this morning. N.C. said he saw you. I wondered if you were going to say anything."

"Anyway. Valery asked me to get in and go for a ride. Connie Walker was with her. She drove to that roadhouse on the Spartanburg Highway that people call the E-lite Tavern only it's really the Elite Tavern." He saw that Eddie was puzzled. "It's spelled Elite, but people say E-lite."

Eddie frowned.

"Forget it. Anyway her brother owns the place and we went in for a hamburger."

"OK, and?"

How much should he say? He didn't want to mention the whisky; that might cause Valery trouble, but at the same time he wanted to include the forbidden.

"Well we had something to drink—think roadhouse."

"You had a beer."

"Something like that, but I don't want you to repeat any of this. I don't want to be the cause of trouble."

Eddie nodded. "So a hamburger and something that will remain unknown, and then?"

"That's it. She took Connie and me home." He sure wasn't going to say anything about swimming.

"How come she asked you?"

"Couldn't help herself I guess."

Eddie smiled. He'd stepped into that.

"What about the car?"

"Terrific. Powerful. Sixteen cylinders purring away."

"Did you ask her to let you drive?"

"Why? She was doing just fine."

Eddie smiled again. Two in a row. "OK smart guy, if she asks you to go for a ride again, tell her you have a friend who could find time to come along."

"And you'd ask to let you drive and to be nice she'd say yes and then my life would be in danger."

Eddie threw up his hands and opened the drugstore door.

At Schauger's a cherry Coke or a chocolate shake bought one unlimited occupancy of a space on the bench seat of one of the six booths, arranged three on each side of the narrow room which led back to the pharmacy window, that vague place that none of the kids ever visited. A share of a booth's bench diminished from full width for the first to arrive on down to a fourth of the bench as the afternoon wore on. The ceiling over the booths was festooned with paper covers from drinking straws, which had first been dipped in a milk shake and then shot upward by a blast of breath from strong young lungs to stick to the ceiling and seemingly hang there forever. So many were now planted that it had become a problem to find a clear space for an addition.

Eddie handed Ben a nickel and headed toward a booth where three of their friends were already seated. Ben detoured by the soda fountain to ask Brother Packard for two cherry Cokes. Brother had just arrived from the graduation assembly to work behind the counter and was fastening his apron. As Schauger's soda jerk, he had landed one of the envied summer jobs. Logic dictated that a boy nicknamed Brother must have at least one sibling and he did, a sister whose voluptuous figure was acknowledged as one of the graduating class's main assets.

Ben took the Cokes and pushed into the booth across from Eddie. Except for Hank Edney, now a junior and wedged in against the wall, the two others were in Ben's class. The topic of conversation was summer jobs. Hank, with some pull through a friend of his father, had gotten the most envied job of all, lifeguard at the Laurel Lake Inn's beach. He would spend the summer getting a great tan while treating himself to free hamburgers and Cokes. Ben thought he was too young to be a lifeguard and was beginning to appreciate the saying, "It's who you know." Bill Lawson would be working at his father's men's clothing store on Main Street as he had last summer. Bill tried to make it sound like a good deal, but Ben thought otherwise. Bill had little to do except dust shelves and whatever dumb job his father could think up for little more than movie money—while having to wear a shirt and tie. It was very like the job Ben had had last summer working for his own father at The Mountain Lodge and he had no wish to repeat that.

Sitting next to Ben was Tim Graham whose family owned a dairy farm five miles north of town.

"You'll be working at the farm, right?" Ben asked.

"Yeah, me and the German prisoners."

"So that's where they were going. See, I told you they were German soldiers. Eddie wouldn't believe me. He said I'd flipped my wig."

Now Eddie was interested. "What do you mean they're working at your farm?"

"They are working in the bean field. Usually about twenty . . . and the officer."

"Ben said they were from North Africa."

"That's right. All members of the same tank battalion."

"I didn't know the army can make prisoners work," Eddie said.

"We can't. These guys all volunteered to work and get paid. The same pay as American soldiers make, which is damn little."

Lawson said, "I don't get it. You mean we actually pay these guys? That's stupid. They should work for nothing, they started the war."

"The way my Dad explained it there is a law that all countries agreed to. You can't make a prisoner work, but you can ask them to and pay them. Last year a lot of the bean crop was lost, because so many men were in the army that there was no one to pick the beans, so someone had the idea of asking the prisoners. The officer told me his men voted and decided they'd rather work than sit around a prison camp. The main camp is in South Carolina. There are about a hundred of them here. They split up and go to different farms. It's a temporary camp out Stoney Mountain Road. Tents."

The boys were silent for a while digesting this information.

"We saw them in a truck on Church Street, but I didn't see a guard," Eddie said.

"There's one guard. He rides up front with the driver. Usually it's Tony. He comes from New Jersey." Tim laughed, "When they're working Tony sits and dozes off a lot of the time."

"Isn't you father afraid they'll escape?"

"No. He says they have no wish to escape. First of all, where would they go? Dad says they are just happy to be out of the war. They're treated well, eat well. They're just waiting to go home when it's all over."

Lawson said, "You said the American guard is from New Jersey; do you think he knows Frank Sinatra?"

They all laughed. Tim said, "I'll ask him."

"Whadya think will be number one this week?"

Sinatra's name had brought the radio program, *Your Hit Parade*, to Eddie's mind.

"*I'll Get By*—once again," said Lawson.

"I think you're right," agreed Eddie. "Sinatra will sing it instead of what's her name."

"And we'll have to hear all those girls screaming and going nuts. Why do they do that?"

"Who knows? Some actually pass out. I mean dead away," marveled Hank.

"Why isn't Sinatra in the Army?" asked Tim with an inflection implying, "He's getting away with murder."

No one had an immediate answer, then Lawson offered, "Maybe he's too skinny for any of the uniforms"

How about *Take it or Leave It,* asked Hank looking at Eddie. "Did your little sister get all the answers right again?" How about the 'Sixty-four Dollar Question?' Did she know that country that Adis . . aba . . something was the capital of?"

"Abyssinia," said Eddie, then grudgingly added, "Yeah, Cookie got all the answers right."

"Does she ever miss?"

"Hell, yes," he answered quickly. "She doesn't know a damn thing about sports—baseball, boxing. She probably knows Joe Louis's name, but nothing else."

N.C. Foster walked up and slid onto the bench next to Eddie. He looked at Ben and was on the point of saying he'd seen him in the Continental, when he read the message on Ben's face that said, "Not now, not here."

Ben asked him, "How about you, have you got a summer job lined up?"

"Nothing good. I guess I'll caddy again."

"You said you hated the caddy master, wanted to club him with a nine iron."

"I do. Ed Wicker, the son-of-a-bitch. But he's gone. The Army got him. The new guy is the greens keeper's son and he's OK, but there's no money. There are only a few members who tip more than a quarter—damn few."

Eddie, who was facing the door looked up abruptly. Ben followed his gaze. Walter Abbot had just come into the store.

Walter Abbot was the town's eccentric. Very eccentric. He was somewhere in his mid-sixties, tall, erect, wore a probably once expensive, once cream-colored linen suit frayed at all terminal points, a rumpled dress-shirt and always the same yellow tie. A black patch worn over the right eye completed the picture. The story was that he was the scion of a once wealthy and socially prominent family. The one fact that everyone knew about him was that he "called" President Roosevelt every day to advise him on how to proceed with his day. Such advise as, "Make sure the tire pressure is correct on the trucks. Most important today." Ben made a mental note to ask his friend Abbie Ransom about Walter. She knew everything about Hendersonville.

Walter lifted his battered Panama hat and nodded toward a booth where several high school girls sat and said, "Ladies," as he continued back to the pharmacy window.

Hank Edney said he had to leave, so the guys on that side of the booth had to slide out and in again. Hugh Bates walked up carrying a chocolate sundae and made six again.

"Well Master Bates! We hear you're joining the circus," said Eddie.

Bates, so accustomed to being called, "Master," hardly heard the tired joke. He returned the "circus" quip, "That's right, the side show

38

in fact. I'm the Strong Man. Wanna feel my muscles?"

And Hugh did have muscles. In spite of the fact that he was the tallest, heaviest and best physically suited in Ben's class, he had no interest in playing football. This was something that neither Ben nor Eddie understood. Eddie regarded Hugh's attitude as a betrayal of the school.

Smiling an acknowledgment of Hugh having bested the exchange, Eddie said, "OK, it's not the circus, but a dumpy carnival. How'd that happen?"

"My sister's boyfriend." He looked around for a sign of recognition but got none. "Yeah well, she's seeing this guy, Lloyd, who runs the octopus ride for the carnival that travels around the western part of the state during the summer. He offered to get me a job there—roustabout. In the circus world he's the guy who gets the dirty jobs. But, what the hell, it pays better than anything else I could find."

"Your parents don't like this guy, right?" Ben said.

"You're right, and I think Lloyd believes getting me the job will influence them, but when my mother heard of it, she immediately heard it as an attempt to seduce me to be on his side and lead me . . ."

"Into a life of crime," supplied Ben.

Hugh nodded. "Maybe she's right. The next time you see me I may have a tattoo and call myself, 'Knuckles'."

"Nasty picture," said Eddie, "All because you couldn't resist a few cents more an hour."

"I gotta admit," said Ben. "Your job sounds more fun than ours. Eddie and I are going to be mowing lawns."

"Really, mowing lawns" said Hugh. "But wait, I can see a future in that. I can see you moving right up into garbage collection."

"Hey that's not nice. What did I say? Did I say that since I can see the direction you're . . . falling, I'd like you to return the flashlight I lent you to go to that scout camporee *last fall*?

The attention of the others became focused, as if gathering to watch a fight.

"That piece of shit. It didn't work. I didn't think you'd want it back, so I tossed it. The first time I tried to use it I was going out of the tent in the middle of the night to take a piss. The light went out as I was leaving the tent, I tripped over a tent stay and the whole tent came down on the two guys from Asheville I was sharing the tent with. During the inspection the following morning we were given three demerits. Those guys will forever think of me as a jerk."

Eddie, laughing at the scene of the collapsing tent, could hardly speak.

"Guys, I think we've kidded poor Hugh enough about his new career. He needs our support."

"You're right," Tim said. "From now on no more 'Master Bates.' From now on it's 'Jerkoff Bates.'"

Hugh, smiling, rocked back and forth with his eyes closed. He opened them, looked at Ben, and in the voice of a moderator doing a radio interview said, "This lawn mowing, how do you go about getting customers, sir? Do you knock on doors and say, 'I couldn't help noticing your lovely grass, Ma'am, I see it hasn't been tended in some time, which is a shame, a nice looking lady like you. I'd like to . . . tend it for you. You'd have no complaints. (wink, wink) Ask any of your friends I service.'"

Ben made as if he was writing this down. "Good stuff," he said.

"Seriously, how do you go about getting customers?"

Eddie looked at Ben and then took the question. "We took over the 'Moses Mows' business. You've seen his old truck with the hand-painted sign on the door, 'Moses Mows.'"

"An old colored guy?" said Lawson,

"Yeah," Ben said, "He had a stroke and can't work anymore, so one of his long-time customers, Mrs. Dickson, got the idea that someone should take over the customers - he had ten - and give Moses a share of the money. We'd be sort of partners. Mrs. Dickson spoke to my mother, said it was a 'Christian' thing to do and my mother volunteered me."

Eddie put in, "And he volunteered me."

Hugh said, "Now I think that's right nice. Wouldn't you say so fellas—right nice."

There followed general agreement. Tim said, "Very Christian."

"Christian?" Hugh said pointing at Ben. "I've never seen him in church." Then he asked, "What percentage does Moses get?"

"Twenty-five," replied Eddie.

"Holy shit!" gasped Lawson. "You do all the work and he gets twenty-five percent?"

"It was Mrs. Dickson's deal. She hustled around and assured all the worried customers that we'll soon be there."

"All Gotham City awaits the arrival of the Dynamic Duo," Hugh said, smiling from ear to ear. "Like Tim said, very Christian . . . Oh, that reminds me. Speaking of Christian treatment, have you heard the school canned Miss Martinez?"

"The Spanish teacher? Fired her? Why? Everyone likes her."

"Not everyone," Hugh said. "The rumor is that Mr. Burdick got some complaints from parents. I've heard it was Jane Simon's and

41

Fran Bishop's mothers."

"Jeeze, I heard Buddy Franklin was off base with some things he said in class. But I never imagined it would mean she'd get fired," Eddie said.

"Franklin's an ass. She was too nice to kick his butt out of class," Tim said. "Anyway it's a friggin' shame. I was going to take Spanish in the fall."

While this was unfolding in the booth, Dr. Schauger, the middle-aged. mild-mannered pharmacist and owner of the store, looked out from time to time on the scene through the small window of the pharmacy. He looked out and pondered a decision; should he take out the booths and put in shelving for the more profitable cosmetics as had the only other drugstore in town? That store, on Main Street, had a small soda fountain and only three tables with the traditional wire-backed soda fountain chairs. The rest of the space was utilized for displaying toiletries and cosmetics. Plus, the other store got most of the prescription business in spite of the fact that Schauger had put in an extra school year to get his PhD in pharmacy. It got the business , he figured (and correctly) because adults who bought drugs were disinclined to run the gauntlet of teenagers in his store.

Schauger liked the kids. He enjoyed their youthful exuberance and their hubris, the self-centered belief that he, Dr. Schauger, was dependent on and desperate for their nickel and dime trade. He remembered being just like them. It was very hard, though, to look out and see the drinking straw covers that hung from the ceiling waving like sea anemones each time the door was opened. He had decided removing those unsightly stalactites would be futile, because that would only create an urgent need for the booth occupants to fill the void. He liked the kids, but money was money and his professional credentials were being discounted. He had a decision to make.

Leaving the drugstore and their friends, Ben and Eddie walked toward Ben's house. One part of the deal was that Moses was to donate his hand mower and Moses's daughter had brought it over to Ben's house that morning.

"Lawson's right, twenty-five percent is a lot," Eddie said as they walked up the Roberts' driveway.

"I don't know—yeah it is—but I do feel sorry for the old guy. How else is he going to get any money? I never talked to him, but he would always smile and wave when he drove by in that old Model A truck of his. And besides it's already agreed. It would be hard to change."

"Yeah, OK." The issue was settled.

They both looked down at the mower that was resting on the concrete apron of the garage.

"Jesus, it's old." Ben observed.

"It must have been made when grass was invented."

Eddie had been using his neighbor's mower to cut both the neighbor's lawn and the White's small front lawn. He knew he couldn't ask for the loan to be extended to include their new customers, so he was looking at his tool for the summer. He gave a sigh of resignation and flipped it over so it would freewheel and started off pushing it home.

"Talk to you later."

Ben went into his house to change his clothes before going across the street to cut Mrs. Ransom's grass. He'd begun taking care of her lawn last summer. The money he received from her and the money Eddie got from his neighbor were outside the deal. The rest of the lawns they'd mow together.

Abigail Ransom, Abbie to her friends, had been a revelation to Ben.

43

She was the widow of Oliver Clyburn Ransom, who had been superior court judge of District 29 forty years until his death six years ago. He was famous for quips he threw at attorneys appearing before him, who didn't know their law. Those remarks were still repeated when local lawyers got together .

Throughout his adult life Ollie Ransom's understanding of the role of judge had been based upon his certain belief that the human community could only live together in harmony if one and only one rule were followed—the Golden Rule. Do unto others what you would have others do unto you. All the rest of moralizing was just hot air. The problem was that the Rule was impossible to follow for two unchangeable reasons. The first was the genetically imprinted fear of the "other." For the sake of survival the human, like other animal species, had to be very careful about who and what to trust. A mistake could be fatal. Trust faded precipitously the more removed the "other' was from one's immediate family. The second unchangeable reason the Rule was impossible to follow was that the human species was not naturally inclined to share, and again this became evident the further removed the recipient was from those who were seen as like oneself: the immediate family, tribe, religion, interest groups, nation. Since thinking and behavior in keeping with the Rule was essential for harmony and that was impossible, the Law was created to correct the inevitable infractions against the Rule. An unstable semblance of harmony was thus achieved that permitted the community to usually function well enough.

Ollie thought of his role as that of gardener. Weeds (violations of the Rule) must be pulled out if flowers were to stand a chance. The moment one stops attending to the weeds, the garden reverts to nature.

When the rule of law is suspended and man finds himself alone and far away from the trusted family, he reverts to his natural state of fear and selfishness. So Ollie Ransom was content in his role of puller of weeds, seriously and insightfully intent on his job, while with good humor he kept the other "gardeners" who appeared before him on their toes to be both competent and fair.

While Ransom believed the basic fear of the other and reluctance to share would never change, he'd discerned that over the many centuries an evolution was taking place in who was seen to be that "other;" More and more the other was coming to be seen as like oneself—like family. Regrettably this happened very, very slowly. Laughingly he forecast that someday "the other" would disappear completely. It would happen just before hell froze over, but it would happen.

Abbie had been busy through those years as a community activist, chiefly in the area of education and child welfare. She had now reached "emeritus" status, and while her name was listed on the stationery of several organizations, she rarely attended meetings anymore. She knew the younger women regarded her as a relic to be listened to politely, but whose views belonged to the past. She remembered thinking the same about Maud Harris, the minister's wife, when she'd herself first become involved in the workings of the community. At eighty Abbie retained the charm that had served her so well all her life. She managed to easily establish intimacy with very few exceptions. Of course many did not follow her views, but she didn't blame them for having learned as they had, and she tried, where she thought it possible, to alter what she considered obsolete notions. "The Baker sisters are so unalike don't you think, quite different personalties—chalk and cheese—and yet, while not identical twins, they are twins nevertheless and therefore their "stars" had to be in the same position at the time of their birth. According to astrology, shouldn't they have the same sort of personality?"

She was tall and thin, kept her naturally curly hair cut to the level of her earlobes and wore a hint of makeup.

Abbie was careful not to appear to be as interested in Ben as she really was. She didn't want to scare him away. Her two children and four grandchildren lived on the west coast and although they corresponded regularly, the truth was that they were far away both in distance and their need for her. She first became acquainted with Ben when he began mowing her lawn last summer. She immediately saw in him a potential surrogate for her absent grandchildren. Her program to secure this relationship was much like one she employed to gain the trust of squirrels and rabbits she fed on her back patio. After finishing his work and coming to the door for his pay, she invited him in for lemonade and cookies. He welcomed this at first, because he was hot and thirsty. Gradually he'd come to enjoy talking with her. Over the past winter months she'd found tasks that were now difficult for her and would ask him to stop by and help her. Now, when she was out in her garden he'd spontaneously stop to chat. From him she could learn about the current interests and attitudes of his age group, while at the same time being provided with a young mind she could influence. She had been so passionately involved with education and community development over so many years that she felt empty without the sense that she was making a difference—with someone. Besides, she liked Ben. He was very like her Ollie in one very important way—new ides had to stand the test of logic. This attribute, to her mind, could only be explained by a unique structuring of the brain. It couldn't be learned. There was no one in her husband's family (God only knew!) from whom he could have learned it.

Abbie missed Ollie very much. It helped that Ben was there. She envisioned a useful role for herself, one which added a measure of purpose to her otherwise uncommitted days. Perhaps she could help Ben sort out his options—avoid pitfalls.

Ben emptied the grass clippings into the trash can then splashed water from the hose on his face prior to knocking on the back door. Moments later he was sitting across from Abbie with a glass of lemonade. He wasted no time getting to the subject that had been on his mind all the time he'd mowed.

"I know Congressman Sinclair has been in office a long time, but I really know nothing about him," he began, "Is he exceptionally good? Why does he keep getting reelected?"

Abbie wondered why the sudden interest in Sinclair and Ben starting right off asking about him, but she answered, "Well, there are several reason. First of all, no one except a Democrat can get elected here since the war between the states. That means the competition is really an intra-party influence thing. The Democratic Party decides who will be congressman or senator, the people don't decide."

"They vote don't they?"

"Yes, but the party sees to it that no one runs against the person it selects. Going against the party spells doom for him who does."

"So, you're saying that some guys in Raleigh sit around smoking cigars and decide who our senators and congressmen are?"

Smiling she said, "For the common good, of course."

"So, Sinclair has good friends in the capitol."

"Um. In the beginning at least. Now he has assumed the status of a law of nature. It would be so difficult to dislodge him that anyone who tried would end up hurting himself, so no one will try."

"I haven't heard any complaints about him. How do you rate him?"

Abbie was still wondering about Ben's interest.

"I suppose he does a good enough job. He hasn't gotten our district much in the way of favors in Washington, but then ours is a relatively poor farming district; except for his vote on the favored legislation of other congressmen, there isn't much Troy Sinclair has to offer in order to collect favors. He claims he got contracts for the paper and textile mills, but with the war, they'd probably have gotten the work anyway. And then there's the airfield the Air Force built at Fletcher; Troy claims credit for that too although the actual work was done by a Buncomb County contractor—out of our congressional district. As far as malfeasance is concerned—wrong doing—I suppose he's no worse than others would be in his place. You may have heard of the saying, "power corrupts." That is after being in a position of power for a while, one tends to believe that rules that apply to others don't apply to oneself. Here she decided to take a chance and add a bit gossip, like a juicy tidbit for a squirrel. "For instance, there's this story that the state's road repair trucks have been seen spreading gravel on roads at one of his farms. This is just between us, of course," she said with a mischievous smile.

Ben thought about this in silence.

"May I ask why you've become interested in Congressman Sinclair?"

He hesitated a moment before saying, "I happened to meet his daughter last night."

Ah ha, thought Abbie. "Ah yes, Valery. I haven't seen her for a couple of years. That was at the wedding of Mary Sydney's granddaughter." Abbie remembered her as very attractive. She delayed several beats before asking, "What was the occasion of this meeting?"

"She asked me to go for a ride in their Continental convertible—along with a friend of hers."

Abbie knew the car. Here was an irresistible combination of two of the most appealing entities to a teenage boy, a beautiful girl and a matching car. Maybe in reverse order.

"What was your impression of Valery?"

Ben was not prepared to answer this question. He hadn't yet reached an answer in his own mind.

"She's different."

"Oh? How different?"

"She goes to a fancy private school in Charleston."

"I see."

His answer sums up a lot, thought Abbie. To Ben Valery was exotic, grown like an orchid in the protected enclosure of an exclusive Charleston greenhouse, the most romantic foreign city in their part of the South. Perhaps exotic to the point of being an entirely different species. Yet she had asked him to go for a ride. Was Valery indulging a whim, a dalliance with an attractive boy—a boy of the citizenry? Abbie could see the makings of a painful life experience for Ben. Were it to begin to look like a fatal experience she would be compelled to act. But at his age, of course, it would not be fatal, only painful. It could feel fatal nevertheless. She could foresee the possibility of first-aid wound dressing.

Ben changed the subject. "I saw some German prisoners today. They were in the back of a truck driving down Church Street. I recognized that cap they wear."

"What cap is that?"

"It goes up in the front like a fireman's helmet. I've seen their pictures in *Life*."

"Yes, I heard that they were being brought in to work on the farms."

"It was so weird. You know, German soldiers were only in the movies—the enemy, like Indians in a Western, then there they were in real life".

"How did they make you feel? Were you afraid . . or angry?"

Ben thought for a moment. "No, I was curious. They were laughing and talking."

Abbie refilled Ben's glass. She remembered that at his age the whole phenomenon of war was still another of the curious activities the adult world could get up to.

"Do you have relatives in the army or navy?"

"A cousin in the Air Force in Arizona."

"Do you discuss the war at home?"

"Some. My father is English as you know, and he has a brother and sister in England, so he talks about the bombing."

"They've been all right?" she asked.

"They live in a small city that's not near any of the targets. Three bombs were dropped on it though. My father figures the bomber had three bombs left over from a raid on Birmingham and dumped them on the way back to its base."

"Did your father become an American citizen?"

"Yes, but he's too old for the Army. He was in the English army in the first war."

"Really?"

"The whole time, four years."

"My, he's lucky to have survived."

"He says more than half of his regiment died."

"That's terrible. Does he talk about his experience?"

Ben thought for a moment. "Hardly at all. I've asked him questions at times, but he changes the subject. And the little he has said makes me unsure I want to hear more."

And here in Hendersonville is that enemy that his father fought against and won't talk about, thought Abbie.

"What is his attitude toward the Germans, do you know?"

"Ah well, he hates Hitler like everyone else, but he has always talked about the Germans in an everyday sort of way. He calls them 'Jerry', like 'Jerry was in the trench up ahead', or 'Jerry sent over some shells.'"

They sat in silence before Ben added, "I've never thought of it until you asked, but he doesn't seem angry with 'Jerry', as if they are only the opposing team. Not like the Japs."

Abbie said, "I guess everybody hates the Japs." She thought to herself that everyone is ready to hate those who seem different—and especially if they don't play fair and bomb you first.

Ben stood up. "I've got to go. Eddie and I have to talk over the mowing schedule."

She walked to the screen door and watched him wheel off his mower. She hoped she hadn't prattled on too much. She didn't want to become a boring old woman.

At home Ben found his mother in the kitchen making a meatloaf for dinner.

"I'm going to take a shower, Mom, then go over to Eddie's. I'll be back before dinner time."

"Your father wants you to wash the car, when he gets home. He has a meeting of some sort tonight."

"Why does he have to have a clean car for a meeting? They're not having the meeting in the car are they?"

"I'm only a conduit, don't take it out on me."

"Yeah, OK. I'm going up to take a shower."

He started to leave the kitchen, then remembered he hadn't asked Abbie Ransom about Walter Abbot as he'd wanted to do.

"Mom, do you know anything about this weird guy, Walter Abbot? I was going to ask Mrs. Ransom, but forgot. Do you know who I mean?"

"Yes, I do. I was at Carson's Cafe with Joan Dickson when I noticed him come in and sit at the next table. He ordered a cup of coffee and drank it and just got up and left without paying. I was surprised and our waitress, noticing my look of surprise laughed and said, 'Oh, that's Walter.'

"Joan said that she'd heard he was sort of crazy and that he calls the President every day. That's all she knew about him, so when Abbie Ransom was over here for coffee later on, I asked her about him figuring she'd likely know. She knew alright. Shall I tell you now or after your shower?"

"Tell me now."

"OK, have a seat," she said as she continued with dinner preparations at the kitchen counter.

"Abbie is a good friend of Walter's aunt with whom he lives, so she knows the full story. Walter grew up in New York City. He was an only child, a withdrawn child who didn't make friends, preferring to be left alone to read. His parents, of course, hoped his life would become fuller as he matured, but when he got to adolescence the opposite happened. He became suspicious and secretive and seemed to be hallucinating, seeing and speaking to someone who wasn't there. Hospitalization was recommended. His parents, as you can imagine, were devastated.

"But then, this amazing thing happened—surprised all the doctors—left them stumbling around to try to explain it, because he suddenly became a totally different person. Not a normal person to be sure, because he thought himself to be a wealthy, sophisticated, perfectly mannered aristocrat. It was as if he'd stepped out of one of the novels he'd been reading. No longer was he reclusive. While he made no real friends, he easily mingled with people, inquiring about their health and their families in the most polished way. He also insisted upon wearing expensive, conservative suits. His parents were well off so they could afford it. It was totally weird, but infinitely better—as far his parents were concerned—to his being confined in a mental hospital. Every day he would stroll though Central Park tipping his hat to ladies and saying, "Good morning" or "Good afternoon," and smoking Balkan Sobranie cigarettes and then he'd lunch at the Plaza."

His mother laughed. "I'm telling this in almost the same words Abbie used. I guess it was because I was so caught up in her story."

She saw that Ben's mouth was literally open in disbelief.

"I think it's caught you too. Anyway, something terrible happened. Both of Walter's parents were killed in a freak elevator accident. Since his aunt was the closest relative, he was brought to live with her here in Hendersonville. He continues to live out pretty much the same delusion as before."

This was the first time Ben had heard any details about a mental disorder. "That's wild. What about calling the President every day?"

"Yes, that's true. The clerks at the Carolina Hotel 'put through' a fake call to Washington so he can advise President Roosevelt about all sorts of things." She laughed. "Strange things. Like when he first came here he told the President that shelters were needed here for all the homeless children. Of course, we have no homeless children, but seeing kids going around freely without their parents was not something he 'd seen in mid-town Manhattan."

"What about that patch over his eye?"

"Yes, Abbie mentioned that too. He says he lost his eye in an accident while hunting wild boar in the Italian mountains. A famous Viennese surgeon did the operation. His aunt says he takes it off to read and puts it back when he puts the book down."

Yes, thought Ben, that was the man he'd seen.

His mother went on. "Although Walter has a room of his own in his aunt's house, he insists on staying in an abandoned realtor's field office in Laurel Park. He calls it his "dacha." That's what wealthy Russians call their country cottages. Abbie thought it has no plumbing, and he can only get away with it, because the whole town treats him like a mascot. The barber cuts his hair. He eats lunch at one or other of the cafes, or picks up an apple at the grocery and tells them all to put it on his account. At the end of the summer, before leaving for Florida for the winter, his uncle stops around to the various businesses in town and pays Walter's 'account.' Most say Walter's even with them. Hendersonville has taken him to its heart and to have him pick your business for his needs bestows a certain prestige. Well, that's Walter's story."

Ben shook his head. Life had just become more mysterious.

At dinner his mother asked, "How did the last day of school go?"

"Good. The seniors were as high as kites going through the graduation ritual, walking across the stage to get their diplomas and then doing that switching sides with the tassels on their caps."

"What do you mean?" his father asked. He hadn't graduated from an American high school, or any high school for that matter, having left the English school system at fourteen. "It's the ritual where the tassel hanging on the cap is moved from one side of the cap to the other—left to right I think—when they are handed their diplomas."

Ben had noticed some seniors did this with an air of having done a momentous thing, while others had a look that said, "Why am I doing this dumb thing?"

"A bit of nonsense isn't it?" his father said.

Ben had engaged in countless rebuttals to his father's ready denigration of American customs. Gradually he came to recognize that nothing resulted from this engagement except unpleasantness, while his father didn't change his attitude a bit. This awareness became the seed from which a lifelong Epicurean orientation would develop—avoid unnecessary, profitless pain.

"It could be looked at that way," he replied.

"The only way it could be looked at I would say," his father pronounced with the finality of a gauntlet having been thrown down.

Ben let it lie.

His father, a good-looking man, a smart man, was a discontented man, never experiencing himself to be following a chosen path, but instead, regarding his work as something temporary, a somewhat grudging participation in paths chosen by others and at less pay than he deserved. He wasn't aware of it, but he externalized this discontentment through an ever-ready alertness to opportunities to disrupt contentment he perceived in others, his family chiefly. Ben was his frequent target. Ben's mother had protectively adapted by simply avoiding any show of enthusiasm in his presence.

"I expect the boys will be going into the Army," his father said.

"Not yet, most are only seventeen. I heard Mack Loman has already got orders to report, but he's nineteen."

"Should I know him?"

"I told you about him. He's the fullback on the football team."

"Ah yes, Big Mack."

Mack had a hard time graduating, but he kept trying. The student body was happy, because it meant he'd be back at fullback another year. Rumor had it that the head of the permissive draft board had been a Bearcat in his day.

"Do you still believe a summer pushing a mower will be better than working at the Lodge?" his father asked, meaning Ben had made a dumb choice.

"So far so good." Again he wouldn't take the bait.

Ernest Roberts was now manager of the Mountain Lodge. He had taken the job when an exclusive Miami beach club where he'd been assistant manager closed for the duration of the war leaving him without an income. The Mountain Lodge had been built upon grandiose expectations of a burgeoning tourist business in Hendersonville thirty years ago, expectations which failed to be realized because of the Depression. The Lodge then limped along until it finally closed its door at the outbreak of the war and the subsequent decline in tourism. A member of the Miami club, a native of Atlanta, bought the property cheaply two years ago, figuring once the war was over, the mountains would once again become a favored vacation destination for southerners baking in the summer sun of South Carolina and points south. He'd known Roberts from the Florida beach club and hired him to put the Lodge in shape ready for the hoped for post-war prosperity.

Last summer Ben had worked at the Lodge. It was true that the work was much easier than pushing a mower—little to do in fact. It had been very trying, however, to be his father's employee. The business plan was one of rebuilding—current occupancy rate unimportant. But whenever a reservation was cancelled, his father would become anxious and Ben could count on soon being criticized for some aspect of his job performance. "Why haven't you cleaned the chairs around the pool yet?" And Ben would answer to himself, "Because you told me to water the house plants first thing this morning." Pure agony that Ben had no wish to repeat.

The phone, which sat on a stand at the foot of the stairs, rang. Ben's mother, who had already risen to get the dessert, answered it.

"It's for you, Ben."

He picked up the phone thinking it must be Eddie. He had planned to go to his house before dinner, but his father wanted the car washed.

"Hi Ben, this is Valery. How are you?" She continued before he could answer. "I'm hoping you can come to my house for lunch tomorrow."

His first reaction was alarm. Something unexpected and strange was happening, like opening the front door and finding Gary Cooper standing there. A moment passed before it registered that he was actually being invited for lunch.

"Ah . . . I have to work tomorrow."

His alarm increased when he recognized just how cold and

dismissive his answer must have sounded. Plain dumb!

"I mean that I'd like very much to have lunch with you, but a friend of mine and I have a job mowing lawns."

"You still have to eat don't you?" Her voice retained its initial friendly playfulness, ignoring his stumbling.

"Well, yeah."

"I pick up and deliver lunch guests - how about it?"

"I'll be wearing work clothes."

"No problem. There will only be the two of us, and our cook. I promise to deliver you back to work in an hour"

Eddie's voice said, "She wants to see you stupid; just say yes."

"OK, great. I'll be at the Henderson's - 320 Justice Street."

"Twelve?"

"Yes, OK."

"See ya."

"Ah, goodbye."

Ben hung up and continued standing, his mind buzzing with what had just happened. That easy confidence was in her voice. Very friendly. More than friendly? Luckily he would be cutting the Henderson's lawn by himself, since Eddie had to go to Asheville with his parents in the morning. He walked back to the dining room relatively unaware of where he was. His parents noticed .

The phone, installed after the war had started and the only option available, was a four-party line. This meant conversations must be brief. No extended gossip with school friends was permissible. Conversations with friends were always and only face-to-face. A phone call was worthy of the family's attention.

When it became apparent Ben didn't intend to comment on the

call, his mother inquired, "A friend?"

"Someone I met yesterday . . . invited me to lunch."

"Lunch? Too bad you'll be working," his father said.

"She offered to pick me up and bring me back to the Henderson's."

"If you just met her, she must not be in your class," his mother said, pushing he interrogation along.

"No, she goes to a different school."

His mother would next ask which school, but his father beat her.

"Just met you and wants to give you lunch; she must be very interested in you."

Eddie's patent line came to Ben's mind and his irritation with his father prodded him into repeating it.

"She's only interested in my body."

This was the most risque´ thing he'd ever said to his parents, His father managed a grunt and his mother a hesitant small smile. It ended the interrogation.

They began eating bread pudding in silence, when the phone rang again. This time the call was for his father. Ben heard parts of his father's side of the conversation.

"Really? Well if you think it's important. It's unlikely you'll be needed in the kitchen the rest of the evening. I'll see you tomorrow."

He returned to the table saying, "That was Rosa at the Lodge. She's supposed to stay until Howard comes on at nine, but she says she needs to leave early. Something to do with the woman who stays at her place. The police want to ask her some questions."

"The police? Ask questions now? At seven-thirty? Ben's mother asked.

He was not really interested in the subject and replied, "Yeah, yeah, but it's OK."

Cut off from that subject, she went on to another concern. "We're nearly out of milk. You'd better go to the farm tomorrow."

"Ben can go," he answered.

The "farm" was the one owned by the Graham's. It was there the unpasteurized milk Ben's father insisted they drink (Pasteurization removes all the nutrients!) could be bought.

"Can I use the car?"

"If you go first thing, I can wait for you to return before I go to the Lodge. I have to be there at nine, though."

If he left the house by eight, he'd be back on time.

"A gallon as usual?"

"Yes. Make sure it's fresh," his mother said.

"I'll make sure it's still hot from the cow."

Detective Kyle Sexton stood at the doorway to Blanca Martinez's bedroom. Rosa Sanchez stood behind him. He had come there to learn more about Miss Martinez's disappearance. As with any unexplained disappearance of an adult capable of possessing plans of their own, the first explanation of her behavior, in the absence of contra- dictory evidence, is that she is pursuing her own damn business and no one has a right to interfere. At what point does the community—the police—become justified, even obligated to inquire? The answer is: "It all depends."

Rosa Sanchez had called that morning to report that her friend and tenant had failed to return home last night. This was duly noted by the dispatch sergeant and wound up on Sexton's desk.

When Sexton looked at the report and noted the woman's age, he thought it likely that this was a case of a young woman who had not yet terminated a night of love. He called the number Sanchez had given the sergeant expecting to hear that the missing friend was no longer missing. Instead, no one answered.

Hendersonville's police department was small, the detective division consisting of Kyle Sexton and Clint Edney, who together handled all the felony cases. The fact that the report about the woman was on his desk and not Clint's was the result of a mental filing system in the brain of Flora Childs, the department secretary, who kept track of which man had got the last case.

Kyle had been with the department for three years and Clint for two. Both were draft age, twenty-eight for Kyle and twenty-four for Clint. Both were exempt; Clint because he was partly deaf in one ear and Kyle because Chief of Police John Bell Housman could safely rely on him to do his work so well that John Bell could put the detective department out of his mind and tend to the things of more vital interest to him such as pleasing his Asheville girlfriend and the local political figures his job depended upon.

Kyle had attended Furman University in Greenville for two years before dropping out to join the Greenville Police Department. He'd made a very good impression during his four years there and was on the cusp of advancing to the detective division, when he'd heard the same job was open in Hendersonville. He preferred the cooler mountain climate and learning to boot that he'd be the whole of the detective division, he'd decided to make the move.

John Bell had duly notified the draft board in 1940 that Kyle was a vital civil servant. That was fine with Kyle at the time, but he'd developed mixed feelings about his exemption when Japan bombed Pearl Harbor. He wanted to be involved in the fight, but at the same time he'd just been hired in a job he very much wanted. There had been moments when he'd had the urge to quit and notify the draft board of his changed status. Then an interesting case would come along to delay that move. He had once again begun to feel the urgency to join the battle before it was too late, leaving him feeling like an outsider in his own generation.

Then Rosa Sanchez called again in the late afternoon to say that she had gone to her house to see if her friend had returned and found she hadn't. She supplied the additional information that the missing woman was a teacher at the high school and managed to impress the dispatcher that her absence without explanation was totally atypical. The call was put through to Sexton. At that point the balance shifted away from, "It's her own business." It now warranted looking into and Sexton told Rosa Sanchez he'd like to meet her at her house at eight o'clock. She'd said she would see if she could arrange it and call him back.

"She has rented a room from me since last September. She is a nice quiet person. She's never been away overnight before. She would never do it I think without telling me."

Sexton walked into the bedroom and gave it a once over; single bed, five drawer chest-of-drawers, small dressing table and a night stand with a lamp made up the furniture. Two stacks of books lay on the chest and another book was on the night stand. Over the bed hung a red, hammered-tin heart with flames coming out of the heart's top. Sexton thought this was probably some Mexican religious symbol. He'd never seen anything like it.

He went to the chest and pulled out and examined the contents of each drawer. Nothing to catch his attention - women's clothing arranged neatly.

"All her clothes are here except what she was wearing," Rosa said at the door.

"And what was she wearing?"

"I didn't see her when she went out last night, you understand—I was at work—but I know her clothes and I can see that her best dress, the one she bought in Asheville two weeks ago, is not here."

"And her best shoes too, I'd guess."

"Yes."

There were two other pairs of shoes in the closet.

"And her silk stockings," added Rosa.

All dressed up thought Sexton. "Looks like she had a hot date. What does it say to you?"

"She always dressed up to go out, even when it was just the two of us going to the movies."

"What about dates with men?"

"I know she went on a date with the basketball coach at the school. That was back near Easter. One of the big bands was playing in Asheville."

"That was the only date since she came here?"

"She didn't tell me about any others. We're friendly but she doesn't talk to me about that sort of thing—about men. You have to understand I come home around nine o'clock in the evening. If she is going out, she has already left by the time I get home."

"And on those nights, what time does she come home?

"A few times after I'd gone to bed, but mostly she'd been to a movie, and I'd still be up when she got back."

On the closet floor he saw a medium sized suitcase, fairly new, made of pressed cardboard. He surmised it had been bought for the trip to Hendersonville.

"Where did she come from?"

"From Houston, Texas. I'm from there too. I know Blanca's aunt."

He closed the closet and said, "I'd like to sit down and make some notes."

She led him back down the hall to the dinette.

Sexton said, "Please sit down. I'd like to ask you a few more questions."

Rosa was basically wary of speaking with the police. It hadn't led to good results back in Houston. On the other hand, she desperately needed help finding her friend and she was helpless on her own. She sat down across from Sexton and waited.

"You told the dispatcher your friend was a teacher at the high school."

"Yes, she was, but she was fired ."

"Tell me about that."

"She told me last week."

"Why was that, I mean why was she fired?"

"She said there had been complaints . . . from parents. They said she did not have control of the class."

"What kind of control? Behavior? Their work?"

"Their behavior."

Sexton thought of a substitute teacher when he was in high school. The poor woman couldn't face-up to the bad actors in his class - name calling - thrown erasers. She only gained control when she broke down and started crying.

"The classes were unruly then?"

"Not exactly. You see she is a - uh - good looking young woman. Dirty things were written on the blackboard . . . and said."

"And they fired her?" Something was wrong with this picture, Sexton thought. You don't fire the teacher because she is attractive and some horny students are out of line.

"She must have been angry."

"Not so much. She knew there was a problem. She talked to me about it earlier. I told her she should send the boys to the principal, but she didn't want to be a . . ."

"Bad guy? A disciplinarian."

"Yes. She was unhappy about not being able to manage the class. She blamed herself and didn't seem to be angry, almost - well as if it didn't matter, as if she had other plans."

"Really? Most people would be very unhappy about getting their walking papers."

"It was like she had more important things to do."

"Like another job lined up?"

"She never said that."

"How long had she had this attitude?"

Rosa considered the question. "I'd say about a month. Before that, I could tell she was worried about school, but then she began to lighten up, I thought things at school had become better. Turns out that wasn't true."

"Sounds to me like something happened a month ago to cause her to change her . . . priorities. Could it be she met a man she became interested in—best dress, best shoes?"

"Like I said, not that I know of."

Sexton took a couple of minutes to write down what he'd viewed and heard. Rosa watched him feeling despair that anything useful had been accomplished by calling the police.

He looked over his notes and said, "You say you know her aunt in Houston. Have you called her to see if she knows anything?

"No."

"Do you have her phone number?"

"She doesn't have a phone. I have the number of a neighbor."

"Can you call the neighbor now?"

"I know she'd be working now. She works in a defense plant. I can call her tomorrow. It's a long distance call."

Sexton thought of getting the number and making the call himself, but figured he might end up talking to someone who spoke no English and might also be wary of talking to the police.

"Look Mrs. Sanchez, ask the operator what the call costs and I'll pay you back. OK?"

She nodded.

"Good. Call our office as soon as you talk to the aunt. Leave a message if I'm not there."

He looked over his notes again.

"You haven't even a slight idea or hunch about where she went last night—you're sure?"

"I have no idea."

"The dress she wore; can you describe it?"

"Yes, it's orange."

"Orange?"

"Well, apricot."

66

"One more thing; do you have a picture of her?"

"Yes." She left him and returned with a snapshot of a smiling, very good-looking young woman of obvious Mexican heritage.

"I'd like to keep this for a while?" he said.

She nodded consent.

He closed his notebook, put his pen in his shirt pocket and stood.

"You'll call me tomorrow, OK? Thanks."

Kyle sat in his car reviewing what he'd just seen and heard. He made himself consider Rosa Sanchez as being involved in her friend's disappearance. He closed his eyes and imagined the woman's tone of voice. No, he didn't think so. She was telling the truth. What facts then did he have? A very attractive young woman had aroused the burgeoning hormones of sixteen year old boys to the level of uncontrolled behavior. She was Mexican to boot—exotic, maybe commanded less respect because of this. She had been fired, until proven otherwise, because she couldn't control a few horny guys. She hadn't reacted to being fired in the expected way—not angry, not depressed, almost as if she didn't care. Now this, as he thought of it, was the strangest part. Other factors he could account for in the scope of his experience, but not this. After all she had little money—few dresses, three pairs of shoes, a cheap suitcase. She hadn't spoken of the prospect of another job and yet seemed to "have other plans." OK, Kyle concluded, even though Sanchez said she dressed up whenever she went out at night, it looked to him as if she'd had a date Thursday night, a date she didn't come home from. She hadn't run off with the guy, because all her stuff was in her room. Sanchez knew of only one man she had dated, Colin Dobbs, the basketball coach. Kyle knew his name, because he had attended the games.

What should be his first steps? He would interview Dobbs and the school principal, talk to her fellow teachers to find out more about her personal life. He would make an orderly inquiry and gather the facts without bias, but the odds said he was going to be looking for a guy, a guy she'd dressed up for, and the odds wouldn't be "the odds" if they weren't usually right.

Kyle started his car and began driving home. The Sanchez house was within walking distance of the school, half a dozen blocks north and west and about twice that distance to his apartment on Main Street over the bowling alley on the corner of Third Avenue. The idea of living over a bowling alley nixed it immediately for most people, thus the rent was cheap. Kyle never disabused anyone of that prejudice. As a matter of fact, the only real business the alley had was on Friday and Saturday night between seven and closing time at ten. Even then the sound was tolerable, because most people played the "rubber duck" pins, the small pins bound with a thick band of rubber, because the bouncing pins produced more strikes. Rubber on rubber wasn't very noisy. Besides, the rear twelve feet of the second floor space, the part actually over the bowling pit, was a storage room for the alley accessed by a rear stairway. So the apartment was cheap and large—the size of a five lane bowling alley minus twelve feet. Kyle had furnished it with hand-me-downs from relatives and an antique, oak dining table he'd picked up at a farmer's market. The origins of this collection sounded unpromising, but the effect was comfortable. It suited him and there was no one else at the moment to please. He took a beer out of the refrigerator, kicked off his loafers, sank into his armchair and emitted an end of the day sigh.

Saturday, June 3rd.

Ben enjoyed driving to the Graham farm. The road meandered through rolling hills covered with the area's many apple orchards. For a long stretch of the way a rapid, shallow stream switched back and forth from one side of the road to the other as if playing tag. Usually coming to the farm to get milk and eggs meant dealing with his friend Tim's father, a nice, but painfully taciturn man. This morning he hoped he'd be talking with Tim . . . and hear more about the German prisoners.

He turned into the farm's drive. Cows, tan Guernseys , were beginning to walk from the large barn to a field that lay to the right. The milking had just finished. Ben scanned the area by the barns for the Army truck, and there it was. He parked next to the open door of what they called the milking parlor.

Hearing Ben drive up, Tim looked out of the barn and left what he'd been doing to walk toward the car where Ben was reaching back inside to fetch two half-gallon bottles he'd brought to fill.

"You on a milk run, Roberts?"

"Yeah, got a gallon you can spare?"

Maybe two quarts," he said grinning, "But I can add two quarts of water and it will be richer than that Holstein milk they sell at the A&P. Aren't you supposed to be mowing lawns?"

"Just as soon as I get the milk home. I see the Army truck. The prisoners must be here already."

"They're here. They're working in the bean field across the branch.

Wanna see them?"

This was a bold idea, a scary idea, getting near the enemy he'd seen so many times in the movies.

"Yeah, sure."

"C'mon then. I have a few minutes before Jesse needs me to help move the milk cans into the cooler."

The two set off on a path that ran along a creek forming one boundary of the pasture where the cows were heading. Over a narrow footbridge and through a gap in a wild hedge they came to the edge of the bean field. And there they were, the Germans, about twenty, shirtless, working steadily with hoes. They all wore the distinctive tan caps he'd recognized the day before. His eye traveled along the edge of the field to where an American soldier sat on a folding chair smoking in the shade of a tree, a carbine lying across his lap. The soldier brought a cup to his lips and drank while appearing lost in thought.

"He's the only guard?" Ben asked.

"Yeah, his name is Tony. Mom makes coffee for him—and the officer."

"The officer?"

"Yeah, on yonder past Tony. Interesting guy. He speaks English better than . . . well better than you."

Ben saw him now, reading a book. "I guess I never thought of a German speaking English. You've talked to him?"

"Sure. He doesn't work in the field. I understand it isn't proper for officers to work with the men under his command."

"What do you mean 'under his command', they're all prisoners, right?"

"Yeah, but they still maintain their rank. Tony explained it to Dad.

The Army wants it that way, since it helps maintain discipline in the camps."

"I'll bet the guys doing the work think differently about it."

"Nah, from what I've seen, they want it that way too."

"What did you talk to him about?" Ben asked.

"Not much, just where he was from, did he have any children."

"Why did you want to know if he had any kids?"

"He asked me if I had any brothers or sisters. After I said that I had a little sister, it seemed natural to ask him about his kids. He's easy to talk to, and he doesn't—have any kids—not married either."

"What rank is he, do you know?"

"He's a major, only they pronounce it 'May-yor' and Tony told me to say 'Hair May-yor.'"

"Major is a pretty high rank to be sitting here in a bean field."

"It's a hell'uva lot better than being shot at. Tony told me his name is Gerhard von Kleist. He was the commander of a tank battalion in North Africa, what they called the Afrika Korps."

"Jesus, the commander of a tank battalion."

"Want to talk to him?"

Ben hadn't planned on anything like this. He was intensely curious, but talking to a German soldier? And also it would make him late getting back home and his father would be pissed.

"I don't know . . . yeah OK."

"Let me check it out with Tony first. C'mon."

Ben stood and waited as Tim spoke to the GI. From the guy's body language he read that there was no problem. Tim came back and said, "It's OK. Let's go."

Minutes before this, Gerhard von Kleist had finished reading a book given him by an American officer. He turned back to an early passage that had affected him. "There was music from my neighbor's house through the summer nights. In his blue garden men and girls came and went like moths among the whisperings and the Champagne and the stars." The softness of the described scene brought back a life alien to him for years, rekindling nostalgic memories long held out of conscious awareness, yearnings suppressed in order to concentrate on the action at hand in order to survive. He glanced up from the book at the scene before him. There he saw his men digging in the soil to cultivate a crop, not digging in the sand to save themselves from mutilating death. He took a deep breath and relaxed one more degree and began rereading the passage as the boys approached.

Although seated, Ben made the man out to be tall and younger than he expected a major to be, maybe mid-thirties. Beside the chair on the ground was a cap, different than the others—more like a motorcycle cop would wear. It rested on top of another book. His long-sleeved, tan shirt was rolled up to the elbows. When the boys were ten yards away, he looked up from the book.

"Ah, my friend, Tim."

Hi, Hair Mayor. This is my friend, Ben."

"Happy to meet you, Ben."

To himself, von Kleist wondered if Ben was the first of Tim's friends who would be brought to view Tim's prize, a living German soldier. He'd had two conversations with Tim. He'd thought that throughout both he'd discerned a holding back, something on the boy's mind he was afraid to say. Von Kleist guessed it was probably the question he'd have in Tim's place , "Did you kill any American soldiers?" And if that were correct, what had held the boy back? Temerity? Good manners?

72

"Do you go to school with Tim?" the major asked.

"Yes, we're in the same class, tenth grade."

"And what courses do you take in that grade?"

Ben had not expected he'd be having a conversation with a German prisoner and certainly not about school courses. "I meant to say we will be in the tenth grade when we return to school in the fall."

Von Kleist, smiling, waited for an answer.

"Ah well, there's English and algebra and I'm going to take Spanish. How about you?" He looked at Tim.

"I'm taking Spanish too. Biology. Gym, of course."

"Is Latin taught?" von Kleist asked.

"Yes," Ben answered, while noting that while the man's English was perfect, there was no doubt that he was German.

"And did you study it?"

"Yes, last year but I'm taking Spanish next year. I want to learn a language that people speak today."

Tim interrupted. "Cookie White speaks Latin and she's only had it one year."

Von Kleist thought Tim must mean that this person reads Latin, not "speaks" it. He said, "So Latin is not compulsory then."

The idea surprised Ben. "No, is it compulsory in Germany?"

As he asked the question he was again aware of how weird it felt to be talking to a German prisoner about school.

"Yes, everyone who goes to a gymnasium, a type of high school, studies Latin for nine years and Greek for six."

Both boys were speechless. They had never heard of anyone studying Greek - and Latin for nine years? Incomprehensible. Always in their minds was the abiding question of what made the Germans start the war. Being forced to take nine years of Latin and six of Greek might be the answer.

"Is this Cookie a boy or a girl?"

"She's a girl, our friend Eddie's sister."

"And you don't really mean she *speaks* Latin after studying it for one year do you?"

"Yeah, she does. She's a brain," said Ben.

"A brain?" von Kleist laughed.

"A brain and a pain," said Tim.

"And a pain?" repeated the major. "Does that mean what I think it means?"

"It means she's always giving me a hard time—teasing me," Ben said.

"Just you?"

"Ben is her favorite target," jibed Tim, nudging him with his elbow.

"I see. How old is this gadfly?"

Ben didn't know what gadfly meant, but he supplied the answer. "Thirteen. She skipped a couple of grades so she's in our class."

A gentle smile stole across the officer's face. It was a remarkable face, a high forehead above deeply-set eyes that could go from soft and understanding to penetrating and dominating as if controlled by a rheostat. A jutting jaw gave the impression he wouldn't turn away from an argument.

"I see, so Cookie speaks Latin in your classroom?"

"Well not in the class," conceded Tim. "She's not a show off, I'll give her that. She and the teacher sit in the cafeteria and jabber away. Looks like they're having a ball."

Von Kleist's young visitors had supplied him with many colloquialisms to be added to his English vocabulary: brain, pain, hard time, show off, I'll give her that and having a ball.

"So, after all those years of Latin, you must speak it too," said Ben.

"Yes, once. Once but not anymore. Sadly unless one uses them, languages can be forgotten . . . and I've had a lot of other things on my mind these past years."

Von Kleist surmised that the novelty of seeing and talking to a captured German soldier was Ben's motive for being there. He wondered how he would handle a confrontation.

"What brings you so early in the morning to the Graham's farm, Ben?"

"Milk."

"Milk?"

"Yeah, my father thinks unpasteurized milk is better for you and Mr. Graham sells us some before the rest goes to the milk company."

"Your father is not afraid, then, of the disease a person can get from drinking unpasteurized milk?"

"He's mentioned something called 'undulant fever'. He says, however, people have been drinking milk for centuries without getting sick."

"Is that what you think?"

Again Ben felt the strangeness of talking to a tank commander about milk.

"He may be right about the odds of getting sick, but there is no doubt a risk, or why go to the trouble of pasteurizing it?"

Interesting, thought von Kleist; the boy is torn between two loyalties, to his father and to logic.

Ben then commented on the book the German had been reading.

"I see you're reading a book by Fitzgerald. I just finished reading one of his novels, *This Side of Paradise*."

"Is that so? *The Great Gatsby* was given to me by an American officer. I've finished reading it. Would you consider trading books with me? *Gatsby* is very good."

Now here was an amazing idea, trading books with an enemy tank commander. Would that be proper? That problem was already solved however.

"I can't, because the book wasn't mine. It was loaned to me by a neighbor and I've already returned it."

"I understand. It was only an idea. But, here, take *Gatsby*. You'll like it and I won't be reading it again—not for many years anyway."

Here was a break in the conversation and Ben knew he was already late getting back.

"I have to go. I've got to take the milk home and then go to work."
"What kind of work do you do?"

"Mow lawns. My friend Eddie White and I have a lawn mowing business this summer."

"Ah, Eddie is already working and I am holding you here."

"No, no. No problem. I liked talking to you and thanks for the book."

"You are welcome and I also enjoyed talking. Maybe on your next trip for milk we can talk again."

Hesitantly, Ben said, "OK" although he wasn't sure. To come to see this man again was like forming a relationship with an enemy soldier.

Gerhard watched Tim and Ben walk away. Nice boys, he thought. They treated him with respect as had the other Americans they'd come in contact with since becoming prisoners. His thoughts went to the young girl, Cookie. His curiosity was tweaked. He thought of her picking on one boy, Ben. He'd bet she had a crush on him. To be able to speak Latin after a year's study, even haltingly, was very impressive. So, a brilliant young girl had surveyed the field and picked out her man. It was his own story. Hilde was smarter—much smarter than he, He had always known this, yet she had found something in him that compensated for this inequality. It wasn't clear to von Kleist just what that something was, and since it wasn't clear, he hadn't known what he should do to keep her love alive. He had not seen her since his division had left for North Africa, now over three years. While fighting there had been little time to worry about her love. He had tucked a certainty of its existence into the back of his mind, not to be brought out and questioned. His survival had required this. But now with empty time on his hands, images of Hilde and the times they'd shared flowed in to fill his thoughts whenever a current task didn't command his attention. He couldn't realistically be certain she still cared for him. Her last letter had been right after the first battle of El Alamein, He carried it with him. The letter was pure Hilde, honest, unalloyed feelings.

He and she had been four years older than this American pair when they'd first met—nineteen and seventeen. She was the daughter of one of his university professors and he regarded her at first as he might a child—her hair worn in a single braid, no makeup. He was just as oblivious as this boy; Hilde knew what she wanted, he imagined Cookie did too.

Apparently Cookie didn't find it necessary to mute her capability for the boy's sake. Neither had Hilde. At only twenty-five she had earned a PhD and joined the faculty of the University of Munich as a junior

77

professor of linguistics—in Germany a very unusual performance at her age. But that was three years ago. It was torture not to know more. He put these thoughts out of his mind once more by shifting his attention to the men in the field. As usual he focused on Gefreiter Karl Hoffmann, his only real problem among them. For Karl the war wasn't over; he still believed in the inevitability of the "Thousand Year Reich." He regarded the attitudes of the other men, that they had fought a good fight and were now just waiting to go home, as being those of traitors to the cause. All of the other men except Karl took Germany's eventual defeat for granted. A small country like Germany was no match for the resources of the Americans and the English, and the Russians since Stalingrad were unstoppable. Hoffmann could not share that view. In spite of being out of ammunition, gasoline and most of their water, he regarded Von Kleist's surrendering the battalion to the Americans as an especial act of betrayal deserving, von Kleist had no doubt, of the death penalty.

Keeping an eye on Hoffmann was his main reason for choosing to come with the men out to the farms.

His father came out of the house the moment Ben drove into the driveway.

"You're late," he called out brusquely. Recognizing this he attempted to soften it with a joke. "Were the cows reluctant to give up their milk this morning?"

Ben could have thought of some easy excuse, but he told the true story. "I took a few minutes to talk to a German prisoner. They are working at the farm. He was the commander of a tank battalion."

Mr. Roberts was taken aback. "Really. I'd heard a little about their being in the area picking beans. A tank commander, huh? How did that come about—talking to this man?"

Ben explained the way it had happened, but not a full account of all that had been said. He held up *The Great Gatsby*. "He gave me this."

"He did?" He thought of asking why, but instead said, "Tell me about it later, because I've got to get going. Oh, and by the way, I talked to Rosa on the phone just now. A woman who lives at her house is missing and Rosa said she is a teacher at the high school. I think she said, Blanca. Do you know a teacher named Blanca?"

"Miss Martinez. Her name is Blanca. What do you mean she's missing? When?"

His father hadn't been very interested and only half listened to what his cook had said. "I think Rosa said last night. Apparently she went somewhere last night and hasn't come back yet. That's all Rosa knew." He started the engine and backed out of the drive.

Ben wondered where she might have gone. Yesterday Hugh Bates said she'd been fired. Maybe she'd left town already.

He hurried into the house with the milk, put it in the refrigerator, called out,"Mom," and getting no answer ran upstairs to get a clean sport shirt and a towel, then dashed outside to get the mower from the garage, flipped it over to free wheel and began running with it along the sidewalk to the Henderson's house. He was late. He had wanted to get the grass cut before Valery came to pick him up, leaving only the trimming to be done after lunch. He started off pushing the mower across the lawn at a run, only to have to concede that it bounced so much the cutting was uneven. He had to slow down and let the day's work unwind as it would. A quarter of an hour before Valery was due to arrive, he took off his sweaty shirt and sluiced down his upper body

79

with the hose at the side of the house. Now came the towel and the clean shirt. He walked out to the street to wait for her. In spite of it being her invitation, he harbored some doubt that she would show up. He didn't understand her and began preparing himself for a possible disappointment.

Summer recess had begun and it was Saturday besides, but Kyle Sexton hoped the principal would still be finishing up tasks at the school. He drove past the athletic field and slowed when he came to the three-story brick building. He had never been to the school building proper, only to the gym, a separate stone structure. Jutting toward the street, a section of the building presented a classic Greek facade, six columns flanking five doorways. Auditorium came to his mind. On the wide lintel supported by the columns he noticed an inscription. He stopped the car to read, "Dedicated to the Sanctity of Child Personality." Surprised, he read it again. "Child Personality." He'd never read anything like that inscribed on a public school. He was sure the administrators of his high school never considered that a child had a personality let alone one worthy of sanctity. If his school had had an inscription it would have read, "Children Should Be Seen and Not Heard." It occurred to him that this might be a pretty good place to go school, even though it had not been a place for a good-looking, Mexican/American woman to get a fair shake.

The main entrance door was farther along and stood open. Kyle parked and went inside. The hallway was empty, but he heard voices. They came from the administration office where a secretary dressed casually in slacks was stacking file folders into a cardboard box. She was talking to someone in an inner office. A man similarly dressed in casual work clothes appeared in the office doorway and noticed Sexton. The man's first impulse was to say that the office was closed, but he concluded quickly that the visitor probably knew that already and had a reason to be there anyway.

"Good morning, we're packing things away for the summer. Can I help you?"

"Yes, I'm Detective Kyle Sexton of the Hendersonville Police. I'm hoping the principal might still be here. I'd like to ask him a few questions about one of his teachers."

"I see. I'm the principal, Paul Burdick."

He glanced toward his secretary. She returned an half surprised, half knowing look. She'd told Burdick only a few minutes earlier that Blanca Martinez's landlady had called yesterday afternoon to ask if the school had heard from the teacher.

"If you'd step into my office I'd be happy to talk to you."

Burdick hoped this hadn't to do with his having terminated Miss Martinez's contract, a sensitive issue for him.

"Please have a seat, Detective. How can I help you?"

"Thank you, sir. As you may have heard a teacher of yours, Miss Blanca Martinez, is missing and I'd like to get some information from you."

Paul Burdick nodded. "Yes, I heard something about that a few minutes ago."

"Only this morning?"

"Yes, my secretary told me the young woman's landlady called yesterday to find out if we had heard from her. I'd already left for the day."

"I see," said Sexton while thinking the call hadn't aroused any urgent concern in the secretary. "We heard this morning from Miss Martinez's aunt in Houston that her family has no knowledge of where she might be, so we are now treating it as a case of suspicious disappearance. My coming here is part of our routine investigation."

"I'm very sorry to hear this. I'm afraid I know nothing that would help you. I hope the reason for her absence turns out to be simple."

Sexton, while pitching his voice to reflect "routine" was focused on Burdick's reactions, his manner, tone of voice. He thought the man's concern was genuine.

Burdick went on, "She is a very likeable young woman. If you don't know already, I must tell you, however, that we did not offer her a contract to teach here next year. This was not because she was not potentially a good teacher, but because she had a problem - ah - maintaining control of her class,"

Burdick sat for a moment trying to pull together a sterile presentation of a hot subject. Realizing such an attempt would appear phony, he decided to relate an unvarnished version of the situation.

"The fact is, Detective, Miss Martinez is a very sexually attractive young woman only a few years older than the boys in her class. This aroused very natural feelings in them. She wasn't able to put a lid on their behavior, which became progressively more . . . inappropriate. Things were said, written on the blackboard before class and so on. I think she was too good natured to slap the offenders down—so to speak. If it had been a problem of class disruption such as talking in class, teasing girls, things like that, she may have come to me for help. I think it was embarrassing to come and say the boys had sexual feelings toward her.

"Anyway, by the time I heard what was happening, the community already knew. Two mothers came to talk to me. One of them was the President of the Parents' Association. Her daughter was in Miss Martinez's class. Both mothers demanded that she be fired immediately. That was about a month ago. They placed all the blame on her."

"And you didn't stick up for her?" Kyle was irritated and it just came out.

"Believe me, I wish I could have. They were both adamant and it was clear they were out for . . . well that they wouldn't take no for an answer. Both had voiced objections against my hiring her in the first place. The situation that had developed gave them the leverage they needed in order to convince other parents that the young woman must be fired. I could see no way that my resistance wouldn't have ended badly for Miss Martinez"

Burdick saw he was not going to get easy compliance from Sexton.

"Anyway, if it makes a difference, I'm not at all happy about what I decided I had to do—seek a compromise that would permit her to complete the school year. That way in any letter of recommendation to future employers I could say her reason for leaving was because she had wanted to relocate. I promised the mothers she would not be here next year."

Sexton heard Burdick saying he had been forced to do what he did for Blanca's good. How about telling the mothers to kiss his ass?

"When did you tell her?"

"Right away, so she'd be able to start making plans for next year. I promised her that she'd get a very good recommendation from me."

"How did she take it?"

"That's a good question. She was surprised at first and looked hurt, but then nodded as if she understood, maybe even expected it and then strangely enough, it seemed to me she didn't really care. That puzzled me, because I knew she couldn't have much money and should be concerned. She just stood up and thanked me."

Kyle sized Burdick up and decided he was probably a decent guy placed in a difficult spot—a difficult spot, because he was afraid to stand up to two parents—a guy who needed to avoid trouble with those with influence, but not from a young woman with none. But then, Kyle thought, maybe he was being unfair. Burdick had given her an opportunity. How many schools around here would have hired a Mexican/American woman?

"You said you told her 'right away'. When was that exactly?"

Burdick took up a calendar on his desk. "A week ago last Wednesday."

"You decided to let her go a month ago and only told her a week ago?"

He didn't ask why. He knew why. The guy was afraid of what her reaction would be. He let Burdick feel his condemnation for a long moment.

"What do you know about her friends here in the school - outside activities?"

"Nothing. She did not establish any relationships with other teachers that I know of. She was . . . well she was foreign of course. That is she was .. "

"And younger perhaps?"

"Yes, very much younger."

"And very sexy."

Burdick allowed uncomfortably, "Yes, that too."

"OK. Thanks for being frank with me. I think I have a good picture."

84

With those words Sexton stood up. "Will you be in town? I may have other questions."

"For the next two weeks, yes. I hope to heaven nothing bad has happened to her."

Sexton left the office and began walking toward the building entrance. He had one more interview in mind here at the school. He wanted to talk to the basketball coach. Rosa Sanchez said he'd taken Martinez to a dance. Kyle followed high school sports—what else was there here in western North Carolina for a spectator—no nearby college or professional teams, only radio. He'd seen the coach at the games he'd gone to, but had never talked to him. He remembered his name was Colin Dobbs. Two boys were walking toward him along the hallway.

He raised his hand in greeting and said, "Can you fellas tell me where I can find Mr. Dobbs, the basketball coach?"

"The gym. I don't know if he's there. School's over. Anyway that's where his office is."

"Thanks, much obliged."

The boys hadn't thought to tell Kyle where the gym was. After all, to them it was one of the earth's centers. And, he did know. He turned left at the next hallway and followed it to the back exit of the building. The gym, a free standing stone structure, lay up a small rise about forty yards away. As he walked there he thought of how Burdick had been uncomfortable when he'd said "sexy." Obviously Martinez had aroused the guy. Was there more than arousal? He filed the thought for later.

The large high-ceilinged gym was empty and the silence was at first surprising, because the other times he'd been here the noise level had been deafening: shouting, screaming, laughing, cheering. There were

85

doors at each of the gym's corners. Which one? He chose the door to his left. He stopped after having taken three steps inside. The strong odor of wintergreen said locker room. He walked to the adjacent corner. The door there was open. A man stood at a desk studying an open catalog. Sexton knocked gently on the door frame and the man looked up—a look not unfriendly, but not exactly friendly either.

"Can I help you?" he asked, as he turned another page of the catalog.

Colin Dobb's good looks could have been used for the poster seen everywhere that stated, "Tell it to the Marines!" The last time Kyle had seen him was at the league championship game. Hendersonville won and the players were going wild. Then Kyle noticed Dobbs reaction. He wasn't joining in with the team's joy. Instead, his was a look of smug satisfaction. Kyle had thought no more of it at the time, but Dobb's present attitude brought back the memory.

"I'm Detective Sexton of the Hendersonville Police. I want to ask you a few questions, but first let me congratulate you and your team on the championship."

"Thanks," was the flat, automatic reply.

He'd heard something else about Dobbs. Parents of players were unhappy with how ruthlessly long and hard he made them practice.

"The reason I'm here is the disappearance of a teacher, Blanca Martinez."

Dobbs turned to face Sexton, leaning back against his desk with his arms crossed over his chest, his expression wary.

"Disappeared you say?"

"You hadn't heard?"

"No. When was this?"

So far Kyle judged the man's surprise to be genuine.

"She hasn't been seen since Thursday and it's beginning to look like it wasn't of her choice."

"That explains why I haven't heard. I've been in Milledgeville, Georgia since last Wednesday—the funeral of an uncle, my father's brother. Didn't get back until this morning. I haven't had a chance to talk to anyone. I didn't know her at all."

A solid alibi, thought Kyle, if true. "I'm told you went to a dance with her a couple of months ago."

"Where did you hear that?"

"It's not true?"

Dobbs delayed answering, but seeing he had no recourse answered, "Yes, that's true. Would you mind telling me if you heard that from anyone connected with the school?"

"From the woman she lives with."

Dobbs nodded. He then unfolded his arms and gripped the edge of the desk, seeming to relax. "Nothing much to tell. She was a very attractive woman. I became, uh, interested and thought . . . you know."

"Thought what?"

Dobbs looked Sexton in the eyes to see if he were only a detective or whether a man-to-man understanding was possible. "Thought maybe I could get me a piece."

Kyle was surprised by the blunt answer. Was this an attempt to manipulate, or was it a raw, undefended reply?

"And?" said Kyle.

"I didn't know what was possible. Blue Barron's band was playing in Asheville. I thought it was far enough away from here and not the kind of thing anyone from the school would attend. We danced a couple of numbers. She was a very good dancer and easy to talk to. But then I noticed three senior boys from school and their dates come into the hall. The shock I felt when I saw them pushed aside any other ideas I'd had and I immediately recognized I was playing with fire—as far as my carer was concerned."

"What do you mean by that?"

"Getting involved with another teacher is a risky thing. That is if you're not headed toward marriage."

"That's so?"

"Right after ministers—no, make that even before ministers—school teachers are the most closely scrutinized people in our society for improper behavior. Well, I had no thought of marrying her."

Sexton raised his eyebrows in question.

"Not my type . . . and she was an outsider."

Kyle didn't need to ask what he meant.

"So, what did you do—at the dance hall?"

"I made an excuse, said we had to leave."

"An excuse?"

Dobbs looked down and away. "I said the only thing that came to mind. Something I'd heard women in movies say. I said I was sorry, but I had a headache."

Sexton managed to suppress laughter but couldn't do the same for a smile. "And so you left."

"Yes, I was embarrassed and I thought about stopping for some food - give the woman something for coming out with me, but I realized that would contradict my excuse, so I just swallowed the whole fucked up mess and took her home. I haven't spoken to her since."

Sexton wondered if this were all true. Another scenario might have been that he'd gotten what he wanted, intended to drop Martinez, who wouldn't go quietly so he silenced her for good. A grim possibility, but Kyle didn't think it likely. He judged Dobbs was telling the truth. Checking out his alibi of the funeral would settle this. He could ask Dobbs for the uncle's address in Milledgeville, but if Dobbs had lied, he would hurry and cover that lie. Sexton thought it likely he'd end up talking to someone at the given address who'd back the lie. He'd check it out another way. One other thing was on his mind, Dobbs kept referring to Martinez in the past tense, "was a good dancer." Any meaning there, or did it just mean she was past history for him?

"Thanks for explaining. I see no reason to tell anyone about this."

"Good and thanks. It's important to me."

"Oh, what was your uncle's name?"

The question surprised him. So he was still a suspect. "Jarrod— Jarrod Dobbs."

Kyle left feeling sad for Blanca Martinez. She had only accepted an invitation to a dance and now she was persona non grata—dead or alive.

Walking from the building, he reviewed what he'd learned. What stood out was the principal's surprise at Martinez's attitude of indifference to being fired. It stood out because it matched Rosa Sanchez's similar impression. It certainly made one think she had other plans other than remaining a teacher at that school.

But here came Valery, right on time driving the family's Mercury station wagon. The relief he felt seeing her told of his doubts. Getting into the car beside her he almost said, "A guy could get used to this kind of service," but realized in time that the remark carried the assumption of continued service, which he was afraid to assume. This left him with nothing to say.

"Been hard at work all morning?" she asked.

Ah, here was a topic. "Only a couple of hours. Early this morning I was talking to a German war prisoner." He went on at length until he wondered, judged by her lack of questions, that it might be more than she wanted to hear, or even that she thought his interest in an enemy soldier was unpatriotic. He ended his monologue with, "Anyway, we have them working."

That was clearly the end of that subject. He tried something open-ended. "And what have you been doing this morning?"

"Oh, getting my clothes in order for the summer—what I can use, what needs to be replaced."

Her mention of clothes caused him to focus on what she was wearing: jersey top that left the midriff bare, shorts with cuffs and sandals. She was as beautiful at mid-day as she was in the evening.

Ben supposed that "getting clothes in order" was a girl thing. He knew what he would wear, the same things he wore last summer: bell-bottom jeans rolled up above the ankle or suntan khakis again rolled to show white athletic socks and with these, a white T-shirt under a sport-shirt worn unbuttoned and outside. The shoes were the ubiquitous Keds or his regular leather shoes with plaid laces.

In the background hovered the question of Valery's motives. Where did they stand, was this lunch to be the "another time." She said there'd just be the two of them. Or was this only a way to retrieve her image after her *savoir faire* had dissolved at the lake.

She turned into the mountain laurel lined drive of the Sinclair estate. The bushes were so dense and high that only an occasional glimpse into the grounds was possible. They emerged onto an open, gravel-covered parking area the size of two basketball courts. Across the lot a wide two-story colonnaded porch reached out toward the visitor. Only the center section of the building was double-storied, single story wings extended on each side. Noon sun reflected brilliantly off the freshly painted white façade. Tall square columns were a bit obviously a tip of the hat to antebellum splendor, but impressive nevertheless. The white Continental rested in the shade of towering pines at one end of the parking area.

"Damn, Daddy's home," said Valery, surprised.

Ben looked over at her.

"I didn't know he was coming back," she said shrugging.

She switched off the engine. Did her shrug mean, "Another time" once more?

"I'll take you on a short tour before lunch."

Once again her role was leader, his was follower. She led him on a flagstone path that skirted the house. They crossed a stone terrace on which stood a wrought iron table with chairs. A French window provided access to the house. Leaving the terrace, the path plunged into the jungle of laurels. From what he's seen so far, Ben figured one couldn't earn much money mowing the grass on the estate.

Now before them as they emerged into full sunlight was the feature Valery had been heading toward, a pond that Ben guessed to be over an acre.

"Daddy's fish pond," she announced in a tone indicating it was his toy. "He had it made."

Much effort had gone into its construction. The natural creek that was its source had been made to enter it over a waterfall. Boulders, some partially submerged in the water, bulrushes and willows managed to look placed by nature.

Ben's scanning stopped at a collection of water lilies on the far side of the pond.

Valery noticed. "Those lilies were given to him by the Japanese Ambassador—before the war," she laughed.

"You said 'fish pond', so there must be fish."

"Lots of fish - maybe too many. They keep breeding."

"What kind?"

"I'm really not the one to ask. We eat trout mostly. As I understand it, the pond is spring-fed and cold. Trout like that."

"And your father catches them for your table?"

"You better believe it. I like trout, but not as often as he'd like us to eat it. Ulla takes most of the fish home to her neighbors—she's our cook."

She waited a moment then added, "Ulla said she'd heard a teacher from your school is missing."

Ben thought, "It's a small community. News travels fast."

"Yeah, that's right, the Spanish teacher. The woman she lives with works for my father. She told him that Miss Martinez went on a date last night and didn't come home."

"Wow, so it happened last night?"

"Yeah. She was well liked by most of the kids."

"Most of the kids?"

"A couple of girls had it in for her'

Valery took his arm and turned him toward the house.

"I asked Ulla to make us BLT's."

"Great. I'm hungry."

Reaching the terrace, Ben saw that two places had been set on the table awaiting their return, also an inviting pitcher of lemonade.

Valery filled their glasses. "Anything else new besides your collaborating with the enemy."

He knew she was teasing, or was she. Could she really be questioning his loyalty?

"No, I can't think of anything," he said despairing to come up with something to fascinate her.

The French door opened and a woman whom Ben judged to be past middle age came onto the terrace carrying a tray. She put a plate holding a sandwich and several slivered carrots at each place.

"Ulla, I'd like you to meet a friend of mine, Ben Roberts. Ben, this is Mrs. Holden."

"Pleased to meet you, Ma'am."

"Pleased to meet you, son."

This marked a significant moment in Ben's life although he wasn't consciously aware of it. He was fifteen and had lived in the south his whole life, yet this was the first time he had spoken to, and only the second time he had been spoken to by someone who wasn't white. Until three years ago his family lived in North Miami, an all white lower middle class community. Which meant that residents did their own house and yard work—no servants or gardeners. His parents and he went to downtown Miami on many Saturday nights, but only Caucasians were in sight. He didn't know if this was true, but the story was that colored people had to be across the tracks in their own neighborhood, Liberty City, before sundown. He'd heard nothing prejudicial in his home. His mother was from Michigan and his father was from England. Race was never a topic, although he knew his mother was strongly against segregation and said on several occasions that all people are alike. His father, he had discerned, was more prone to discrimination, but those he singled out were the Irish.

This was the second time he had been spoken to by a non-white. The first time had been only a month earlier. He had previously ridden the city bus from downtown to his home on two occasions. Both times he had climbed in, dropped his dime in the box next to the driver and taken the first seat he'd come to. Each time there had been no more than four other passengers sitting in the front rows of the bus, but he had noticed several colored women sitting in the very back. This banishment to the back of the bus was one of his mother's targets of outrage. As a result, on both if these rides he had felt self-conscious to be sitting up front, as if he were guilty of participating in a great wrong. The third—and certainly the last time—he'd take the bus, he had just emerged from Cam's Sport Shop where he'd heard Cam tell him that he had a "perfect athletic build" and was destined to be a star on the high school football team. An objective adult listening to Cam and at the same time viewing the object of his praise would no doubt conclude that Cam was a good salesman. Ben was not usually prone to solicit or believe praise, but on this occasion he bought it enough to leave the shop feeling pumped up. He didn't have his bike and was about to start the walk home, when the bus pulled up at the bus stop right in front of him. Jauntily he swung aboard and dropped a dime in the box. An old guy occupied one of the front row seats. At the rear, Ben saw four colored women sitting in the very back. In the next second he found himself cockily walking to the back where he sat down across the aisle from one of the women.

His had not been a well thought out move rooted in deep conviction or with a calculated purpose of protest. Being temporarily full of himself, he was thumbing his nose at convention while serving as his mother's knight-errant. He was unaware, of course, of the complexity of his motives. He had done a brave and good thing—until the driver, having noticed Ben's action in the mirror, yelled to him.

"Hey boy, you don't belong back there. Come back up here."

There was irritation in the driver's voice. Ben heard himself being reprimanded by an adult, a fat, not very bright looking adult, but an adult nevertheless, and Ben heard adults as just that until he could get far enough away to relegate them to insignificance. He didn't know what to do. To obey the guy would be an embarrassing loss of face. He continued to sit there.

"Boy, I ain't moving this bus until you do what I'm tellin' you!"

The old guy in the front row looked back and scowled.

Now the situation had become more problematic; if he didn't move the bus wouldn't either. What he did now affected the other passengers. It would still be a loss of face to obey the stupid driver. He now felt incapable of moving.

"Boy, you better hear me," the driver threatened.

It was at this point that the woman across the aisle spoke to him. He would never know if what she said was true, or if she had just come to his aid.

"Honey, do what the man say. I gotta get home to my kids."

She had handed him a "get out of jail free" card. As he walked forward it came to him that he didn't have to obey the jerk of a driver and take a seat up front, he could get off the goddamn bus. And he did.

"Thank you, Ulla, and thank you for the carrots," said Valery with irony. She turned to Ben, "Ulla insists that unless I eat carrots, I'll go

95

blind, and as you see, it hasn't happened yet."

"You won't be laughing young lady if you have to get glasses before your time." She said this with the weary acceptance of the teacher who knows she is burdened with a recalcitrant student.

She shifted her gaze to the carrots on Ben's plate. He quickly picked up two slivers and tossed them in his mouth.

She smiled. "What you become depends on the kind of company you keep. Perhaps there's hope for you yet, young lady."

With that Ulla left the terrace.

The sandwich was delicious and Ben was very hungry after his full morning of work. He had just taken a second bite, when a tall, heavy-set man burst through the French doors.

"Let me have a bite of your sandwich," he said and strode to Valery's chair and commandeered half of her sandwich.

"I'm Val's father," he offered in Ben's direction, perhaps as an introduction and perhaps as an explanation.

Ben felt he should respond although his mouth was filled with the large bite he'd taken. He pointed at his chest and said, "Ben Roberts."

The congressman swallowed, "Pleased to meet you, sir." and held out a large hand.

Shaking hands, Ben was conscious of twin thoughts: This is the famous congressman, and that it was the first time anyone had called him, "sir."

"I'd guess you're a Bearcat—football. Am I right?"

"Ah . . . yes, sir."

"I was a Bearcat a long time ago."

"Yes, sir, I know."

"You're a sophomore and an end, right?"

96

Ben laughed. "Right again. How did you know?"

"Elementary my dear Watson. You look the right age to be a sopho-more. If you're not playing football for Hendersonville you should be. The way you pointed to yourself says confidence, so you're on the team. An end? You're tall, rangy, have good hands."

Ben was overwhelmed. All he could return was a helpless chuckle.

Troy Sinclair held up the half sandwich. "Have Ulla make you another. I've got to run." He looked at Ben. "Nice meeting you, Ben. I'll look for you on the field in the fall. I can brag to my friends that I know you." With that he rushed through the door into the house as if he was late for something.

Valery studied Ben. What was his reaction to the phenomenon of Congressman Sinclair. Probably typical, she thought. Ben now was firmly in the Congressman's camp.

After the sandwich came a slice of Key lime pie. At his last swallow, Valery stood. "When I invited you, I promised to deliver you back to your mower in an hour. I keep my promises."

She said that while laughing, but Ben had the feeling he was being ushered off stage in order to move on to the next act. Was she dis-pleased, because her father being home had upset her plans? Or, did she feel he'd up-staged her? She remained an enigma. Maybe that piqued his interest, this promise of intimacy that failed to advance beyond cordiality - cordiality with a hint of volcanic possibility.

They had just consumed the midday meal: fried chicken, boiled potatoes and a treatment of green beans that seemed to be a staple here, cross-cut and cooked to death with pork fat. He was beginning to like the beans. He took his chair into the shade at the side of the bean field. At his feet was the copy of *Tom Jones* given him by the American commander of the camp in South Carolina. It was a used copy the American had bought for him when he'd heard von Kleist say that it was his favorite English novel. He picked up the book and surveyed the field before opening it. The noon sun caused scintillations of heat to rise from the raw earth distorting the men's shapes as in a surrealist painting. It felt unnatural to be separated from them. He ate with the men, but they parted when it came to physical labor. The men truly wanted it this way. With the exception of Karl Hoffmann, he was a hero of almost mythic magnitude to the other men—equal no less to Rommel himself. His tactical brilliance, his unerring judgement of the possible and his audacity on the battlefield had kept the battalion intact, making it possible for most of them to survive. This he'd managed while—for the greater part of the campaign they believed—they'd also bettered the enemy. This last meant a great deal to how the men felt about themselves and how they were able to accept defeat—defeat after their last round of ammunition had been fired.

The morning had been difficult. Hoffmann had been in a provocative mood. The other men tried to ignore him or humor him, but they'd reached a point when even the most even-tempered of his men couldn't resist a comeback. That, of course, was what Hoffmann sought. Open fighting would surely have followed if Gerhard hadn't stepped in forcefully. Fortunately, Hoffmann still followed von Kleist's shouted order to cease. *Schweigen Sie!* A charged silence followed this command with Hoffmann's vitriol blocked and the other men still wanting to deck him. Gerhard could report Hoffmann's behavior to the American commanding officer—problem solved. Although he was a pain in the ass, the men still thought of him as one of theirs. His expulsion would be seen as a betrayal of sorts. The situation had to be tolerated.

Gerhard had tried to put himself in the man's mind, to understand what stoked his hatred. He had tried to engage Hoffmann in expressing himself in a calm way, but to no avail. It was clear the man needed to preserve his grievance. Gerhard suspected his demon had little to do with his stated reasons, but sprang from deep within his personality.

At the beginning of the war, some of the men in the battalion had been whole-hearted believers in Hitler's vision. Over the last years, however, their zeal had cooled to lukewarm and had finally arrived at a resignation that it had been a bogus vision from the start, but they'd been true to their comrades and that knowledge had made it possible to retain their self-esteem. To a man, with the exception of Hoffmann, all they wanted now was for the war to end speedily and for them to be able to go home. For those who had hated the Nazi gang from the outset, as he did, the insufferable conflict of being made to fight for Hitler's objectives was over. The experience of working together as a unit under the command of a leader they admired, fighting natural fear to do what was required and sharing the grief of losses as well as occasions of elation was what they would carry home.

The memory of their experience could not really be shared with anyone else except these other men and they would soon be going their separate ways. As much as they yearned for their homecoming, it was mingled with sadness for the anticipated dissolution of the unique bonds they'd formed. This parting would come sometime soon. Germany's defeat was sure. American news media, which Gerhard believed to be fairly reliable, told the story of inevitable retreat from the Soviet Union and the certain fall of Italy to the Allies. Germany needed to surrender and avoid unnecessary destruction. So far Hitler showed no sign of such sanity.

What would Gerhard take away from these past years? He knew that war was man's fall into primitive absurdity—a primordial subcortical reflex. His own ironic saying was that war was, "the ultimate failure of discussion." Yet at the same time, the life of his battalion had provided the most intense and unalloyed experience of community that he'd ever likely know; men working together in harmony and trust to preserve each others lives and at the same time earning each other's respect. In the midst of battle he'd only been aware of total concentration, total application to the desperate demand of the moment. And yes, although it was a confession that belied his preferred notion of himself, he had felt brief visceral exhilaration in destroying the enemy. It was only afterward that the cost was reckoned. The momentary elation of thinking oneself smarter and braver than the other side brought a flood of joy, which was always followed by the pain of the reality of the death and horrible maiming of comrades and the indelible image of the ghastly destruction of good men of the other side. Repeated was the memory visual and tactile of kneeling beside his good friend Hans Kuhn whose arm had been blown off at the shoulder by a bomb. Desperately, Gerhard had tried, but failed to stop the pulsing arterial bleeding that gushed between his fingers, his bare hands the only means of applying pressure, while Hans looked up at him appealing for him to save his life.

He'd assured Hans over and over, "It's going to be all right," until his eyes lost focus and his breathing stopped. Gerhard knew this vivid image would be with him for the rest of his life. Alma Halfa, the name of a unremarkable rocky ridge was a name more engraved in his brain now than that of the most beautiful places he'd known. Repeated also was the image of the British soldier emerging from his burning tank to run totally engulfed in flames before collapsing in death. During battle he'd been able to quickly place these thoughts in a locker to be considered later. Since their surrender there had been many moments for those "laters." Grief and shame were now familiar companions. He knew now that it was not alone about the horrors of war that made many veterans reluctant to talk. They were also afraid to open paths to shame.

So how was it that we can permit ourselves to repeat the madness of war? He thought, sitting there in the shade, he'd caught hold of the answer to that question just as it was attempting to slip away into hiding once again. He felt the strong pull toward dimming and suppressing the image of the burning Brit. This is what we do, isn't it? We repress the bad image and install in its place a whitewashed version, memories of good times with friends, moments of victory. Some years ago he had undertaken an alpine adventure with three friends. The goal was to climb one of the minor peaks, one bested many times by other climbers, but still a difficult challenge. Unwisely they had setout at the shoulder off the climbing season with the increased chance of unpredictable weather. They experienced an early winter storm that immobilized them for four days of perfect hell, during which frostbite caused two of his friends to lose toes on both feet. Immediately afterward, during the rescue by the mountain emergency team and treatment in the hospital, the awareness of their pain and their stupidity stood front and center in their thoughts. But apparently this memory of pain couldn't be tolerated long psychologically and it began to be repressed leaving in its place memories of comradeship and the notion of having done something "macho."

There was even talk of assaulting another even more difficult peak. That never happened, but it could well have. Was this the reason we are willing to consider, even favor, getting into another war? We repress the abject idiocy of the experience we've just had and in its' place we substitute a self-congratulating fiction. War, Gerhard knew, could be driven by national policy of greed or hatred, but if it were not for this human trait to repress the memory of pain and guilt, those wishing to go to war would find no followers. The would-be soldiers would shout, "Go to Hell!" But then, he reminded himself that youth had no memories and so was ever ready to offer itself as cannon fodder.

He believed he was right, but he didn't want to think about the subject any longer. He opened *Tom Jones*.

Later that afternoon, Ben climbed the steps to the White's front porch and knocked on the screen door. A few moments later, Cookie was looking at him through the screen.

"You don't go to church," she said out of the blue.

"What?"

"You don't go to church like everyone else . . . why?" she said opening the door and coming outside.

"Now where the hell did that come from?"

She cocked an eyebrow. "You're not answering the question."

No one had ever asked him that before. That wasn't exactly true; his third grade teacher on Monday mornings had made all those who had been to Sunday school raise their hands and she recorded this on a chart fixed to the bulletin board. He'd never gone, but he knew what was expected and always raised his hand. He may have been the only class member with a perfect attendance record.

"How do you know if I go to church or not?"

"I just do."

Ben was stymied. He didn't want to discuss this.

"So?" she persisted.

"Why do you want to know?"

"I just do."

She didn't say that she wanted to know everything about him.

"You've got a sunburn. Didn't wear a hat did you?" she said.

"Ah." He put his hand up to his face,

Her expression hinted at the combined affection and resignation of a mother whose child had once again lost his or her gloves.

Ben shook his head as if baffled. "Where's Eddie?"

"Out back."

Still shaking his head, Ben began to retreat down the porch steps as she continued,"Eddie's in the back yard swearing at the mower Moses lent him."

Ben found his friend on his knees next to the mower, which he had partly dismantled.

Eddie looked up at Ben standing over him. "I don't know how Moses managed to use this fucking thing. The drive gear is so worn that it only catches on every third cog."

Eddie's use of the "f" word was jolt. Not that Ben was offended, but it was unusual to hear it. Among his friends, one almost never heard it—not even in the football locker room. It took a desperate level of frustration to free the word up.

"Not good," Ben offered. "I noticed a mower repair place in

Asheville. Maybe they'd have some parts."

"Maybe. It would have to be a salvaged part. I'm sure they don't make parts for a mower this old. You can't even tell what brand it is."

Cookie materialized. "Confucius say man who start lawn-mowing business should first have working lawn mower."

Eddie raised his eyes slowly to study her, saying sarcastically, "Thank you Confucius."

If not prejudiced by his charged sibling feelings, Eddie would have seen a slender, taller than average, attractive, dark-haired girl whose intelligent face featured soft, understanding, brown eyes. Adults would recognize in the facial bone structure of this pubescent girl a promise of future beauty and they'd be impressed by her solid sense of her own worth. She wore sandals, shorts and a checked blouse worn outside. There was no gawky adolescent clumsiness in her movement. The opposite was evident as she floated down stairs two and three steps at a time. Once in movement, she rarely touched the handlebars of her bike. Unfortunately there were no high school team sports for girls. Girls only played basketball during gym. A girl could hold the ball for three steps and then she had to pass it—proper southern ladies didn't run—or sweat or throw the ball with force or accuracy. The sport she loved was horseback riding, but could only manage to do it every week or two. Her aunt had an apple orchard and two riding horses on a farm twelve miles away. She would happily ride that distance every day, but riding a bike that far alone was not permitted for a girl. Still, when she and Tinker Bell reunited it was a meeting of lovers, forehead to forehead, whispered words in Tinker Bell's ear.

For the school, Cookie presented a problem. None of the faculty had ever dealt with a student of her intelligence. She had been moved up only two grades, because the principal was afraid that further advancement would harm her social development, but all her teachers knew she was capable of so much more. They confided in each other that she knew more about the subjects they taught than they did, and so they could not do much more than encourage her. Which they were happy to do, because none left feeling their effort hadn't been appreciated. This courtesy didn't extend to her brother.

Cookie said, "Don't you think finding a replacement part for this ancient thing would be like looking for a needle . . . but then you'd never look for a needle."

Eddie gave her an irritated look and then went back to studying the defunct machine.

"Staring at it won't magically repair it," she said.

Ben had begun observing the sparring as he might watch two boxers circling each other. So far Cookie had been jabbing, Eddie taking a few soft ones on the chin while trying to look unfazed.

Cookie continued, "I'm sure you're aware that old Mr. Collingsworth, who lived at the end the block had a stroke and is now residing in a nursing home in Arden. His house will be sold and his daughter, Mrs. Stevens, who lives on 5th Avenue, now has to dispose of his furniture and other belongings."

Eddie looked at her in disbelief as if she had lost her mind or suddenly started speaking in tongues. "What in the world does that have to do with anything?"

"I'd say it's obvious. Old Mr. Collingsworth used to mow his own grass before he had the stroke—you must have observed that. Doesn't that suggest something to you?"

Eddie didn't reply. He was used to her provocative questions. He waited.

"His son-in-law now has two lawn mowers, his own and the old man's."

Ben watched Eddie as he first let himself consider what she had said and then begin to credit it. Before acknowledging the value of her contribution to the solution of his problem he needed to play for a little time.

"How do you know that?"

"I asked."

"You asked?"

"Yes, I took a jar of my blueberry jam over to Mrs. Stevens and asked if she had disposed of the mower yet. She said, 'No, do you know anyone who needs one?' I said I might."

Eddie said nothing. He noticed once again that his sister led a different mental life—related to people differently than he.

Cookie intuited what he was thinking. "My world is larger than a football field and there are people in it who aren't football players."

"Big deal."

"A simple thank you would suffice."

Ben had enjoyed the exchange. He got a kick out of Cookie's steady refusal to accept the role of little sister that Eddie demanded. He watched as she sauntered over to the herb garden to pick some mint for a sauce she'd said she was making for dinner, no doubt sure in her mind that she'd won the bout.

Eddie changed the subject. "I heard Miss Martinez is missing. The police believe she went on a date and didn't come back."

"Yeah, Dad told me. The woman Miss Martinez lives with works for him. Where did you hear about the date?"

"Mrs. Reilly next door told Mom. You know her old man is the mayor, and he got it from the police, of course."

Eddie dragged the old mower to the garage and leaned it against the wall. It was apparent he was taking Cookie's advice.

"I had lunch at Valery Sinclair's house today," Ben said trying to sound matter-of-fact.

Eddie stood looking at him until Ben had to smile.

"I'd call that a 'shit eatin' grin'," Eddie said. "At her house, huh?"

"Yeah, she called me last night and asked me. She picked me up at the Henderson's and brought me back."

"I can't believe this. Are you trying to tell me she's really interested in *you*?"

"I'll have to let the facts speak for themselves."

Putting the fencing aside, Eddie asked, "Was anyone else there?"

"Val thought there would just be the two of us and the cook, but her father was there unexpectedly."

"Did you meet him?"

"Yeah. He seems like a nice guy. He said he'd played football for the school."

"Is the house big?"

"Yeah, but I didn't go inside. We ate on the patio."

"So that was it—you ate lunch and left?"

Ben nodded.

"When are you seeing her again?"

"I don't know."

"You didn't ask her to do something?"

"Like what?"

"I'm beginning to see the picture. She asks you two times in a row to get together and you're waiting for her to make the next move."

Eddie then delivered his version of a country accent, "S'matter with you boy? You need hit'n over the head with some lumber?"

Ben knew that if Eddie had been aware of the skinny-dipping he'd be screaming at him. He now saw the situation as his friend did. He'd been experiencing Valery's attention as an inexplicable phenomenon that was happening to him and not an interaction in which he could— and should—be an active party.

"What can I ask her to do . . . go to a movie?"

Now Eddie began to address the problem. "Nah, a movie later maybe, but now you need to get her alone. Take her someplace like . . . like Crystal Falls. Maybe she hasn't been there."

"I haven't been there. Where is it?"

"Not far. Couple of miles past Flat Rock. There's a place to park and then you walk back into the woods for a quarter of a mile until you come to the falls. I've been there twice and it was deserted each time."

Ben imagined standing next to Valery looking at the falls, slipping his arm around her waist and kissing her. The problem was getting the car, but then she seemed to have no problem having a car. But how to contact her. Out of curiosity he'd already looked up her number and found none. Obviously the congressman wanted it to be unlisted. Riding his bike to her house and knocking on the door was a kid's method. He needed her phone number. Eddie was looking at him for a response to his suggestion about the falls.

"That's a good idea - get her to the falls. I'll call her."

Kyle sat in a booth alone at Carson's Cafe on Main Street. He'd

skipped lunch and had only eaten one of the homemade oatmeal cookies Flora had brought to the office that morning. He'd ordered a
hamburger, coffee and a piece of banana cream pie. The waitress was
new yet seemed experienced, and in more ways than waiting on tables
he guessed from the seductive way she lingered over pouring his coffee.

Yesterday, when he'd first picked up the dispatcher's report on
Blanca Martinez he'd been skeptical about her absence being serious.
After the information he'd gathered since then he was afraid it was a
very serious matter. He was feeling pessimistic that the outcome would
not be tragic.

His hamburger arrived. The waitress hung around smiling and
wanting to be sure he had any and all the condiments he wished. When
all she could get was his assurance that he had all he wanted, her smile
faded and she left him to his rumination, which centered on the question of where in the small city Blanca could have been taken on this
date he was sure she'd had. There were the two movie theaters, the
State and the Carolina. Restaurants: the Rosebud out on the Asheville
highway, the Hendersonville Inn around the corner on 2nd. Avenue,
and the more expensive and exclusive Country Club and the Mountain
Lodge. Sanchez worked in the kitchen of the Lodge and would have
known if Martinez had been taken there. He mentally crossed the
Country Club off the list. What member would take a Mexican woman
there for dinner?

Where else? The Elks Club? What did he know about the Elks Club:
only that they served illegal liquor and the Chief had told him and the
other cops to ignore that fact. The Chief belonged to the Elks. Was it a
place to take a young Mexican date? No. That about covered the available nightlife. Then there were the three sets of tourist cabins on roads

leading into the city. Asheville was another matter. Many possibilities there. He'd consider it after he'd checked out the local places. It was Saturday night, so he thought most of the staff that had been on duty Thursday night would be working tonight as well.

He paid his bill, went to his car to get his notebook and the picture of Martinez and began his round of inquires with the Carolina Theater.

At ten-twenty, he parked his car behind the bowling alley having received negative replies from everyone he'd talked to. The waitress at the Hendersonville Inn wasn't working, but the hostess who'd seated everyone Thursday was sure no one had been wearing an orange dress. He went home frustrated and even more worried about the young teacher—as well as being uneasy about his own performance.

Sunday June, 4th.

Johan Frisch, the chaplain, gave the closing benediction of the Sunday morning service. Gerhard walked up to him and shook his hand.

"Very apt sermon, Hans: You advised to work with the hand you're dealt, while keeping in mind that you are alive and this is one of your God-given days. Or as you phrased it much better, "You only have a few days. Don't piss on one.""

Frisch smiled. "Thanks, Major. I know you appreciate elegance of speech."

Although a non-believer, Gerhard's regular weekly compliment was sincere, since he credited Frisch with dependably mature common sense. At the very outset of his time as a commander, a senior officer had recommended—knowing of von Kleist's absence of religious belief—that regular, respectful attendance at the weekly service would help both him and those under his command. Help him, because he would be identified with the traditional authority of the church and God and this added to his own authority when giving orders, and help his men since it would enhance their feeling of security thinking their commander had the support of the Almighty. Gerhard had followed that advice and endorsed its wisdom. Besides, Frisch was a pleasant fellow with a good head and worth listening to.

The canteen coffee was strong and bitter, but good enough. He got a cup and went to his tent to get his copy of *Tom Jones* and a canvas folding-chair. In the angular space between the perimeter fence and an oak tree he had established what was recognized as the "Major's place." Removed as it was from the flow of the camp's foot traffic, he could relax and read without interruption, while still being part of the group. Making relaxation more possible on Sundays was Karl Hoffmann's feverish love of soccer, which he played all day and which rendered him exhausted at the day's end. Already, ahead of the others, Hoffmann was out on the rudimentary playing field awaiting them, juggling the ball in the air with small alternating kicks with each foot.

Gerhard sat for a moment and looked over the camp. He was tired of this strange role that had been forced upon him. Once he had accepted the role of commander of a single tank until he commanded a whole panzer battalion, he had given his all to performing the duties that came with the role, for his own self-esteem, the welfare of those entrusted to his command and to uphold the honor of the family name in the Panzer Corp. But, commander of men was not the real Gerhard von Kleist or at least not what he thought of himself nor wanted. He had as a young man prepared himself for an academic career and had happily joined the faculty of Anthropology of the University of Munich in 1935 as an assistant professor, *Akademischer Rat*. Three years later things were going very well for his reputation in the department, his research into the movement of early people in Europe and most importantly, his love life, when, on an early March day his promising life fell apart.

Just three weeks before this fateful day Viktor Heinz had replaced Leon Rothmann as head of Anthropology. No reason was given and Leon had departed from Munich in a matter of days leaving the impression of a situation where a person had egregiously broken the rules and had fled the humiliation which would follow. To consider that possibility only brought sad confusion, since Rothmann had enjoyed an unblemished reputation as a scientist and warm affection from the department faculty. That he should be dismissed was disheartening, but shocking was the news of his replacement with Viktor Heinz. Gerhard and his colleagues, in fact the great majority of scholars in the field, regarded Heinz with derision. He had written a paper in the early 30's promulgating a hierarchy of racial intelligence that placed white, northern Europeans at the head of the order. He wasn't alone in German academia promoting this idea, but he had become the flag bearer. He based his claim on his dubious measurements of cranial capacity. Credible international scientists disregarded him and his paper as laughable and his data as bogus. Publicists for the National Socialist German Workers Party, the Nazi Party, however, repeatedly cited the paper in their effort to portray Jews as an inferior, mongrel race. And now here he was Chairman of the Anthropology Department, one more proof, if one were needed, that the University was under Hitler's thumb. Several years earlier all the Jewish faculty had been dismissed, as part of the general persecution of the Jews. While angering Gerhard and causing him to openly express his outrage, this hadn't touched his department where there were no Jewish members. Now with this absurd action, it was clear that everyone was expected to be on board with the Nazi Party.

The day that changed his life began with the morning announcement by Heinz that Gerhard's research would be put on hold since his time must now be spent expanding Heinz's own theories. At lunch Rudi, his best friend in the department had given him an alert.

"Anna, our secretary, told me this morning that over a week ago the Gestapo knocked on her sister's door and took her husband in for 'questioning.' Yesterday they discovered that he was down the road in the Dachau camp."

"What is the charge?"

"There is no charge. Anna's brother-in-law had been outspoken in his Nazi criticism. They are making it clear that no criticism will be tolerated."

"Come on, such thinking follows panic. "

"Normally I'd agree. But before you act on that conclusion and do or say something that will get you in trouble, I advise you to be cautious. Actually, it is generally known what you think of the National Socialists. You may be closer to serious trouble than you think."

A mood of panic was incubating among those not aligned with the Nazi ideology and he figured his friend had caught the bug.

"Good. I'll remember your advice."

It was Friday and Hilde and he were both finished at the University at the same time and would meet at the fountain outside the main entrance on Ludwigstrasse. On that day, he paced back and forth by the fountain awaiting her, wanting to pour out all his angry, conflicted thoughts. He saw her coming, her joy at seeing him evident and he felt his usual excitement at seeing her, an excitement springing partly from love and partly from the wonder that she was really excited to be with him. The impatient wish to tell her all that had happened that day was quickly tempered by her smile. He shouldn't burden her with his anxiety, confusion and indecision.

As she walked up, her expression sobered.

"What's wrong?" she asked.

"Is it that obvious?" He laughed, kissing her.

She'd put her arm through his and they'd begun walking along Ludwigstrasse toward the Siegestor as he poured out his concerns.

"I don't see how I can continue at the University if I have to take part in this charade. It's a fraud. It's the opposite of everything I want my career to mean."

Immediately on both their minds was a major consequence of his quitting his job. They would not have the money to marry.

"It's rotten. Everything is becoming rotten. My department is unaffected yet—what can the Nazi's do to linguistics?"

"Don't be so sure. They can order words of Semitic origin to be purged from the German language."

"You mean like Messiah?" They both laughed but knew it was no joke. "I'm frightened to think of where we're headed."

"We're headed toward war," Gerhard said. "Hitler is only toying with the British and French."

At Schackstrasse they turned toward the library. Hilde squeezed his arm and held it close. "If you feel you must leave the University, you can find another job and continue your research on your own. Remember I have access to the library."

He'd stopped there, embraced her and kissed her.

He held on to that memory as long as he could now sitting under the shade of the Carolina oak tree. But then pushing aside that wonderful memory came the memory of the evening of that same day. It began with a soft rapping on his apartment door. He'd opened it to be faced with the commanding figure of Manfred Stolz.

"Manfred!"

"You're right, it's been a long time."

Stolz was a friend from his gymnasium days in Brandenburg. He and Stolz had been good friends back then, yet they had never been really close; their interests were too different. Manfred was the extrovert athlete/leader, while Gerhard's interests ran to the bookish/artistic. They both attended the University of Berlin where they would run into each other. Through those infrequent contacts Gerhard learned his friend intended to join the Berlin police after graduation. So it was a surprise to open the door here in Munich and see Manfred's large body fill the doorway. Manfred wasn't smiling. He moved quickly forward into the room forcing Gerhard to move aside.

"I haven't much time. Close the door."

Before Gerhard could ask about his friend's presence in Munich, Manfred answered the question tersely.

"I left the Berlin police a year ago to join the Gestapo. I was assigned here four months ago. I came to tell you that you are in grave danger. I'm going out of my way—taking a huge risk coming here—because, as they say, for 'old times.' You, my friend, have been very foolish in broadcasting your dislike of the Party and in particular of the Führer. You have been quoted calling him a 'delusional clown.'

"Understand, I don't agree with you. I believe the object of the Party is to lead Germany into the changing world. I know you my friend, I know you must think our methods crude. Maybe so, but that can't be helped just now."

Gerhard had heard this excuse often. It was license to do anything no matter how immoral. He was depressed to hear it coming from someone with whom he had shared part of that unlimited friendship of youth.

Manfred knew and accepted that there existed now a great gulf between them. He had not come to advocate, but to warn.

"It's like this my friend; you are to be arrested for 'crimes against the state.' I don't know what you are supposed to have done, but Helmut Müller, the Gestapo Chief of Operations, issued the order himself. Have you been fucking his wife, Gerhard?"

Stolz paused, taking von Kleist by the shoulders and giving him a single shake. "Now listen to me. You are to be arrested immediately. I didn't stay around to hear the details. I didn't want to appear too interested and I didn't want to waste a moment coming here. You are to be an example to the intellectual elite here in the city, especially the University crowd. Criticism will not be tolerated. Anything can happen to you after they arrest you, I hope you understand that."

Gerhard was in shock, but a life-long trait had always enabled him to move mentally from a surprising experience to a controlled, rational response.

"You said immediately; how soon exactly?"

"I don't know. Helmut Geiger was the one given the assignment. They may be on their way here now. However, I heard Geiger making a date earlier with a woman. He may delay coming here."

"What should I do?"

"Get the hell out of the country. Grab your toothbrush and go immediately to the Hauptbahnhof and catch the first train to the west: Switzerland, France . . . or join the army. The Wehrmacht is still fairly independent. Hitler wants to maintain good terms and is not interfering in the army's internal affairs. I know you have contacts there. Just get out of this apartment now! Leave things as they are—as if you just stepped out to meet someone for a beer. It will take a day for them to figure out that you're on the run.

"I have to go," he said abruptly, turning and walking to the door.

With his hand on the knob and without looking back, he said, "Good luck." He opened the door, glanced quickly into the hall and left.

Gerhard stood looking at the closed door for only a moment before reminding himself of how emphatic Manfred had stressed the need to act rapidly. He had to stay calm and think. Leave the country? He didn't like that idea. Hilde was here. He'd be abandoning her to what-ever happened here. The army? It was true, he did have contacts. Each generation of his family since Frederick the Great had had members in the officer corps. Gerhard's father had been an Oberst, a colonel. His father had died, however, when Gerhard had been in college, but his father's younger brother had retired only two years ago as a brigadier general and second in command to General Heinz Guderian, the com-mander-in-chief of the panzers. Manfred had handed him two options he could not think of another. He opened his address book and looked up his uncle's number.

Max von Kleist heard the tension in his nephew's voice and lis-tened intently as a field commander listens to a report of enemy troop movements. He replied, "What is you phone number? I'll call back as soon as I can."

Gerhard went to the closet to get his suitcase, then remembered Manfred had said to leave everything as is. From the bookshelf he got the book in which he kept his money—one hundred forty-six Reichsmark. That and the twenty in his pocket was all he had.

Waiting for his uncle's call was beginning to unravel his calm. Fear began to mount, fear and the awareness of the total, unimaginable disaster that had seized his life.

The phone rang and he snatched it up. "Hello."

His uncle's even, unhurried voice said, "Gerhard, you are expected in Munster tomorrow. That is the Munster in Lower Saxony, the Panzer Training School. Report to Hauptmann Roeper. We love you." The phone clicked off.

Gerhard hung up and walked out the door and locked it. He walked several blocks in order to leave the neighborhood before looking for a telephone booth.

"Rudi, this is Gerhard. I must talk fast. I'm leaving to join the army. I -"

"The army?"

"Just listen. I have been talking to you about this for a while, understand? I have become disillusioned with an academic life and anthropology. My reassignment to research in which I had no interest clinched the matter. I've decided to follow the path of my father and join the army. Since I was undecided, I asked you to say nothing to others about this . . . until now. Goodbye Rudi. If things work out, I'll be in touch." He hung up.

The second call was to Hilde. "Darling, don't talk just listen to me. I'm leaving the city tonight. If anyone asks you, I have been thinking about joining the army. I'll call you soon. Goodbye." He knew he was leaving in a total quandary the person in the whole world he wanted least to hurt or confuse, but this way she would be telling the truth when she said she didn't know where he was.

He'd flagged a taxi and rode to the main train station. He had never heard of a Munster in Lower Saxony, only the city in the Rhineland. Looking through a railway timetable at the station he saw first that he had a long way to travel and second that a train with a final destination of Hamburg, the shortest route, wouldn't leave until 6 a.m.. By that time the Gestapo could have departing trains watched. In

119

fifteen minutes a train left for Stuttgart. It was out of the way, but out of Munich. He bought a ticket.

A cheer from the soccer field interrupted his rumination. His thoughts shifted to the constant question he couldn't answer and about which he was helpless to act: How was Hilde? What was she doing?

Another cheer brought his attention back to the camp. He watched the action for a minute before turning to *Tom Jones*. Molly's juicy introduction didn't help temper his longing for Hilde.

Ben got behind the wheel of the family Plymouth. He adjusted the mirrors and started the engine. The "Sunday drive" was about to begin. While his parents would have made this a weekly event, gas rationing forced a twice monthly cap. In addition to the Plymouth's "A" rating allotting four gallons per week, the Lodge had a station wagon, which was rarely used but was entitled to a "C" rating as a hotel vehicle. That added eight more gallons a week. The government had forbidden sight-seeing trips and the speed limit was set at 35 mph. No one observed either rule.

Ben had mixed feelings about these Sunday drives. He was allowed to drive part of the distance, which was good, but that really translated into a long driving lesson, which was not good. Smoking seemed to be a required part of the experience for his parents, both heavy smokers. They were considerate enough to open the windows—unless it was raining or cold. Bad weather didn't effect the need to smoke, only the need to roll up the windows. Some of the places they'd been to were interesting like Chimney Rock, but others were only OK like Lake Lure. A meal in a restaurant was part of the package. For his parents, this seemed the best part of the trip. His mother enjoyed having someone else provide the work for a change. Ben understood this, while his father's behavior puzzled and irritated him. Ben imagined his father experiencing himself as part of the gentry being waited upon by servants. His voice altered to an appropriate tone for addressing underlings—or so it seemed to Ben. This was odd, because his father treated his employees as equals. Ben supposed it all had to do with the English class system, a way of viewing society that was deeply embedded in his father's mind.

Ben didn't like to sit and wait for food. He liked it best when his mother said dinner was ready and he'd help carry things to the table, reliably good things. He rated this particular Sunday lunch the best so far: fried chicken, mashed potatoes, corn bread and beans cooked with bacon fat. At home his father wanted the beans cooked until rendered tasteless. This style really extended to all vegetables. Ben pictured eating in England to be a grim event. The rustic place they'd stopped at, Tucker's Home, served family style, large platters put down on long tables for all to help themselves. A request for more water was answered with, "Tap's over yonder." His father actually relaxed and enjoyed it.

The destination that day was a waterfall in the Nantahala National Forest about fifteen miles from town. To get there, one had to leave the highway and drive five miles down a dirt road.

"Slow down," his father yelled when a rock flew up and hit the underside of a fender. He said it in a tone that meant it wouldn't have happened if he'd been driving. Ben slowed to 30 mph. His father didn't like to creep along either and was impatient, but he'd set the pace. The road came to a fork. The branch to the left was closed with a padlocked chain, and a sign read, "Authorized Vehicles Only." A sign pointing down the other branch read "Cherokee Falls and Star-Crossed Rock 1/2 mi." Along this way the road passed over a fast-flowing creek and ended in a parking area large enough for a dozen cars. Ben parked and set the handbrake as he'd done for his driver's test the year before. Except for the flying rock, he'd made it through without a scolding.

A notice board covered with a small roof stood at the edge of the parking area, where a trail could be seen entering the woods. Ben and his parents stood and read the map displayed on the board. It showed that after .3 mi. the path divided. To the right was Cherokee Falls. The hike was graded "easy." To the left was the way to "Star-Crossed Rock" graded "steep grade 1.5 mi."

Along side the map was written; "According to Cherokee legend, when a princess and a brave fell in love but were forbidden to marry because of their family's different status in the tribe, they joined hands and jumped to their deaths from a cliff that white settlers named, 'Star-Crossed Rock.'"

"Hey that sounds like a gas. Let's go see," Ben said.

"Not after that lunch. Maybe another time," his mother quickly countered.

"Your mother's right," his father said. "You know it will only be a cliff anyway. We'll go to the falls like we'd planned."

"And a waterfall is only water falling off a cliff," Ben thought in rebuttal.

So, it was to the falls they walked. In addition to the growing thundering sound, Ben was aware of the coolness as they approached the crashing water. Gripped by the sight of the full cascading stream, he wondered what there was about it that so affected people the way it did. He thought the roots of the awe must lay deep in the human mind. He imagined a guy wearing a bearskin standing next to him staring upward as awestruck as he.

Kyle Sexton opened a can of Spam and cut two slices off the block. He fried them and a couple of eggs. The coffee rationing that had been enforced had been lifted the year before, but it had never been a problem for Kyle, since the Police Department, designated as a"vital" government facility, suffered no shortage of coffee and so neither had Kyle. He finished off breakfast and lit a cigarette and settled back with his cup. There was but one thing on his mind, what to do about the investigation of Blanca Martinez's disappearance? As of that moment he had zero leads. If she had been taken any place where there were other people, someone must have noticed her—hot looking Mexican woman - orange dress. He had a thought; if you lose a pet, you advertise. He knew a reporter on the staff of the Hendersonville Times-News. Don Howard. Come to think of it, Don was the only reporter you could know, the only one the paper had. Kyle had met him a year ago over the smoldering remains of the Baptist Church at Five Points. The question of arson had them there for different reasons. They'd hit it off and had gotten together for coffee several times. It was Sunday morning and normally not a time for business, but news and crime knew neither calendar nor clock.

Kyle looked up Don's number and called thinking it likely he'd be at church. Don answered.

"Good. I caught you at home. This is Kyle Sexton, Don. You can do something for me and in return I have something for you."

"The last time I heard that I was given the clap."

Kyle laughed. "My offer isn't that good."

"I'll bet your gift has something to do with a missing teacher."

"Damn, someone in our department must be on your payroll."

"Not someone, Kyle, everyone. How else can a city employee put bread on the table? What's the deal?"

"I need the paper to run a front page piece describing the woman and asking anyone who saw her, particularly last Thursday night, to contact us. I've got a picture of her that you can use. Looks like she had a date Thursday."

He then added a detailed description while Don took notes. As his half of the bargain, he promised to keep Don in the loop regarding any developments.

"I take it you've already shown her picture around at the date spots in town."

"Right. No luck."

"Well, ours is a small pond. I'll throw a line in the water. Orange dress on sexy señorita. One couldn't ask for better bait. Get the picture over to me."

"I'll want it back."

"Let's see. Meet me at the office in half an hour with the photo. I'll have a plate made for the half-tone and get the photo back to you tomorrow."

"Can you get the piece in tomorrow's paper?"

"No problem. I already told the printing room to save space on the front page for an article on the missing teacher."

"How did you come to know about this?"

"My daughter was in her class."

"From what I've learned so far, it sounds like she got a raw deal."

"My daughter would second that."

Sitting by herself beneath an umbrella-shaded table on the terrace of the Hendersonville Country Club, Valery Sinclair absentmindedly gazed toward the players finishing up on the eighteenth green. She wore the same outfit she'd worn the night she went swimming with Ben. An empty plate and a half glass of Coke were in front of her. A young man wearing the uniform of an Annapolis cadet walked up to her table and spoke. Reverie broken, she looked up with the dawning expression of recognition. Someone she knew but hadn't seen for a while. He said something that made her laugh. She motioned toward an empty chair and he sat down, removing his cap and placing it on the table. He waved the waiter over.

Monday, June 5th.

The morning had been frustrating. Clint Edney, who made up the other half of the detective squad, had been away all morning investigating a report of a stolen prize bull from the Wakefield farm near Dana. So, Kyle sat alone in the office and smoked, then paced and filled yet another cup from the percolator, all the while reviewing his options for advancing the Martinez investigation. He'd called the Milledgeville police and confirmed Dobb's alibi that he was at his uncle's funeral. The State Police? What were they likely to do that he hadn't? It would be time for them once he had some evidence their lab could help with. The FBI? They'd only come in if there were a kidnapping and there was no evidence to support that yet—no ransom demand. Besides they were busy with matters like espionage. And then there was Asheville. Kyle had a casual relationship with two of their detectives, but had never worked on a case with either. How much effort could he expect them to expend making inquires around the city about a young Mexican/ American woman? If he got no response from the newspaper story, he'd call them.

At noon he walked to Main Street and Carson's Cafe. Sitting at the counter he ordered an egg salad sandwich, coffee—even though it was dishwater compared to Flora's—and a piece of chocolate cream pie from the new waitress. She appeared to be overwhelmed by the lunchtime rush. Showing sympathy with her plight, one of the other customers without comment got up and fetched the silverware she'd forgotten. Kyle told himself to be patient. Bert Carson came out of the kitchen and seeing Kyle waved and went to the jukebox and jacked in a nickel to play his obsession, Ella's, *Those Little White Lies*.

The talk he overheard down the counter was that the Allies were about to take Rome. Good news, which also carried a disheartening meaning for him. This war would be over before he could play a part. At that moment, an idea asserted itself, a conviction; he'd finish this case—find Blanca Martinez—and then resign from the Police Department and join the Air Force! His mood soared.

He was working on the pie when the waitress came by and poured more coffee. She smiled and lingered again as she had last night. Flooded with his good feelings, he smiled back. She's not bad looking, he thought. He might have taken her up on her offer, but his newly confirmed resolution swept him right past momentary pleasures . First the missing teacher and then into the fight! He paid his bill and left.

Back in the office he found that Don Howard had sent over a proof of the front page of the paper which would be circulated later in the afternoon. The picture of Martinez was a little darker than in the snapshot. Her features were clear enough to make an identification. The text of the article gave a straightforward report off the facts. Now he just had to wait and hope.

Clint Edney walked through the door and sailed his hat toward the hat rack, missing.

"You used to play some baseball didn't you?"

"Yeah, I tried out with the St. Louis Browns."

"I see why you dropped the idea."

Clint picked up the hat and hung it on the rack. "Hell, haven't you caught on yet that I miss so my clumsy partner won't get depressed.

We all know you're a fragile case." He sat down. "Anything new with the teacher?"

"Just waiting for the paper to come out. What about this stolen bull? And why are you investigating a complaint from a farm? Shouldn't that be an issue for the sheriff?"

"That's what I was thinking until I looked at the map." He gestured toward the large wall map of the city. "The Wakefield farm is in the county, but the house is in the city—so I went to see what it was all about. Mrs. Wakefield started right off spewing out the story so fast I had to get her calmed down before I could make head or tail of it. The situation was this: her hubby and son had gone to Greenville to a livestock show taking the hired hand with them. They weren't coming back until tonight, so she was home alone. They've got some pure bred Angus cattle and this bull, Geordie, that won first prize at last years's state fair. When she went to bed last night the bull was in a small pasture right off the barn where there's a door to a sheltered space reserved for him. Walking out to the barn this morning, she noticed Geordie wasn't in the pasture where she'd normally see him grazing. She looked into the space inside the barn and he wasn't there either. She freaked out. It was clear to me there was a family problem here where the men don't trust her not to fuck up. She was scared shitless of what would happen when they got home and found the bull had been stolen right from under her nose.

"Well I got her to sit down and take some deep breaths and said I'd go out and look 'round. To make the story short, I found the bull in the milking room with a heifer. She had scratches on her side from where he'd mounted her. In a patch of bare ground just outside the door of his stall, I could see where at least two men maybe three had been walking 'round. Inside the milking room were four cigarette butts. I figure some boys, knowing the Wakefield men were away, got the bull in there with the heifer and milked themselves some prize bull sperm."

"What do you mean?"

"It's something new—'round here anyway. They get the bull to mount a cow and then with some device they intercept the sperm into a container and then inject it into another's cow's vagina using a gizmo. I've heard tell it's like a drinking straw."

"Wow." Kyle thought a moment. "Why did they leave the bull in the milking room? If they'd put him back in the pasture, no one would have known."

"Good question. I reckon ole Geordie had had enough of them and became pissed. A pissed bull is someone to leave alone."

"Yeah right. So what is your next move—by the way that was some good sleuthing, Sherlock."

Clint smiled. He thought it was good detective work too. "Not much I can do. Nothing special about the boot prints. I found tire tracks where a truck had been pulled off the pavement in front, but the tread was like that most trucks 'round here—bald. The cigarettes had been hand rolled. Again, like those most farm boys smoke. I sniffed the tobacco in one of the butts and I'd say it was Bull Durham. Almost every farm hand in this part of the state has a pouch of Bull Durham in his pocket. About the only thing I can do is inspect all calves born in our vicinity nine months from now. Not something I'm gonna recommend."

"I expect Mrs. Wakefield will get hell anyway."

"Nah. The bull was quiet, so I led him out of the milk room and into his pasture and put the heifer with the other cows. I gave old lady Wakefield a look, which she understood."

"Nine months eh, same as humans?"

"Yeah, there might be a joke there, but I'm not gonna touch it," said Clint. "Anyway, my dance card is vacant now, so if you need a hand with the teacher, I'm available."

"Good. Don Howard at the Times-News is running a story about her disappearance and her picture this afternoon asking anyone who saw her Thursday night to call our office. I'm going to be sitting around here the rest of the day waiting for a call - waiting at least until it's past everyone's bedtime."

He felt it was now urgent to contact Valery. Eddie had clarified the role he had assumed with her: she was dominant, the one leading, while he was attendant, waiting to see which direction she would lead. That might have been OK for a start, but he now agreed with Eddie that she would no longer tolerate that arrangement without losing interest. He knew what he would say to her. He would propose an adventure, a new experience, a waterfall in the woods. He would take charge . But, how to make that contact? A bike ride to her house and knocking on the door was out—kid stuff. He had to call her. He needed her number.

It was by accident the answer came. He and Eddie had knocked off mowing at twelve, because Eddie had to help his father in the afternoon. Ben rode his bike to town to buy new shoelaces at Woolworth's, when he saw Congressman Sinclair get out of the family station wagon and enter the four-story building next to the courthouse.

Her father! That's it! He had hit it off with the congressman. He'd ask him for the telephone number. He parked his bike near the building entrance and went inside. He had never been in the building before, but had heard that lawyers and doctors had offices there. He'd had no need for either. He'd never been to a doctor in his life apart from being born. The lobby was empty. How could he find out where Val's father had gone? A directory faced him on the wall across the lobby. This was the first time he'd ever encountered one of these, but he understood when he read the list of names that it would answer his question. Congressman Sinclair was listed in room 301. Other office numbers were also in the hundreds. There weren't a hundred offices in the building, so 301 must be on the third floor. The single elevator returned to the ground floor and an old man sitting inside on a stool slid the door open. He wore a dark blue uniform jacket too large for him with "Elevator Operator" embroidered over the pocket. Ben stepped inside and said he wanted to go to the third floor.

"Where you goin' boy?" the man asked as if he didn't trust a kid.

"Congressman Sinclair's office."

Still unsure of the likelihood that Ben should be allowed to go to that office just because he wanted to, he hesitated weighing the question. Reluctantly he slid the door closed and turned the wheel that started the lift. When Ben got out, he continued to watch him until he opened Sinclair's door.

The room Ben entered was large and well lit from a tall window in one wall. Sinclair's secretary sat at a desk opposite the door, typing. A large portrait of President Roosevelt hung on the wall behind her. Ben judged her to be about his mother's age, but much more glamorous, a platinum blond like Lana Turner.

She smiled like Lana Turner also. Her "How can I help you?" dazzled him.

"I'd like to speak to Congressman Sinclair, please."

"And what business do you have with the congressman today?"

"I'm a friend of his daughter, Valery. I need to get in touch with her . . . I need her telephone number."

There were a number of possibilities here, thought the canny secretary. This naïve appearing boy might, as he said, be Valery's friend. On the other hand, he might not, maybe wishes he were her friend. She didn't want to blunder, give out the number if Valery didn't want him to have it. While her boss expected her to handle most of these kinds of issues, this was one she was going to pass on.

She got up saying, "What is our name, sir?" When he answered, she said, "Just a minute," and knocked on the inner office door and then entered.

Ben noted this was the second time he'd been called, "sir" in two days. He felt he was being catapulted into adulthood.

In his office Troy Sinclair looked up from a letter he'd been reading.

"Boy outside named Ben Roberts says he's a friend of Valery's and would like to have her home telephone number."

Sinclair thought, Ben Roberts? Oh yeah, that boy she had over for lunch. The high school football player. So, Val hadn't given him our number. Didn't want him to call her? Or forgot to give it to him? Hell, it's not my business to decide this. If she didn't want him to have the number she should have told me. He seemed like a good kid. Not her type, surprised she'd had him to lunch.

"OK, Beverly, I'll see him."

When Ben entered the office, Troy got up and extended his hand enthusiastically. "Good to see you, Ben. My secretary tells me you need the home number. No problem."

He picked up a pen and wrote the number on a note pad and tore it off and handed it to Ben.

"Tell me you've started running some every day like I advised you."

Ben, surprised, said, "No sir, but I'll start . . . today."

"Good. Now is there anything else I can do for you today?" Troy had walked around his desk and was turning Ben toward the door.

"No sir. Thank you very much."

"Hope to see you soon."

Ben was smiling when he came out of the office and said good-bye to the secretary. She judged by the short time Ben had been in Sinclair's office just how he'd handled the situation. She'd made the right decision.

Ben waited for the elevator trying to remember the congressman telling him at lunch to "start running some every day."

A pair of eyes fixed on the photo on the front page. The article asked for information from anyone who'd seen her on Thursday night. His heart beat faster. He reviewed in his mind who might have had that opportunity. He could think of no one. Still . . . .

It had never been discussed how they would go about keeping records for their business. They were meeting at Eddie's house in the late afternoon to work on it. The business now had a name, "The Grasshoppers." Several names had been tossed around in a giddy, silly session while mowing that morning: "Lords of the Lawn," "Blade Battalion," "You Bet Your Grass" and "U Mow No Mo."

While still in motion, Ben swung his leg out and over the bike's seat, hopped to the ground, dropped the bike on the White's front lawn and bounded up the porch steps in one unbroken motion. He raised his fist to rap on the screen door as Cookie pushed it open.

Surprised, Ben said, "Hi."

"Hi yourself." She wore shorts with a peasant-top blouse. Barefoot. "Is Eddie here yet?"

"No, just little ole me. They went to Mrs. Rutledge's. Dad needed help moving some furniture for her. Eddie knew Mom and Dad would want to stay and talk so he rode his bike."

Ben began to search for something to say to her.

"Do you think God exists?" she asked in a serious, even tone as if she were asking if he'd like a glass of water.

With those words a unique experience began for Ben. Up until now the basis of his relationships with others had been mostly established incidentally by proximity. On the first day of school he might find himself sitting next to someone he hadn't met. "My name is Ben," "My name is Bill." As the days passed an unconscious judgement was made; I like to hang out with Bill and my friends do too. Girls had been invisible until recently when it became exciting to sit next to one of the girls in his clique at the Saturday matinee. Their scent was intoxicating. Of course, he knew it was perfume, but it seemed to emanate from the girl herself, each with her own enticing aroma. What did they say when the lights came on? Damn little. He left as fast as he could with the buddy he'd come with.

Now the guys talked about girls a lot, how they were "stacked," would they "put out" (as if the guys knew). No one mentioned any positive feeling about a girl beyond, "I'd like'ta." Ben didn't know of any friends having a serious conversation with a girl—or other guys either for that matter.

Relationships with friends, while strong, tended to lack one dimension usually present in adult friendships—ideology, what they believed beyond one's stand on which was better, a Ford or a Chevy.

Now here was this kid, his friend's little sister, practically demanding that he do something he'd never done with anybody—explain his beliefs. Had anyone ever looked at him in just the way she was regarding him now, unguarded, unblinking and inviting him to be open with her. He felt like running.

His experience said that everyone was a Christian. It was assumed by the other person that you were too. He was willing to have that assumption made, since he knew that explaining his belief, or more accurately his lack of belief would be very unpopular to say the least.

The first words that came to mind after she'd asked the question were, "It's none of your business." He didn't say them. Something kept him from pushing her away.

"Why do you want to know that?"

"Because I'm curious."

"Yeah, but why are you curious?"

"You're stalling. Look, if you don't want to answer me just say so."

Here was a critical moment for him. He had a dawning awareness that he was being offered a kind of relationship he'd not known before. He was blind-sided that it was Cookie who offered it. She was Eddie's kid sister; that had been the sum of it. But in that instant he saw her as a person in her own right, and he became aware she was offering herself as a sharer of flat-out honesty. Her unwavering expression was frank, not smarty or teasing. A frank, honest reply was required if he were to keep the path open toward . . . what? A surprising thought

135

came to him; maybe she was the only one with whom he could become true friends. He and Eddie were close, but theirs was a working relationship. They shared events. Cookie held out the possibility of a depth of contact with another person involving something more . . . what? . . . more complete? He could tell he wasn't prepared or ready for that, but he couldn't break contact with the serious offer in her eyes.

He played for time. "But why are you curious?"

She sensed his hesitancy, but knew she had to make a commitment also. "Because I'm interested in what you think."

"What I think?"

"Yes . . ."

Little things had been evident in the past that should have caused him to recognize her keen interest in him, but he'd been unaware. How was he going to respond? Certainly none had said that to him before, "I'm interested in what you think." His reflex reaction to such a confrontation was to joke in order to avoid exposing himself. An inner voice that he'd heard on other occasions such as when on the point of quitting some hard task like running laps at football practice or neglecting a tiring obligation he'd agreed to, now warned him not to take the easy path and decline her offer, or he'd risk passing up something unique. Caution began to dissolve. He relaxed and shifted his full weight to a new base as if stepping off a dock to board a moving boat.

They were standing in the open doorway. He motioned with his hand to the wicker porch chairs. Cookie's picked up her cat that had been sleeping on a chair and put it on the ground, then sat down crossed-legged on the cushion.

"Sorry Pyrrho."

"I've wondered why you call her that, Peero."

"Him. Because he's such a skeptic. I named him after that Greek philosopher."

"Oh." Ben didn't know what she meant.

"You see, when I explain something to him he looks me in the eye giving me his full attention, and then he just walks away unconvinced."

"Yeah, that's cats for you," Ben said.

The exchange had thrown him off balance. Where was he now? Yes, she'd asked if he thought God exists. She'd said the other day that he didn't go to church; he'd start with that.

"OK, I don't know why the question of whether or not I go to church is important to you . . ."

"Not whether or not you go; I know you don't go."

"Yeah, OK, why I don't go." He was about to repeat that he didn't know why it was important to her, but dropped it. He saw that she was quietly waiting for him to continue. "It's like this, my family never went to church . . . well we did drive to Miami Beach one Easter for sunrise service, but I think that had more to do with it being beautiful on the beach at dawn than anything to do with religion. My father had been raised in the Church of England, but never attended church after the last war. My thinking is that what he saw—all that stupid killing that God did nothing to stop made God unimportant to him. I asked him once if he believed in God and he had to think for a minute before saying, "Well, I guess so.""

"God had become irrelevant," she said.

Ben nodded. He'd never heard that word used by friends, but he knew what it meant. Cookie tended to speak a different level of English than his friends—she had more words. Ben had found in past conversations with her he tended to deviate from his usual vocabulary, using

137

some words he'd read but never spoken—like playing Ping-Pong with a better player will raise your own game.

"When I asked my mother the same question," Ben went on, "she said she believed heaven and hell are here on earth, and if there was a God he was in all things. I remember once she said she was a 'free thinker'. I didn't ask her what she meant; I figured it meant she was free to think what she liked. Aside from that, religion was never mentioned in our home. I wasn't encouraged to go to church or stay away—something like I could decide when I was older."

He studied Cookie's face at this point to judge her reaction. She was fully attentive and he could discern no sign that she was arming herself against what he'd said, but at the same time she looked uneasy.

"You're saying you had no religious instruction."

He nodded.

"Can we know the truth without being told what it is?" she said.

Here was a hypothetical question he'd never dealt with before, at least not head on.

"I don't know," he ventured. "We learn some true things by being told them, but you can also be told things that aren't true."

"My parents told me about God. Would they have told me something that wasn't true?"

"Probably not. Neither would mine except when they knew what they said wasn't true."

"I don't understand."

"For instance, mine told me the stork delivered babies."

She laughed. "Mine said you got them from Sears and Roebuck."

He returned to the point. "But haven't you found that some things your parents thought were true turned out to be false?"

"Give me another for instance."

He searched for an answer. He smiled remembering a recent conversation. "Take our milk for instance. My father won't have us drink pasteurized milk. He says the good vitamins are destroyed by pasteurization."

"He thinks that?"

"Yeah, he thinks it's true. No one I've mentioned it to agrees and I've come to think they're right. Others say that he's exposing us to a disease that cows can have. He says that's nonsense, since people have drunk unpasteurized milk for centuries and he's known no one who became sick."

Cookie said quietly, "As far as he knows. That doesn't make it true."

"Exactly. That's my answer to your saying that parents wouldn't tell you something that's untrue. If my father can be wrong about pasteurized milk, can't your parents be wrong about God?"

Cookie burst out, "Wait a minute! Whether a person can get sick drinking raw milk is hardly on the same level as the question of the existence of God. Forever people have believed in the existence of God."

"And forever people thought raw milk was harmless."

With the hint of a smile she leaned forward and touched the front of his shirt with her finger. He looked down and found he'd fallen once again for the old trick as her finger came up across his nose.

"Hey!"

Her smile was friendly. "So you want me to believe there is no God, because your father had his facts about milk all wrong."

"No. I never said I wanted you to believe anything. I don't care what you think."

"Sure you do. Every argument begins on the assumption that the other person must agree or show their ignorance or stupidity"

This kind of sounded true - or was it?

"Yeah . . maybe, except I'm not arguing with you. You asked if I thought God exists and I'm trying to answer that."

When he was eight he'd first come to his conclusions about God. He'd told a couple of friends. They'd both reacted with anger and called him crazy. One boy avoided his birthday party even though it included a trip to the beach and plenty of ice cream. He also avoided Ben from then on. Any idea he had of converting others to his view died quickly. Those friends treated him as if he had revealed a bad thing about himself. He didn't want that. Besides he could see that there were too many people to convince and the promise of life after death was hard to compete with. As far as his experience told him, he was part of an infinitesimally small minority. In fact, it was a minority of one. His mother, the only person he'd known who didn't step right up and claim there was a God, still hadn't said there wasn't one. "If there is a God, he is in all things."

Now with a teasing tone Cookie said, "I've read warnings about blindly accepting the opinion of authorities, but I've never come across the pasteurized milk argument."

He fell into the spirit of her jibe. "I'm rally surprised. Maybe you should read deeper books."

They both laughed. He decided to take another chance.

"I don't mean to match the depth of my thinking with what you've been reading, but I'll tell you about my own . . . I'll tell you what happened to me."

Ben felt buoyant at that moment, because of his growing trust in their friendship. Perhaps he would be able to discuss his ideas with someone of his generation and not expect to be judged. He could expect open minds from his mother and Mrs. Ransom, but he experienced them as tolerant adult listeners who wanted to guide his thinking.

"I had a stamp collection when I was eight, " he said,. "We all did. Did you?"

"No, I never did."

"For some reason my parents had bought me a large album, one that had pages for pretty near every country in the world—those that had stamps at least. You could buy an envelope of stamps from all over the world for very little money, like two hundred for fifty cents. They were used stamps, of course, with postmarks. I had a small globe, so when I came across a stamp from a strange country I'd find it on the globe. After a while I knew my geography pretty well; there were many countries and many different people.

"I can see by your expression that you're wondering what my stamp collection has to do with the existence of God."

"Hmm."

"On one of the stamps from India there was a picture of a guy with a fancy headdress and four heads and four arms. I asked my mother about it. She didn't know much about Hindu religion, but knew they had a lot of Gods and this was probably one of them. Later I learned the God was Brahma. On my globe, my mother pointed out which areas had different religions. Here was the space where people were Jewish, in this area were the Mohammedans, over there were the Hindus . I wondered why these other countries would choose a religion other than Christianity, since that's what everybody around me believed. After all, it was supposed to be the true religion. My mother said all people think their religion is the true religion.

"That ended our discussion, but I began thinking about it on my own. First I was impressed with the spacing of the religions. I concluded that what determined which religion a person would follow was a matter of where they were born and grew up, who their parents were and had nothing to do with whether or not the religion was the true one. It was a simple matter of geography.

"Do you see what I mean?" he asked.

"I'm following you."

"Well next I reasoned there could be only one "true" religion—or none. I decided that if there were a true God who was all powerful, one who could do whatever he wanted to do, he would want everyone to know he was the true God. Why let people live in ignorance of the truth if you could have it otherwise? Why let some people go to hell simply because they happened to be born on one side of the mountain instead of the other, or say India rather than Europe. That just didn't make sense. A true God would have made sure everyone had it right. That hadn't happened. That meant to me there was no true God. God didn't exist! People seemed to need to believe there was a God, but that had to do with their own needs and didn't prove God existed. My friends seemed to think they'd be punished if they didn't believe. I nervously took a chance and said out loud, 'There is no God!' I said it in a loud voice. I wasn't playing it safe." Ben laughed. "If there was a God, he knew then and there where I stood. But nothing happened. No lightning bolt. No warning voice from the clouds. I was the same as always and so was the world."

Cookie was silent. Finally she said, "That seems too simple. I mean from what I've read this question has been taken up and argued at length by brilliant people. Thomas Aquinas wrote an extensive 'Five

Proofs' for the existence of God and you deal with the question like deciding what to have for breakfast. It sounds like something you'd find in a Cracker Jack box along with a Jack Armstrong decoder ring." She stopped, realizing that her last words had been insulting. "I didn't mean that. I mean can it be that you've never doubted your reasoning since you were eight?"

"My reasoning? I've thought my reasoning was airtight. I did think about the question from time to time but my reasoning continued to satisfy me. I never heard or saw reasonable evidence that I was wrong. I haven't given the question much thought lately, but I'm constantly aware that my thinking is out of step with everyone I know. Back then, I told two friends what I thought and they avoided me, thought I was a bad person. I've come to see it a little differently now.

"It's like there's this big pile of sand, no better, a large pile of used bricks left by a builder. A group of kids come along and one kid says, 'Look, a castle' and the others agree and they play 'castle' for a while - capture the castle, defend the castle and so on and then they leave - lunchtime say , and another group of kids comes along and someone says, 'Look, a mountain' and they play climb the mountain until the first group comes back and argues that it isn't a mountain it's a castle. They get in a big fight. Then a guy comes along and says, 'Wait, it's neither a castle nor a mountain, it's a pile of used bricks.' Neither group likes that. They call him stupid. What he said is worse than competing stories of castle and mountain, because what he said undermines the whole game of make-believe that they've enjoyed."

"So different religions are 'castles' and 'mountains', make-believe notions that groups of people agree on. Whatever value they get from the 'game' depends on everyone believing, so any questioning of the agreed upon story endangers whatever enjoyment they're having."

"That's about it."

"A person who says, 'That's just a pile of used bricks,' must be silenced."

Ben nodded.

"So, since this early stamp episode, you've lived with the guilty secret that you're a spoil sport."

Ben laughed. "Yeah, only it's not like a guilty secret. I don't feel guilty. It's like I'm sitting in the visiting team's section of the bleachers. If I keep my mouth shut they'll think I'm one of them, but if I slip up and cheer when my team scores, I'll immediately become . . . I don't know, excluded I guess is the best word . . . maybe worse."

"How about reviled," she suggested.

Ben didn't know the meaning of "reviled", but it sounded severe and she'd selected it. Did it mean it was what his story had produced in her?

"Do you revile me?"

No, his story hadn't caused her to reject him. He didn't know it, but only a betrayal of trust could damage her feelings for him.

"No, not that. It confuses me. Disturbs me. I've had questions of my own you see. That's why I asked you if you believed in God. There are things that don't make sense to me either—prayer for instance." She laughed. "I don't mean silly prayers like praying that one's team will win, as if the other team isn't praying for the same thing." She mimicked the solemn voice of God. 'Both sides are praying to win, but I'm going to pick Hendersonville, because I like their colors better.'

"My serious doubts began with that bus accident on the Asheville Highway last year when six people died. I went to the hospital with my friend, Martha, to visit her cousin, Jody, who was badly injured. Jody's family was at the bedside praying he would live. But, so was the family of the man in the next bed, who had also been in the accident. Jody lived and the man died. Everyone gave credit to the prayers for saving Jody. I asked Mom if prayer was able to do that, why hadn't it done the same for the man? Mom said God must have wanted it that way. So, God wanted the man to die and leave his family in grief?"

Ben said nothing. He'd long ago been able to dispense with prayer as magical wishful thinking.

She went on. "Do you remember in the same accident a couple was killed, but their three-month old baby escaped without a bruise?"

"Yeah, I remember."

"They attended our church and everyone at church agreed that a 'miracle' saved the baby. 'God's will made manifest' the minister said in the sermon. I think it was a coincidence pure and simple that the baby wasn't hurt and the parents died."

She continued, "I've had doubts like those, but never have I doubted God exists. As you describe that sequence of logical reasoning about geography it seems so simple. Why haven't I been led to the same kind of conclusions? I mean I'm as . . ."

Had she been going to say "smart?" He knew she was so much smarter than he was. "I think this might be an answer. You see, I didn't have any belief to overcome at the time—the time I had my stamp collection. I had never been taught there was a God. If a person is raised to think—to believe—something and taught it with great certainty and that it must not be questioned like kids are taught about God, warned not to be a game questioner, then it's hard to do any rethinking. But, if you hadn't had that prior instruction, you just follow your logic. If I told you right now that I drove to California on one tank of gas, you'd simply turn to what you know about cars to logically conclude that what I said couldn't be true. You wouldn't have to unlearn anything to figure out the answer. See what I mean? In other words, those people through history like you mentioned who were having a hard time deciding about the existence of God already had strong beliefs to undo from childhood."

She studied him, choosing directions.

"You're not worried that you might be wrong?"

"Worried about what? Do you mean that God might punish me? The idea of a god who would punish you for using the reasoning he'd given you is another logical mistake. What would you think of the teacher who threw you out of class because you tried to answer a question and got it wrong? But that's not the reason I'm not worried God will punish me," he said archly, smiling. "I'm not worried, because, after all, there is no God to punish me."

An idea came to Cookie and a challenge brightened her face. "Wait a minute; your conclusion that there is no God is based on the idea that God would want everyone to know the one and only 'true religion' and would see to it that everyone did. Since that hadn't happened - ipso facto - no God. But what about a God who created the universe and then went his own way not caring at all about homo sapiens, or what this one species of animal might do or believe—the God preferred by some Enlightenment philosophers, 'The Master Clockmaker.' What does that do to your logical conclusion?"

A smile appeared on her face as if she'd just said "checkmate."

Looking over Ben's shoulder, she said, "Eddie's here."

Ben had opened up and revealed himself. He hoped he had judged correctly and wouldn't learn he'd been sitting in the visiting team's bleachers.

Cookie got up from the chair and went into the house. She went in, however, thinking she had been mean. She could see that Ben hadn't known what she meant by Enlightenment philosophers or Master Clockmaker. She'd indulged in one-upmanship. She wished she could go back and redo that last bit.

He hadn't had time to digest what she'd said, but he felt that her final remark had pulled the rug from under his certainty.

Ben left the porch and walked around to the back of the house to where Eddie had ridden his bike. He had put the bike away in the garage and was ready now for the first business meeting of The Grasshoppers, where they ruled several pages of a notebook Eddie had bought into five columns: one each for customers names, date, amount due, money received and the final column for Moses's share.

"Anything special you're going to buy with your money?" asked Eddie.

"I'll buy a War Bond like I did last summer—that's eighteen seventy-five. I really need new football shoes. Mine were too tight last fall."

"Mine too. What size are yours?"

"Ten."

"Same here. They aren't making them anymore, only army boots now."

"I know and I've heard the sport stores in Asheville don't have any."

"Maybe we'll have to wear sneakers," Eddie said.

"Or army boots."

The business meeting drifted into whether or not to see *"Three*

147

Men in White" at the Carolina.

Riding home, Ben's thoughts went back to his talk with Cookie. He saw her point. He hadn't fully realized that his logical dismissal of God rested solely on the premise that God would desire all humans to know his true nature and worship him in the same manner. Take that assumption away and his argument collapsed. She mentioned Enlightenment Philosophers and a Master Clockmaker. He'd come across the Enlightenment in world history class, but what he remembered dealt with the rise of science and not ideas about God, so he didn't know what she was talking about. Having his argument undermined didn't in any way cause him to regard religion as more valid. The God cookie suggested brushed religion aside. The God she talked about had no use for religion or humans for that matter. He needed to think more about it. He had ridden home and put his bike away without being fully aware of what he was doing. It wasn't until he opened the kitchen door and encountered his mother that he returned to the present.

"Do you know anything about Enlightenment philosophers?" he asked.

"Enlightenment philosophers?" She shrugged. "Not much. Why?"

"It just came up."

"Gosh, let me think. I haven't thought about the Enlightenment since I was in school. It was also known as 'The Age of Reason.' It was a time when the church's authority began to be questioned and people began to look to science for answers. I don't recall the names of any philosophers. Well, there was this famous one . . . but I can't think of his name at the moment. I do remember from American history class that those philosophers had a big influence on the men who wrote the

Declaration of Independence and the Constitution. Thomas Jefferson, for instance—or so the teacher said."

"What about 'Master Clockmaker' - heard of that?"

"Master Clockmaker? No, afraid not. What's this all about?"

He walked down the hallway toward the stairs trailing an answer, "I've got to find out."

Quitting time came for Sexton. The newspaper had been out for two hours and there had been no calls so far. It was still early. The department had an officer on call all night, but Sexton wanted to take the call himself. The way the caller was handled could make a big difference. He was going to stick it out until he figured any possible responder to the article had gone to bed.

He played three games of solitaire then went to the john. He started down the hall toward the coffee machine for yet one more cup before he remembered he'd emptied the carafe on his last trip. The phone rang and he jogged back to his desk.

"Detective Kyle Sexton speaking."

"I'm callin' 'bout what the paper said—said 'bout that missn' woman."

"Yes."

"I seen her coupla weeks ago and I think I seen her coupla nights ago."

The woman was anxious, as if she'd been undecided about calling. There was music in the background making it hard to hear her.

"OK, Please give me your name," he said trying to make his voice unhurried, casual, trying to calm her.

She ignored his request. "Seen her sittin' in Hunter Sinklair's truck outside the E-lite."

"I appreciate your calling," he began, wanting to lead her into a conversation, but he realized he'd just heard the connection being broken. She'd hung up on him! It was like having a whopper on the line, seeing its size briefly through the water before feeling the line go slack. Hunter Sinklair? He opened the desk drawer and took out the telephone book. No one named Sinklair. The name, Sinclair, was familiar, however. The gasoline brand and the congressman. He checked the book again. No Sinclair either; the congressman would have an unlisted number. But wait a minute—the music!

"Shit! Carson's Cafe!," he yelled, coming out of his desk chair as if on springs.

He'd heard that music every day since it first went on the jukebox. Bert Carson was addicted to it: Ella's *Those Little White Lies*.

Carson's was three blocks away. He jogged the distance, stopping to catch his breath outside the door before going inside. Customers were sitting at three tables. Janice Carson, one of Bert's daughters was filling a showcase at the register with cigarette packages. He sauntered up to the counter and waited for her to straighten up.

"Evenin' Janice."

"Kyle, how ya'll?"

"Fine. Just fine. Janice, do you happen to know if someone placed a call on your phone in the last ten minutes?"

"My phone?"

"The restaurant's phone." He motioned toward the instrument on a counter behind her.

She looked nonplussed. "Not that I know of."

At that moment the new waitress came into the room through the swinging door to the kitchen.

"Have you been here at the register all evening?" he asked.

"Mostly. Except I just went into the back to get some cartons of cigarettes."

He said abruptly, "Thanks Janice, I need to ask the waitress something."

Sexton waited until the woman placed pieces of pie before two diners and intercepted her on her way back to the kitchen.

"Excuse me. I think you called me at Police Headquarters a few minutes ago. I'm Detective Sexton."

She looked stunned. Kyle took her elbow and gently steered her toward the kitchen.

"We can talk best in here."

The cook looked up when they entered and then went back to his work.

"You were telling me about seeing the woman whose picture was in the paper."

She wanted to deny it, but his air of authority overwhelmed her. She nodded. He guided her to a bench against the wall.

"What was the man's name you told me on the phone?"

"Hunter Sinklair."

This was his caller all right. "OK, What is your name?"

"Marie Boyes."

"Take your time, Marie. Tell me what you know."

"What about the customers?"

"Janice can handle them."

She surrendered. "I used to work at the E-lite Tavern down past

Saluda. I went outside on a break and I passed Hunter a'comin' in the door. Then I noticed his truck parked there with this Mexican woman inside. After I come back inside, he left again."

"What makes you think it was the woman you saw in the paper?"

"Looked like her, that's what."

"What time of day was this?"

"On about ten o'clock."

"What day?"

"Can't be sure. Like I said, it was coupla' weeks ago."

Sexton thought a while about what she'd said. He'd never been curious about the congressman's family, but he believed he'd heard he had a son.

"Is this Hunter related to the Congressman Sinclair?"

She gave him a "You're shitting me" look of disbelief.

"Well hell yes."

Kyle ignored the rebuke. "What was he doing at the tavern?"

"What would he be a doin' there. He owns the place don't he?"

"Owns the place?"

Marie Boyes shook her head in wonder at the depth of some people's ignorance. Her experience in life had been one of each person taking advantage of another if they could. She now felt an advantage over this detective and showed it through an affected smugness.

Kyle paid no attention; he was too busy with a dawning awareness that the case had taken on a new and promising dimension.

"Why are you working here now?"

Marie took time answering. "Too far. I live here in town and didn't have the gas."

Sexton weighed this. What she said was reasonable. The tavern must be fifteen miles away. She'd only have an "A" ration card. Four gallons a week would be a stretch for her. He took out his notebook.

"You said you saw her 'a couple of nights ago' also."

"I only think it was her. I was walkin' ta work from my place. Walkin' along 7th. Avenue and I just come up to King Street, when the light changed an' the cars waitin' for the light pulled away. I think the passenger in the first car was the Mexican. I didn't see who was drivin' good, but it coulda been Hunter."

"You said, 'car', so it wasn't the truck you'd seen before?"

"No. Just a car. Dark color. Least ways not white."

"What time was this?"

"I was on my way to work so near five-thirty. Shift starts at six. I only work four hours Monday through Thursday."

"You're saying it was one of those days?"

"Well come to think, it had to be Thursday, 'cause it was my first day on the job. Yeah, Thursday."

Kyle withdrew the picture of Blanca Martinez he had in his pocket.

"Take a look at this. Is this the woman you saw?"

"That's her."

"Give me your address. I appreciate your calling in tonight."

Kyle walked back to Headquarters feeling he'd made progress. He had a name of a man seen with the teacher—in whose car she'd been seen. Who that man was might be a problem he realized. Questioning the big man's son would no doubt displease Chief Housman and Mayor Reilly. Both were politicians first and whatever else came second. He'd run it by Housman tomorrow.

That evening Ben sat with his parents in front of their Philco radio as was every other family in town, waiting to hear one of President Roosevelt's "Fireside Chats." That afternoon on the car radio they'd heard that the Allied forces had taken Rome and they expected this would be the subject of his talk. They were right.

He began, "My friends, yesterday, June 4th. 1944, Rome fell to American and Allied troops. The first of the Axis capitals is now in our hands. One up and two to go." He then went on to extol the virtues of the Italian people, their role in Western civilization, arts, culture and Christianity and how the Italian emigrants have been valued American citizens. He spoke of how Italians had suffered under the fascists and the Nazi and said American forces were hurrying to bring aid to the almost starving people of Rome. He ended assuring eventual victory and talked of "Nazi soldiers nervously awaiting our assault" on Western Europe. His listeners were to discover that while celebrating a major victory, the speech was also a ruse, mentioning as he did a *future* strike against the European continent, when in fact that strike was already underway even as he was speaking.

Tuesday June, 5th.

At seven a.m., Ben's father stumbled downstairs in his pajamas to answer the persistently ringing phone. Howie Philips, the night manager of the Lodge, was calling to tell his boss to turn on the radio—the invasion of Europe had begun. He did this and then woke up his wife and son.

The news was incomplete. The earliest reports were taken from intercepted German radio broadcasts describing paratroop landings and the bombing of the ports of LeHavre and Dunkirk. The American War Department had not confirmed the story yet. The Roberts were glued to the radio for an hour. Mrs. Roberts brewed coffee and made toast. Then they learned from a BBC broadcast that leaflets had been dropped on French costal cities warning people of the heavy bombing and advising them to immediately leave the cities and walk to open country and not collect in crowds. There was no doubt now—the big show was on. It was only later in the day they learned it had a name, D Day. The same bits of information began to be repeated. They turned from the radio, which was left on, to each take up their plans for the day.

"Ben, your mother says we need eggs. We should have thought of it when you were at the farm on Saturday. Come up to the Lodge with me and get the station wagon and drive out there for her."

At the Lodge, his father went through instructions for driving the 1941 Ford wagon, the "Woody." Ben had never driven this car alone, it belonged to the Lodge and his father was afraid of damaging it. It was good to learn of his father's increased confidence in his driving, but it was still hard to pay attention to what his father was saying, because he was eager to get going and the instructions were essentially the same as those for the family Plymouth.

Out of sight of the Lodge and his father, he speeded up, swooping around the banked curves like a diving hawk. Once off the mountain, he decided to stop at Abbie Ransom's house. When he'd told her of the German major's interest in swapping books, she'd said Ben should take *This Side of Paradise* and another book they'd select together the next time he went to the farm. He pulled to the curb at her house and ran to the back door.

The first thing Sexton did when he got to the office in the morning was to write up the conversation he'd had with Marie Boyes at the cafe. He remembered it word for word, because he'd reviewed it many times before falling asleep. This done he got a cup of Flora's first brew of the day, then sat killing time, then got up and sharpened three pencils, then spent more time lining them up carefully on his desk. Finally, at five to ten, he heard Flora's greeting, "Good morning, Chief." In his mind he saw the man hanging up his hat, unbuttoning his coat and finally sitting at this desk. Flora passed down the hall with Housman's morning cup and returned to her desk—the moment he'd been waiting for had arrived. He walked down the hall and rapped with a knuckle on the door frame of Housman's office.

"Good morning, Chief."

"Mornin' Kyle, c'mon in."

As soon as Sexton was seated Housman said, "I couldn't pull myself away from the radio. Reporter talked from Rome about the people cheering our boys. Makes ya proud!"

"And how."

"And the invasion. Son-of-a-bitch, it's about to be over. We'll get that bastard Hitler and hang him by his balls."

"You bet, sir."

Kyle waited a couple of beats for Housman's euphoria to ebb a bit. "I wonder, sir, if you saw the piece in the paper yesterday about the missing high school teacher, Martinez."

"I did. Did you get that put there?"

"It was a cooperative effort. We owe Don Howard over at the paper a favor."

Housman responded with a grunt.

"The thing is, I did get a response to our request for information. A woman claims she saw Martinez sitting in a truck outside the E-lite Tavern down Saluda way."

"The Chief laughed. "The E-lite! Yeah, I know about the E-lite. So some young buck took her there did he?"

"Well . . . You see the woman who reported this said she was a waitress at the tavern. She said she saw Martinez sitting in a truck in the parking lot. It was about two weeks ago—not on the night she disappeared. The woman said the truck belonged to Hunter Sinclair."

"Said what?" Kyle had the Chief's full attention now.

"And on the night she disappeared she thought she saw her again here in town. She thought the man she was with was Sinclair again."

"'She thought, She thought.' Sounds like she's a fuckin' airhead. You can't take that kind of testimony seriously. 'She thought!'"

"I showed her the photograph and she was sure she'd seen the teacher, just not sure who was driving last Thursday."

"Well that doesn't prove nothin'."

Kyle thought to himself he'd been right about Housman not liking this news.

"You're right Chief, it doesn't prove Sinclair had anything to do with her being missing, but it is the only positive thing we have."

"What do you know 'bout this woman, this waitress? You can't go questioning Hunter Sinclair on some floozie's say so." Housman shook his head as if it were the craziest idea ever heard.

"All those Mexicans look alike," he continued. "And they have dark skin. You can see that in the newspaper picture. Could be the woman in the truck had dark skin and that's why the waitress made the mistake. After all there are a lot of people around here with dark skins who aren't Mexican."

"You mean Negroes?"

Housman realized what he'd just suggested and he sure didn't want to be quoted inferring that.

"No I mean . . . What time was it the waitress saw her in the truck?"

"About ten at night."

"See, I mean it was too damn dark for her to be sure of anything. It means to me this waitress has it in for young Sinclair for some reason.

Sexton rubbed his chin and stood up. "It's like you said, Chief, we need to check out this waitress."

The Chief wondered if he'd said that. He nodded nevertheless.

Sexton wasn't about to do what John Bell Housman wanted— forget about anything connected with Hunter Sinclair. He was going to have to explore his lead very carefully, as carefully as a kid playing Pik Up Stiks.

"Thanks for your help, Chief."

Coming back to his office, he found Clint studying his arrangement of carefully aligned pencils on his desk.

"Kyle, I think you're overqualified for this job."

"What can I say."

Kyle motioned for Clint to sit down. He then related the story Marie Boyes had told him and the Chief's reaction.

Clint said, "I can just hear ole John Bell, 'Who is this damn woman anyway?"

"Good imitation, but that's also a good question."

"Tell you what. I'm a now and then customer of the good old E-lite. I can linger over a beer tonight and find out what the bartender, Edward, or Edard as he says it, can tell me about the waitress and maybe the Martinez woman. He knows me pretty well and will talk to me. Whereas if you were to ask questions he'd likely only think 'police' and become careful about what he remembers."

Sexton was itching for action. At last he had a solid lead to follow after feeling impotent for days, but Clint was right.

"Do that Clint."

Ben knocked on Abbie Ransom's back door. Abbie got up from the kitchen table where she'd been drinking coffee and listening to the news. She was dressed in her bathrobe. On the way to the door, she ran her fingers through her short, curly hair and readjusted her robe.

"Ben," she said surprised. "You're certainly up and out early."

In his joy over having the car he hadn't considered the hour until he saw her bathrobe.

"I hope it isn't too early. I'm driving to the Graham's farm and I thought I could take the books you'd suggested I take to the major."

"Of course. Please come in."

"Did you hear about the invasion?"

"Yes," Abbie said motioning toward the radio. "I was just listening. I'm so afraid for our boys."

She led the way into her den and stood studying the book shelves. "Which book beside the Fitzgerald book should we pick for him? You said he liked Fitzgerald so we'd better steer away from someone like Henry James." With a mischievous smile she said, "Let's have him try this one on for size."

She picked a book up from her desk and handed it to Ben—*Farewell My Lovely*.

Ben had never read anything by the author, Raymond Chandler, but he'd heard of him.

"Isn't that a detective novel?"

"Yes, the protagonist is a private detective - a 'private eye.'"

Abbie's choice puzzled him. Was she playing a trick on the major? And what about the fact that she read detective novels?

"You look surprised, Ben. Chandler is a very good writer. He has introduced a new, bold style. You need to read it when he returns it."

She read the doubt that was still on Ben's face. "Yes, perhaps it's not the best choice."

She looked back at the shelves. "I know. He has probably read Hemingway, but he's unlikely to have read *For Whom the Bell Tolls*, since it was published after the war started."

She glanced at Ben; his look of doubt was gone. She took the book off the shelf.

They walked back through the house to the back door, where Ben paused.

"Something else," he said. "The other day a person I was talking to mentioned the Enlightenment and some philosopher's idea of a Master Clockmaker. I've got some idea now about what the Enlightenment was, but not the Clockmaker. Do you know about that?"

"Really, the Enlightenment? How did you come to talk about that?"

Now here was a problem. Ben didn't want to discuss the existence of God with Abbie Ransom. He guessed she was a standard Christian like everyone else and it could only hurt his relationship with her. He mentally kicked himself for not being more careful.

"It just came up," he answered weakly.

"I don't want to be nosy, but I'd think that to be an unusual subject to 'just come up.' Whom were you talking to, if you don't mind telling me?"

"My friend Eddie White's little sister. She was talking about these philosophers and . . . "

His voice trailed off into a mumble, but Abbie was thinking her own thoughts. She had never seen the girl, but her good friend Trudy Burns knew the White family well and she'd described their daughter with pleasure, laughing at the girl's surprising and precocious comments. Yes, Abbie could imagine. Her name was something odd.

"What is her name, Eddie's sister?"

"Cookie."

Yes, she thought, here is Ben talking to this precocious younger girl and it's clear he hadn't asked her what she'd meant about the mysterious

Master Clockmaker. Had he not asked because he didn't want her to know of his ignorance? Was it because she was younger and he didn't want to yield the advantage of his supposed elder wisdom, or was there something additional, not wanting to forfeit her admiration?

"Well, I remember a couple of the philosophers - Voltaire and Montesquieu, but the 'Clockmaker' stumps me, and I don't know how you'd go about looking it up. You could read about the Enlightenment and see if you come across a reference. I'm sorry I don't have a book that deals with that period. The public library has a set of the *Encyclopedia Britannica*; my husband and I donated it—11th edition as I recall."

Gerhard heard a sound coming from the direction of the barns. He turned and saw the boy—the one to whom he'd given the book—what was his name? Yes, Ben. He had two books in his hand. Was he returning Gatsby? He'd given him the book to keep.

"Good morning, Ben. Back for more milk?"

Ben walked up and greeted him, "Good morning Herr Major. I came to get eggs this time, but I also brought you *This Side of Paradise* that you were interested in reading and another book that Mrs. Ransom thought you'd like. It's Hemingway, but a new one, at least not one she thought you'd had a chance to read. He held out *For Whom the Bell Tolls*.

"Thank you. No, I haven't read this and I like Hemingway. Did you like Gatsby?"

"Very much so far."

Books were not on Ben's mind, however. It was the invasion

and von Kleist's reaction to it. He didn't know how to bring up the subject. It seemed like asking a losing candidate for office about his reaction to losing. Instead a substitute subject was readily at hand.

"Talking about books reminds me of talking to a friend who mentioned the Enlightenment and a Master Clockmaker. I didn't know exactly what she was talking about. The Enlightenment I know something about now, but I haven't been able to find out about the Clockmaker. Would you happen to know?"

Gerhard, like Abbie, was a little surprised that Ben and a friend were discussing the Enlightenment and he was more interested in that question than the answer to Ben's question.

"May I ask how you got into this discussion with your friend?"

It seemed that no one was willing to answer his question directly before first quizzing him about the circumstances. He discovered that he wasn't experiencing his usual wariness of revealing his religious non-belief. Maybe it was because the major would be going away and Ben's secret would go with him.

"We were talking about whether God exists and she brought up these philosophers and the Master Clockmaker."

"She? Did you happen to be talking to Cookie?"

Ben nodded, surprised that von Kleist remembered Cookie's name. Gerhard had begun thinking along the same lines as Abbie had; Ben didn't want to admit his ignorance, and he wanted to find out about this bit of information before he talked to her again. Gerhard understood this, because he had experienced the same dilemma with Hilde—many times. He wouldn't ask Ben about the question of God's existence; the boy would talk more about that if he wanted to. In the past years, he'd learned to be patient when one of his men came to him with a problem and let the man indicate how deeply he was ready to delve .

"I believe I can help you with this question. I wrote a paper about the Enlightenment when I was at the university. Some of the philosophers, Voltaire was one, believed God created the universe, but afterward was no longer involved with the affairs of his creation—had better things to do I guess. So, the religions such as Christianity were merely man's creation and rituals and dogma associated with the religions such as prayer, sin, redemption, heaven, hell and so on were purely man-made and had no connection with God. One only had to look at the marvel of the universe to be in touch with God. These philosophers were called 'Deists.' The Master Clockmaker was an analogy to God, who'd made the clock and was finished with it." He laughed. "This clockmaker didn't make clock repairs."

Any question Ben had had was answered; he knew now what Cookie had meant.

"Thanks, I understand now."

But, Gerhard noticed Ben's body language wasn't that of someone who had come to get information and was now ready to leave.

"Was there something else, Ben?"

"Yeah, did you hear about the invasion?"

Of course that would be on the boy's mind. "Yes, we heard on the radio at camp this morning."

He figured the boy was curious about his reaction to the news.

"What do you think of it, Ben?" His tone was neutral inviting an honest answer.

"It is . . . well, exciting."

"Yes, I understand. As if your team has just scored a goal."

Ben nodded.

"And my reaction, as well as most of my comrades, is that the opposing team has scored a goal. Not a happy feeling. We German soldiers knew, of course, that at some time an invasion would be made along the Atlantic coast. But, when it came it was still a surprise. I probably know some of the men facing the invasion. Many will die. That is very sad, but I hope this will convince our generals that the sane thing to do is surrender and save as many lives as possible."

Ben didn't know how to respond to this. He began to recognize, however, that he wanted a relationship with this man. He found that it was easy to look to him for knowledge of a man's world, just as he had been able to use Abbie Ransom for answers he'd been unable to ask his parents. They were the parents of childhood, and good ones, but there was something about the quality of being childhood parents that disqualified them for what he wanted now.

"My father was in the last war—in the British Army. He was in the trenches for four years in France. He almost never talks about it. When he says anything, even though it isn't much, you can tell what he's thinking about is scary. I've wondered . . ."

And were afraid to ask, Gerard thought. Yes, his father has much that is very scary to tell. Gerhard had been able to talk to an uncle and ask the questions he'd not been able to ask his father, so he heard Ben's appeal for information, information to fill a large gap in his imagination about his father. Of course, Gerhard couldn't provide that, but he could make it so the boy didn't feel so on the outside.

"The things that happen in war are very bad and you can understand that a man wants to shield his children from that," he began, while thinking to himself, and especially from those acts he is not proud of doing.

"But, at the same time, the friendships he makes and the experience of working together with others are some of the happiest times he will ever know. You are working together to preserve each other's lives and this makes for very strong bonds."

Ben was totally engaged with a concentration close to what Gerard had just described. Gerhard judged he had said nothing so far that should disturb the boy.

"I was not always a soldier, Ben. I was a professor of anthropology, the study of human societies and how they developed. I joined the army, because . . . I saw it as the best way to have control over what happened to me rather than wait and take a chance on getting a bad assignment (Dachau). I joined the panzers, because I knew someone with influence to help me get into an officer training school. Otherwise, serving in the army would have been the last thing I would have chosen for myself. As I said, you form very strong bonds with your comrades. You go into battle with the great need to be dependable. In the back of your mind is the dread you might let your friends down—this group that has become the most important in your world. Once into the fight, everything is driven by the fear you and your friends will be killed and that gets transformed into anger and a surging wish to . . . win. And so you kill rather than be killed. If it weren't for that war would be like any game. After an agreed upon elapse of time a winner would be declared. The evil of war is that young men are put in the position of killing or being killed."

Gerhard stopped, wondering if he had gone too far. Yes, perhaps.

Ben asked the foremost question on his mind, the one he'd been afraid to ask his father.

"Have you killed anyone?"

Had he led the boy into a topic, which was not his place to lead him? Or, had he only made it easier for him to voice a question the avoidance of which had formed an unseen barrier to a fuller relationship with his father? For he knew Ben wanted to know, but had been afraid to ask his father—afraid of the answer—whether or not his father had killed someone. The societal agreement is that the act of killing, which children are taught since old enough to understand, to be the worst crime possible, will be expunged from the record of soldiers returning home from war. It is agreed, magically, that no returning individual has killed anyone.

"From the beginning, Ben, I was a commander, first of one panzer then of several and finally of a whole battalion." He gestured toward the men working in the bean field. It was not my job to look down a gunsight and pull a trigger (a compromise with the truth), but I directed the killing of many."

Although fully expected, the answer disturbed Ben. Here was a man whom he had wanted to like and although he didn't know it, use as a model, who had just admitted he was a killer and a killer of Americans. Perhaps it was von Kleist's frank, open expression, making no excuse for his participation in war's madness that led Ben to begin to accept him, and his father now as well, as fellow humans caught in one of life's sticky, contradictory conflicts. An understanding began to emerge that his and his friends' perception of adult stupidity hadn't taken those conflicts into account.

"Well, I've got to get back with the eggs," Ben said.

"Nice to see you, Ben, and please thank Mrs. Ransom for the thoughtful loan of these books."

Jack Simmons had just finished his junior year at Brevard College and was taking advantage of the school's summer pilot's training course. The college was one of over a thousand programs across the nation that were recognized by the War Training Service to provide flight training to young men who would later become pilots in the Air Force, Navy and Marine corps. Jack couldn't believe his luck. Since he'd seen his first airplane fly overhead as a small child, he'd wanted to learn to fly, but thought it would be a long time before he could afford that luxury. And now here he was learning to fly at the school's expense—the government's expense. The college, located 25 miles west of the city, used the Myers Airfield and the Myers Flying Service in Hendersonville to provide the instruction and hanger space for the school's lone Piper Cub.

Jack was also taking advantage of a perfect day for flying. The morning news of the invasion had him pumped up imagining himself strafing retreating Germans. With luck he'd be in the Air Force by the end of the summer. He brought the plane into a long left turn preparing for another strafing run. Buddy Farmer, his instructor, relaxing in the rear tandem-seat, had other thoughts, a third of his attention on the view out the window, a third on Jack's handling of the plane and a third on his plans for the evening.

Jack already had completed fifteen hours of flight time and had a natural talent for flying. Buddy would be comfortable after the kid shot a few more landings to let him solo. Jack brought the joystick back to the neutral position and now straight ahead and below them was Laurel Lake.

"Jack, take her down to eight-hundred feet as you pass over the lake. I want to see if my girlfriend's car is in the parking lot."

Jack began the angle of decline to accomplish this.

"Keep to the left side of the lake so I can get a good look at the lot."

Buddy pressed his head against the window as they approached the lake, focusing his gaze on the parking lot. He didn't see the car he was looking for, but in that brief moment his peripheral vision caught sight of a reddish-orange object in the fringe of the bulrushes along the lake's shore. Something about the shape alarmed him.

"Jack, I'm going to take the controls for a minute. I want to have another look at something down there."

He flew on half a mile and then executed a 180° turn and began a run back over the lake, this time flying even lower.

"Jack, look closely along the edge of the lake where the bulrushes begin. I saw something orange."

Buddy held the light plane so they had an excellent view of the lake edge.

"There it is," Buddy shouted. "See it?"

"Yeah. Orange. Beach ball or something."

Buddy was lost in thought. "Yeah . . . something like that," he mumbled, then said, "Jack, take the plane up to three thousand and do the stall recovery and then we'll call it a day. You've done good."

Simmon's landing was perfect. They'd shoot takeoffs and landings tomorrow and then he'd tell the kid to take it up on his own. Buddy liked to "solo" students this way, surprising them, not giving them time to worry. They walked back to the office where Jack filled out his flight log and left.

"Oscar," Buddy called to his boss. "I've got something I want to

169

check out. I'll be back in an hour or less."

He got into his '39 Ford convertible and drove back to Laurel Lake. The orange object he'd seen nagged at him. He parked on Lake Drive at a spot he judged to be where he'd seen it. He got out and walked along the road looking down into the bulrushes until he saw a tiny speck of orange through the dense growth. Tall weeds and brambles covered the steep bank making the climb down to the water's edge difficult. He parted the bulrushes and . . . there it was, the floating body of a woman—just as he'd feared.

At a quarter past eleven, Kyle Sexton, coffee cup in hand, stood in Flora's office pondering Clint's planned interrogation of the bartender later that night. He took a sip from his cup. Good coffee, not like the swill detectives in fictional police departments were forced to endure. The Chief had Flora buy Bokar from the A&P. The Chief was good for some things.

The phone rang and Flora answered it. She handed the receiver to Kyle saying, "You'd better take this."

His face became hyper-alert as he listened.

"OK. I'll be right there."

Sexton parked his car behind the Ford convertible. A young man, who'd been leaning against the front fender of the Ford, walked up to him as he got out of his car.

"Hi, I'm the one who called you, Buddy Farmer."

"I'm Detective Kyle Sexton. Show me what you found."

"It's right down the bank there, at the water's edge. You can see the path through the weeds where I went down. I don't care to go down there again, if it's OK with you."

"But you think it's a body, right?"

"Yeah, I'm sure. I'm a flight instructor. I saw it from the air and came back to check it out."

"Did you tell anyone else?"

"No. I drove over to the Inn and asked to use their phone, but no one overheard my call to you."

"Good. We could have a crowd here."

Kyle left the road and followed Buddy's path through the weeds. He got as close as he could to the water and leaned out and parted the bulrushes.

"Shit!" he murmured as he looked down on the body in the orange dress.

He was hoping the guy had been wrong. He wanted to find Blanca Martinez, but sure as hell not like this. A sinking sadness swept over him. After a long moment he came back to considering the problem he faced. You don't go for a midnight swim in your best orange dress. It was definitely a murder case now. He looked back at the steep bank. There was but one path where the weeds had been bent down. Four days had passed since she'd gone missing. Could the weeds have straightened out in that time? He doubted it, and the guy would have been dragging a body. She was put in the lake some place else and floated here. OK, now to get her out.

"Thanks for the help," he told Farmer when he climbed back up to the road. He wrote the flight instructor's information in his notebook.

"You can go now, and I'd appreciate it if you said nothing about this for a couple of hours until we can get her out. We'll have a mess of gawkers otherwise."

Buddy nodded. "Right."

Sexton went to his car and picked up the radio microphone. He paused to ponder how best to proceed. He'd call the two officers on duty. He pictured the three of them trying to grab the body and pull it out. Not a reassuring picture. They needed some kind of equip - That was it - the fire department. They had ladders, ropes, stuff like that. He switched on the radio. The desk sergeant answered.

"George, this is Kyle, see if you can get me one of the fire guys. I have a floating body in Laurel Lake and I think they are best equipped for the job of getting her out of the water."

"OK, and good luck with that."

Through the static, Kyle heard, "Fire Department, Richards speaking."

"It's Mike isn't it? This is Kyle Sexton from the cop shop."

"Yeah, sure. What's up?"

"We've been looking for a missing high school teacher and -"

"Yeah, I read about it."

"Well, I'm pretty sure we've found her floating in Laurel Lake. The body is up against the bulrushes and down a steep bank. Thing is, I think you guys are better equipped to retrieve her. We'd probably end up in the lake with her if we tried. And I'd like to get the body out as intact as possible to preserve evidence."

Richards didn't respond immediately. "I see your point. We've noticed your problem . . . sure, I'll get a couple of guys and come in one of the trucks. Give me directions."

The two police cars were the first to arrive followed by the fire truck. The firemen surveyed the scene and decided to lay a ladder down on the bank and run the end out next to the body.

"I found a use for your skills," Richards said to Kyle. "The three of you can sit on the ladder, hold it in place."

Richards carefully worked his way along the ladder rungs until he was beside the body. A basket stretcher with ropes tied to the corners was manipulated into place under the body and the other firemen began hauling the stretcher up onto the ground.

The Fire Department ambulance had arrived during this process. So had a dozen curious people who had spotted the activity from the Inn's beach. One of the cops shooed them thirty yards down the road.

It took six men to carry the stretcher up the steep hillside to the road and the ambulance. Kyle had a chance now to look more closely. She lay face down as she had in the water, but in spite of the limit to what he could see, he had no doubt he was looking at Blanca Martinez. It was then he noticed a cord had been tied around her ankle. It was simple sisal twine such as is used to tie a package, about eighteen inches long and frayed at the loose end.

An unexpected feeling of protectiveness arose in him as if the young woman had been his sister. He would catch the bastard who did this. Then, as if the idea of an orange dress suggested the cheap and showy, he asserted, "That dress isn't orange, it's apricot!" - causing puzzled looks all around.

Clint Edney had picked a time when he judged the bar at the Elite Tavern would not be so busy the bartender wouldn't have time to casually chat, while at the same time not being so deserted that their conversation might be overheard by other drinkers—seven o'clock. The guys stopping in for a drink after work had thinned out and the crowd out for an evening hadn't yet arrived. Six stools on the left side of the bar were unoccupied. Edney took the stool on the end, giving

173

him a five-stool distance from any eavesdroppers. He lit a cigarette and settled down like a man at ease with the world looking forward to several drinks. A copy of the *Asheville Citizen* lay on the bar two stools away. He reached for it and looked over the front page. Nothing he hadn't already heard about the invasion. No official report yet of where the landings were made, only the German reports he'd already read.

Edward, the bartender, gave change to a customer down the bar and approached Clint reflexively wiping the bar along the way.

"Hey Clint, How'er they hangin'?"

"Don't ask, Edard."

"That bad? Then I'd say you need a drink. What's it gonna be?"

Clint winked. "How about a glass of Coca Cola with ice?"

"Stickin' to your favorite."

"Old friends are best."

The bartender motioned at the newspaper. "Helluva thing."

"You can say that again."

Edard glanced down the bar to see if he was wanted, then turned back.

"Any excitement in the detective business?"

"Yeah. Did you read about the missing teacher?"

"Yeah, I heard."

"She's not missing anymore. My partner, Kyle Sexton, found her today floating in Laurel Lake."

"No shit? Drowned?"

"Hard to say until the autopsy."

A guy down the bar called out, "Edard, when you're finished gossiping, people over here are dying of thirst."

Edard signaled "one minute" with a finger to Clint and left to dig two beers out of the cooler. He checked the other customers and then slipped a sleeve on a glass and beneath the counter poured a double shot of rum over ice cubes and added a full six-ounce bottle of Coke. He set the glass on the bar in front of Clint.

Clint slid the picture of Martinez across the bar. "This is the teacher. Do you recall seeing her in here—last Thursday night say?"

Edard studied the picture, then shook his head. "Why Thursday night?"

"She had a date that night and never came home."

"I'm sure I'd remember her. Mexican? Don't get many here."

"My partner was talking to a waitress who works at a cafe in town, who says she used to work here and saw this woman in a truck parked outside—coupla weeks ago."

"You mean in the parking lot? Well, I never saw her inside here. Who is the waitress? Gotta name?"

"Let's see, what did Kyle say? Oh, yeah, Marie, Marie Boyes."

"Marie Boyes? That bitch! She was fired a week ago for stealing cigarettes. The dumb bitch had a carton under her skirt fastened to her leg with a garter. It came loose when she was leaving work and dropped right in front of the boss. Fired her on the spot."

Clint's affected nonchalance evaporated. "No shit? I think she told my partner she quit working here, because she didn't have enough gas for the drive here."

"That's a laugh. She hasn't got a car. The dishwasher gave her a lift every day—for services rendered for sure."

"Son-of-a-bitch. So much for her information. You said the boss, did you mean the manager or the owner?"

"Barney Youngblood, the manager. Sinclair had gone before that shit hit the fan."

"I dread telling my partner about this. He had his hopes up."

Clint thought about mentioning that it was in Sinclair's truck the waitress said she'd seen Martinez, but that was dicey. Better let it lie.

Edard was called again to the other end of the bar. Clint took a last full swallow of his rum and Coke, put it down on top of two dollars and left.

"How long are you going to be talking? Shall I go ahead with dinner?" Ann Edney asked her husband, who was dialing the phone.

"Yeah, go ahead. This will only take a minute."

She had started taking the meatloaf out of the oven and then put it back in. She was used to Clint's "only a minute."

Clint lit a cigarette waiting for Kyle to pick up. When Sexton answered, Clint recapped the conversation at the bar.

"So the question is," Clint put it," Did she really see Martinez in Sinclair's truck, or was she angry over being fired and wanted to cause trouble for the E-lite?"

"What's your guess?"

"Well I've never seen her as far as I can recollect. You saw her. Is she someone you'd trust?"

"I wouldn't bet a day's pay she was. It's a question of motive—to cause trouble as you suggest, or did she want to be a responsible citizen?"

"Responsible citizen, Ha! More like did she want attention?"

"Yeah, what's our next move do you think?"

Ann Edney poured herself a cup of tea and sat down at the kitchen table and started thumbing through a *Ladies' Home Journal.*

"I know what we have to do," Clint said.

"We have to haul her ass into the station and confront her with her lie," said Kyle.

"Took the words outa my mouth. Both of us sittin' there staring at her like we mean to toss her in jail and throw the key away. Her reaction should tell us what we're dealin' with."

There was silence on the line while both men had the same thought. Clint verbalized it. "And if we decide she's tellin' the truth, how do we go at the congressman's son?"

"That's easy. You bring him in and give him the third degree," said Sexton archly.

"I have a wife and a child to support. If John Bell fires you, you can thumb a ride north and get a job at the Ford plant making tanks."

Here was an opening to tell Clint about his newly formed intention to resign and join the Air Force, but he didn't say it. Kyle was afraid that news might dampen Clint's sense of them being a team. Clint was fully committed now to help find the killer. Kyle didn't want to alter that.

"I'll contact her and set up a time."

"Sounds good. What about the autopsy?"

"The pathologist is coming from Asheville tonight. I'm going to sit in."

"Let me know what he finds. Gotta go; Dinner's on the table."

Sexton had Rosa Sanchez come to the basement morgue at Parham Hospital to make the formal identification of the corpse, but there was no doubt about who was lying there on the dissection table and also no doubt that the bruises on Blanca Martinez's neck meant she'd been

177

strangled. The question was, had this caused her death, or did she drown? One way or another it was murder for sure. One doesn't go for a recreational swim in one's best dress with a cord tied around your ankle.

He was waiting until Dr. Henry Bryant could come down to Hendersonville from Asheville to perform the autopsy. Bryant was the only board certified pathologist left in the area and he was turned to whenever there was a suspicious death. Tonight he wouldn't get to Hendersonville until eight p.m., which meant a long day for Sexton—for the Doc too.

It wasn't until eight-thirty that he arrived. From the hospital lobby Sexton watched Bryant park and get out of his '41 Buick and stop to light a cigarette before continuing to the hospital entrance. Sexton walked to the door and held it open.

Bryant was a tall man with heavy, sloping shoulders. His suit coat was thrown back over one shoulder and held by a finger through the neck-loop. His face expressed a permanent notion that life was a farce he'd wandered into, couldn't find his way out of, and had decided to make the best of it.

"Good evening, Detective. I haven't seen you since Christmas, How've you been?"

"Can't complain, Doc. Yourself?"

"Tired. So many of our staff have been taken into the service. But, hell with the invasion let's hope it will soon be over. Let's not keep the patient waiting."

Bryant knew the way to the morgue. Sexton followed uneasily. He was like most when it came to autopsies. Could anyone ever get used to cutting people open.

178

Blanca Martinez lay uncovered on the stainless steel table. Bryant usually wrote up his post-mortem findings after he'd completed the work, but Sexton, wanting to eliminate the possibility that a defense attorney might claim the report was written "from memory" and therefore subject to error, had arranged for a court reporter to take Bryant's dictation as the exam proceeded. She followed them into the room and took a seat against the wall. Bryant walked to the table and stood for a long moment. He turned to the hospital orderly, who was going to assist him and took the rubber apron he was holding and put it on. The man held open the surgical gloves Bryant would use and the doctor slipped them on. Bryant stepped up to the table and began talking in a workman-like fashion.

"Here we have a young woman of probable Mexican heritage. My impression is mid-twenties.." He looked at Sexton.

"Twenty-four. She's originally from Houston."

"OK, Mexican/American. Healthy appearing, normal weight . . . well built," Bryant said, smiling.

"Roger that," Said Kyle, stepping forward to take a place beside him and watching closely as Bryant made a careful examination of Blanca's scalp and face. After prying open the mouth with a tongue blade, he did the same to the inside of the mouth. Then came the ears and exterior of the eyes.

"Scalp, ears and eyes unremarkable," he said in his dictating voice.

"Notice these bruises," he said, pointing to areas around the corners of the mouth.

"Three points of ecchymosis each 2 centimeters in diameter 3 centimeters laterally from the mouth. One point over the right mandible and 6 centimeters from the midline," he said, casting a glance toward the reporter to be sure she had heard him.

"Nothing else remarkable about the frontal aspect of the head except skin changes from immersion in water for many hours—I'd guess a week. How long after being reported missing was the body discovered?"

"Ah, four days."

"Was she floating?"

"Yes."

"How cold is the water in that lake?"

"I don't know exactly, but comfortable to swim in."

"Then that's about right. Bacteria begin decomposing the body causing gas to form in the tissues which causes the flotation—usually a week, but sooner if the water is warm. Of course, if there is air in the lungs it enhances flotation. We'll see about that."

Bryant's attention then went to the neck, where deep bruising was obvious.

Measuring with a ruler he said, looking toward the secretary, "The cricoid cartilage appears broken on superficial examination." Aside to Kyle, he said, "I'll make an incision and check that later, but let's turn her on her side for a moment."

The orderly held the body on its side while Bryant examined the back of the neck.

"Posterior aspect of neck is unremarkable."

Speaking to Kyle he said, "Looks like someone placed one hand over her mouth, pressing hard enough to cause the bruising we see, and pressed down with the other hand on her neck with enough force to break the cricoid cartilage—here just below the thyroid cartilage or Adam's Apple."

"Strangled her," said Sexton.

"Well yes, the act of strangling. Whether or not it was the cause of death is another matter. I have only seen half a dozen cases of death by strangling. In all cases, there were thumb marks in front over the trachea and finger marks on the back of the neck." At the same time he was saying this, he demonstrated the action with his hands. "This is different—hand over mouth and pressing down on the neck."

"I got it."

Bryant proceeded to examine the rest of the exterior body in silence before calling Kyle's attention to the left ankle where the skin was broken.

"Something tied around her ankle?"

"A piece of twine, sisal twine eighteen inches long and frayed at the end. Probably tied to something heavy in order to keep her at the bottom."

"Certainly not the kind of rope one would choose if there were a choice. Anyway, the damage to the skin is likely post-mortem, no bruising."

"So, you're saying she was dead before being dumped in the lake."

"That would be my guess at this point. After I look at her lungs we'll know. If I remember correctly it is about this point in an autopsy when you recall that you have important paper work to attend to," Bryant said wryly.

"You read my mind, Doc. I'll catch you before you leave."

Sexton returned to the morgue an hour later and saw that the doctor was still at the table. He waited outside the room and smoked for another half hour. When Bryant came out, he walked with him to his car.

"She was dead before she was put in the lake. There was no water in her lungs. I saw no other pathology except what you saw. I took a vaginal swab, but after being in the water for days, absence of sperm won't prove anything."

"Would you say she was killed the same night she went missing?"

"Looks that way to me."

They shook hands at the doctor's car.

"Thanks, Doc. Let's hope we don't meet again like this soon."

Bryant took a moment to light a cigarette then opened the car door and said, "Good luck with you investigation, Detective."

Wednesday June 7th.

When Ben came downstairs, his father was sitting in front of the radio. He saw Ben and said, "The invasion's going well. We're as much as fifteen miles inland along a one hundred mile front. The Air Force flew 13,000 sorties yesterday.

"Jeez. 13,000. That's great."

"Yes, but the weather is not so great, which means it's difficult to land supplies and troops and air support is hampered. The announcer said the German air force was 'more effective.' We're still very much in the 'keep you fingers crossed' stage."

Ben laced up his Keds and walked to the kitchen window to check the weather. Sun shone on the leaves of the oak next to the house and through the leaves he saw nothing but blue sky.

His father noticed what Ben was doing. "The paper says it will be warm with scattered showers."

Ben turned from the window. "I've noticed that almost every day they include 'scattered showers.' in the forecast. That way they can't go wrong. If it rains they can say 'I told you so.' If it doesn't rain they can claim the showers were scattered somewhere else."

He was eager to eat and join Eddie.

His mother poured coffee for herself and his father, who was eating a bowl of corn flakes while he continued to read the *Asheville Citizen*.

"Everything, of course, is about the American troops. Nothing about where the British are. Are they out ahead, or are they being held up on their front? Nothing."

His irritation was evident in the way he nearly knocked over the coffee Ben's mother had just poured.

"They are probably keeping side by side," Ben said.

"Oh, how's that?"

"They wouldn't want to expose their flanks by letting one army get far ahead of the other," he said spreading peanut butter on toast.

Mr. Roberts was surprised by Ben having a military opinion, and not a little put off by Ben pointing out the issue of being "flanked." Something he hadn't thought of.

"And how do you know that?" he challenged.

"Cookie said so."

"Cookie? She's your friend's little sister isn't she. And where does she get her information?"

She said "Napolean would never allow that to happen."

Ben's mother laughed. "I hope our generals know their history."

Ben had finished the milk and put the last bit of bread in his mouth. He spoke through it. "Do they say anything about casualties?"

"Light. Lighter than expected."

Ben held up crossed fingers as he went out the door.

"See'ya later."

The Thurkell's lawn wasn't easy to mow. Mrs. Thurkell loved azaleas and had planted the bushes in randomly placed islands, making a long run with the mower impossible. It was push, pull, push, pull. He was developing a blister at the base of his thumb. He was working on automatic pilot all the while, because he was focused on the phone call to Valery he was going to make at lunch-time. He would start by thanking her again for lunch on Saturday. He would work in a "water" theme, mentioning the swim on their first meeting, the fish pond on the second and his proposal to drive to see a waterfall on the next. At the end of the next mower lap stood Eddie with his hand up. He had a milk bottle filled with water, which he held out to him.

"Yeah, good, thanks."

Eddie had the invasion on his mind. "Fifteen miles. That's a long way. Hell, it's like from here to Asheville. That's how far they've advanced in just one day. The fighting must be fierce. The paper said four thousand ships took part. I can't even imagine four thousand ships."

Yanked from his thoughts about Valery, Ben began putting together an image of the fighting. His images were drawn from all the many movies he'd seen. The faces of the men invariably resembled Robert Mitchum, John Wayne, William Bendix and their actor buddies. His father had said the Germans were bringing up reinforcements. Could we land enough men in time?

Ben took a swig of water and handed the bottle back. "Yeah, but my father says the Germans have the advantage. They are already in position, they have men and tanks already there. They can bring in supplies over many roads and railroads."

"So that's where you get that."

"Get what?"

"That way you have; if we score a touchdown and go ahead, we both shout for joy, but then you'll say, 'But there's still five minutes to go and they have that jackrabbit, Nolan.'"

Both went back to work, Eddie trying to resurrect his feeling of victory and Ben fully given over to the planned phone call to Valery.

By eleven the edging was completed, the grass clippings swept up and Eddie was turning from the Turkell's back door, cash in hand. Their next lawn, the Erb's, was farther west on Eddie's side of town. They'd meet there after going home for lunch. Walking together pushing mowers ahead of them, they came to the intersection with 5th. Avenue as Valery drove by in the Continental. Ben shouted and waved, but she continued looking straight ahead.

"She didn't see us," Ben said, disappointed.

Eddie wasn't so sure.

The room was one that served as a linen closet for the jail and with the cupboard doors closed, as the interrogation room for the two detectives, who sat now on one side of a table glaring threateningly at Marie Boyes. Marie was frightened just as they'd wanted her to be. She was also puzzled, since she had come there expecting to be rewarded for her information about the dead woman.

"We have testimony that you tried to steal cigarettes from the E-lite Tavern, but were caught in the act and fired on the spot." Sexton spoke the words with the note of finality expected from a "hanging judge."

Marie's head snapped back and her eyes widened. She looked toward the door as if she might bolt.

"What do you have to say?" asked Clint as if this would be her last chance before mounting the scaffold.

She became angry. "I was owed them cigarettes. I was cheated outta my tip money. The waitresses gotta turn all tips over to that fuckin' bartender, Edard. He's sposed'ta divide it and give it out at the end of the shift. He screwed both Shirley an' me. I was only takin' what was owed me."

"After they caught you and fired you, you were really pissed and wanted to get back at the E-lite. Right?" Kyle's tone did not brook argument.

Marie visibly sagged. "I was mad as hell an' I'da kilt that piss-ant Edard an' the stuck up manager, but I had no beef with the owner. I hardly ever saw him." A shadow of sadness came over her. "I just felt sorry for that young Mexican woman. I heard she got fired just like me. I thought I could help."

Kyle and Clint felt like they had just broken down a door and come charging into a room with guns drawn only to be faced with a child playing with her dolls. Here was an awkward gear change.

Kyle began. "Yeah, well we appreciate that . . . that you called. Uh, now if you seldom saw him, how did you know it was Hunter Sinclair's truck you saw the woman in?"

"I seen him drive inta the parking lot with that truck. Hit's a white un an' hit's got one of them spotlights on top'a the cab. Hard ta miss,"

Yes, Clint thought; he had seen young Sinclair in just such a truck getting a fill-up at Stern's garage.

"What time was this you saw the woman in the truck?" asked Sexton.

"Like I tolt you before, I seen her in the truck and maybe in a car on King Street and 7th Avenue."

"I mean what time of day? Both places.."

"Hit was near on ten at the E-lite an' I was on my way to work here in town so 5:30."

From a folder on the table, Sexton withdrew the picture of Blanca Martinez. "Look at this again carefully. Is this the woman you saw?"

Marie studied the image as she had done at Carson's Cafe. She nodded emphatically. "That's her. No mistake!"

It was dark at ten o'clock; how can you be sure?"

"The light over the entrance shines inta the lot. When I came out the door the woman looked up and right inta the light."

Remembering Chief Housman's argument about dark skin tone, Sexton said, "She has dark skin in the picture. Could it be that you saw a dark-skinned woman in the truck and that's why you think she was the woman in the picture?"

"What? Hell Mister, I ain't blind. Hit was the woman in the newspaper."

"And you're just as sure she is the woman you saw here in town last Thursday?"

"No. You don't listen worth a damn. I said I thought it was her."

Kyle looked over at his partner who shrugged.

After signing a quickly typed statement, Marie was dismissed after being thanked again for her help. This left the two detectives handling a fairly hot potato. Marie Boyes had told the truth.

"Hunter Sinclair had Blanca Martinez in his truck outside the Elite Tavern as recently as two weeks ago, and he was probably with her on her last day alive."

"Until proven otherwise, he's our man!"

The woman answering the phone sounded to Ben like she could be the Sinclair's cook.

"Hello, Ma'am. My name is Ben Roberts, I'd like to speak to Valery, please."

"She's not here, son. She said she had a golf lesson this afternoon."

He was so expecting her to be home having seen her a few minutes ago heading in that direction, that he was speechless.

"Ah . . . Please tell her I called and I'll call again later."

"I'll do that. Goodbye."

So she'd been going to the country club, a foreign country.

Ben put down the phone deflated. It was as if you'd got up your nerve to dive off the high board only to look down and see they'd drained the pool. He wandered out the front door and saw Abbie Ransom working in a flower bed in her side yard. Disconsolately, he crossed the street.

Abbie straightened slowly with a groan and saw Ben approaching and pasted a smile on her face.

"Ah Ben. The fight goes on. Neither of us will give up. Why don't the weeds catch on they're not wanted?"

Ben forced a smile and nodded.

"I'm taking a break to have lunch. Have you eaten?"

"No, I haven't." The thought of food had vanished with the failed phone call.

"I made some egg salad earlier. How does a sandwich sound?"

"I'd like that."

"Right this way."

Sitting opposite Ben at the kitchen table she asked, "How is your business venture going?"

"OK, we've had good weather." After a pause, he added, "I had lunch at the Sinclair's house on Saturday. Valery asked me."

"Is that so?"

"She showed me a fish pond her father built - a big pond."

Abbie smiled. "Anyone fishing?"

He saw she was joking. "Not when I was there, but she said her

189

father fishes a lot. I did see him while I was there. He came out on the patio where we were eating and grabbed half of Valery's sandwich. He seems like a nice guy."

Of course he did, thought Abbie. He never fails to win hearts.

"There is something I'm curious about, but didn't want to ask Valery. Where is her mother? She wasn't there and Valery never mentioned her. Is she alive?"

"Oh yes, very much, but Hendersonville isn't her cup of tea."

Abbie saw that his answer had only raised his curiosity.

"I'll explain. You see Troy Sinclair was a poor boy from here, Fletcher actually. His father worked at a saw mill there. The mill owner saw that Troy was smart and athletic and had potential to achieve more than the rural school there could offer. He arranged for Troy to live here in town and attend the high school. He did well, got notice as a football player and was offered a scholarship to Clemson College in South Carolina. He did well there too—star tailback—until he had a knee injury. I think it was his junior year. That ended football and his scholarship. He didn't have the money to continue school without it, but what had already happened is that he'd met a beautiful girl named Lorelei Folsom and they'd fallen in love. She didn't go to the school—it was all male, still is. She went to a women's college in New England, but her brother was Troy's roommate. The Folsum family was rich and very influential in South Carolina politics and thick as thieves with the Calhouns. You've heard of John C. Calhoun haven't you?"

"Is he the guy we read about in American History? Let's see . . . 'the defender of southern values in Congress.'"

"Is that what they teach you? I'm not surprised. Fiddlesticks: he was a staunch advocate of slavery. Anyway he was a powerful politician and big land owner. Clemson College is built on land donated by the family.

"I'm straying from the point. As I said, his injury would have meant leaving college, except he and Lorelei ran off and got married. Now Troy probably wasn't the kind of young man the Folsoms had in mind for their daughter, but the marriage was a fait accompli. The family then had to make him into one of theirs by getting him through college and then law school . . . and smoothing his way toward his eventual seat in the U.S. Congress."

"But that family is in South Carolina and he's a congressman here."

"But they are all Democrats you see, one hand washes the other in politics."

She realized she had to connect the dots. "That was a long way around answering your question about the absence of Valery's mother. My goodness boy, she's South Carolina aristocracy. Her social world is Washington, D.C. during congressional sessions and South Carolina the rest of the time. Troy's office is only icing on the social cake. She makes an appearance here during the election campaign every two years to smile and wave at the crowd and she does precious little of that. But, I'm not being fair. There's no reason she has to like our little city. Her life is elsewhere."

So, Ben thought, Mrs. Sinclair hasn't much use for Hendersonville and Abbie Ransom has little use for her. He thanked Abbie for lunch and left to retrieve his mower from his house and meet Eddie at the Erb's.

Ever since their conversation about the existence of God, Cookie wondered how her parting shot of a God who had created the universe and then moved on had affected Ben. She was impatient to find out. She was handed an unexpected chance.

"Cookie, would you do me a favor?" Eddie was standing at the kitchen door looking in through the screen.

She walked over. His tone was the one she heard whenever he wanted a favor. "What is it?"

"I've got to sharpen the mower blades. I had to make a double pass with it all morning. Ben is meeting me at the Erb's house on Ehringhaus Street. Would you ride over there and tell him I'm going to be late?"

"Why sure, dear brother, nothing would please me better."

There was no sarcasm; he was puzzled.

She found Ben, as Eddie had said, busy at work. She walked her bike up onto the sidewalk and waited straddling the frame until he finished the run he was on and turned in her direction. When he did, she saw his expression was glum, his attention seemingly intensely focused on the grass in front of his mower. She waved as he came to the end of the run only a few feet from her. Still he didn't notice her. She shouted. He paused and looked around as if the voice had come from the clouds.

"Oh, it's you," he said re-entering the present and exiting the one in which there were only questions about Valery.

"Yes, just little ole me."

He left the mower and came to the picket fence that separated them. It came to him that there was something he wanted to say to her. He dove right in.

"When we talked the other day you brought up the Enlightenment and some philosophers who had ideas about a Master Clockmaker." He hesitated a moment before admitting, "I didn't know what you meant at the time, but now I know."

She quickly said, "I'm sorry I didn't explain myself."

Ben believed his previous logical deduction of the non-existence of the God of organized religion still held true, but it didn't suffice when it came to the Master Clockmaker.

"Well, the thing is you're right. Given that description of God, one who made the earth and then left it behind like a clockmaker makes a clock and moves on to other business, can't be disproven with my argument. But, at the same time you can't prove he does exist. My question is, why bring in the idea of a God at all? Why not just say we don't know how the universe was created. He warmed to his argument. "Look, we don't know the cause of cancer and people say, 'We don't *yet* know the cause of cancer. People don't say, 'We don't know what causes cancer, therefore God causes it.' In other words, there's no reason for bringing in a notion of God unless you just feel the need for one—makes you feel better in some way."

He searched her face to discern if she understood his point. "See what I mean?"

"Perfectly," She was smiling more in the pleasure that he had cared enough about her rebuttal to his argument to spend time mulling it over rather than from any satisfaction in his conceding her point.

"I'm curious about how you went about finding out about the Master Clockmaker?"

Her question meant she knew he'd have a difficult time learning about the phrase. There had been no way to look it up. He could be perplexing too.

"Major Gerhard von Kleist."

Cookie laughed out loud. "Who is Major Gerhard von Kleist?"

"He's a German prisoner of war. I met him at Tim Graham's farm."

"And you know this prisoner well enough to ask him about the Enlightenment?"

"Yes, and he was a university professor before the war."

"That's interesting. Tell me more."

Ben looked out over the expanse of the lawn. "Yeah sure. Another time maybe."

"Of course, the lawn mowing; that's why I rode over here. Eddie had to sharpen his mower and wants me to tell you he'll be late."

Happy with the whole exchange, she stepped down on a bike pedal while mounting the seat and called over her shoulder, "See ya later."

Mostly gained through shooting the breeze with other members of the department, Kyle and Clint built up their knowledge of Hunter Sinclair. He was a guy who enjoyed, even seemed compelled to test the limit of the law. Everyone knew he served liquor at his tavern, which meant he bribed the neighboring Polk County officials not to notice. Then there were women who'd made complaints that he forced them to have sex against their wish. (Rape was a term reserved for brutal physical attacks). But these were the type of women whose complaints were deemed below the consideration of decent people and ignored. They also learned Hunter owned a small house near the tavern in Saluda where he sacked-out when too drunk to drive back to Hendersonville. It was also a place where he took women and so it was of great interest to the two detectives. They were together now in Sexton's car driving slowly past the house.

"His neighbors must love him," Kyle said observing the tall weeds that made up the front lawn.

"Hell, the man favors the natural look and nature favors weeds."

"How do we get inside to check it out? Nobody's going to give us a warrant for a search, that's for certain," said Kyle.

"I'd hate like hell ta get caught in there without one. It's been said I've done that kind of thing before when I suspected stolen property was stashed inside some scumbag's house, but this is different, this is Sinclair territory."

Sexton drove the short distance to the Elite Tavern. At the rear of the parking lot was a white truck that had a spotlight mounted on its roof. They looked at each other.

"Closer look?" Clint said.

"I say yes, but what's the chance he wouldn't have scoured the inside if he'd used it to transport a body?"

He parked his car to block the direct line of sight from the building to the truck. They got out and each quickly went to the truck, each opening one of its doors. They were looking for anything connecting the truck with Martinez. Anything: gum wrappers, tissues smeared with lipstick, a piece of twine, perhaps a favorite barrette. What they came away with was disappointment.

Ordinarily, the next step would have been to question everyone on the tavern staff about the teacher and their boss. That option was off the table, it would only rile John Bell.

The two returned to Sexton's car. They sat for a long moment before Clint said, "Break into his shack-up shack?"

"Tonight?"

Mrs. White filled a pitcher at the kitchen sink for watering house-plants. As it filled she glanced out the window into the backyard where Cookie was taking clothes off the line. Several minutes ago Eddie and his friend, Ben, had walked past, their day's work done. Something bothered her about what she'd observed, bothered her, but hadn't taken a definite shape. Her daughter had interrupted her work to say something to the boys and they had stopped and replied. What was there about that exchange that had caught her attention? There had been a quality in Cookie's movement, the way she spoke to Ben. Water overflowed the pitcher and she turned off the tap. She concentrated on that earlier scene. There was something different about Cookie. For contrast she called to mind Cookie's usual behavior when around those boys. Typically, she was on guard or on the offensive. Yes, on guard against her brother's jibes, while at the same time trying to maintain her dignity in Ben's presence.

A more precise understanding of what she saw new in her daughter's behavior began to form and she felt uneasy. She'd noticed that Cookie moved forward to stand nearer Ben. In the past, Mrs. White could expect Cookie to be actively asserting her opinion, pointing out Eddie's error, but just now she'd been comfortably sure of herself without the need to pursue her opinion. And when Ben had seemed to agree with her on something they were talking about, she smiled at him in a . . . possessive way. That's it! Her manner was possessive.

A shock sped through Mrs. White's whole body. It would take time to fully express the implications of this simple action she'd observed, but intuitively she knew what it implied. This was a woman who had moved into a comfortable intimacy with a man. This was a woman sure of her man. In Mrs. White's experience, this meant they'd entered into sexual intimacy. Yes, what she was viewing were two young people who were doing it! No. This must not be. Cookie was only a child. Mrs. White had never considered the two subjects together - Cookie and sex. She had not shown the slightest interest in sex. Yes, she had begun her periods, but she was only thirteen. Her sole interests seemed to be her role in the home helping her mother cook, caring for her pet rabbit and cat, working in the garden and school work and reading. Beyond personal hygiene, she had not been noticeably concerned with her looks. Yes, Mrs. White had noticed that she treated Ben differently, her attention perking up when she'd heard he was coming to the house—a childhood crush perhaps.

Then a fact elbowed its way forward. Thirteen was old enough.

The pitcher lay forgotten in the sink. She was now faced with a problem that demanded immediate attention. She had to talk to her daughter. This thing with Ben had to end. This would be very difficult to discuss. She must do it correctly. She and Cookie had a wonderful relationship, something that made up a large part of Mrs. White's personal happiness and the last thing she wanted was to damage it.

She began to rethink, to challenge the conclusion she'd come to. She reviewed her recent observation. She compared Cookie's body movement to that of other young women she'd known who'd crossed the line. There had been no touching such as was the usual case, not being able to keep hands off each other, but Cookie's face showed the comfort that attends that same depth of involvement between a man and a woman. She sighed. Much as she'd like to believe otherwise, she had to listen to her intuition.

Cookie came into the kitchen and put the clothes basket down next to the cellar door. Mrs. White had intended to broach the subject slowly. Instead, when she began to speak the words quickly became pointed.

"Young lady, is there something we should talk about?"

Puzzled, Cookie answered, "What?"

"I know you very well. You are an open book to me. I would rather not have to accuse you. I would prefer that you were honest with me."

"Honest about what?"

Mrs. White put her hands on her hips, exasperation on her face.

"Honest about what you and Ben Roberts have been doing."

There, she'd said it and hated having said it. It meant the end of a perfect period of untrammeled trust and understanding with her daughter, a period that began with Cookie's birth, continued in open innocence and ended this moment.

Cookie was stunned. She also was aware that a change had just occurred in her relationship with her mother. This was the first time her mother had implied she was not honest. She was bewildered.

"I don't understand. You say, 'What I've been doing with Ben.'" And then it came to her that her mother must be referring to the discussions about God she and Ben had had. But that didn't removed the confusion, for how could her mother know that? And what could she say to her? It would be impossible for her mother to be sympathetic to her changing ideas about religion.

Mrs. White realized then that her voice had had an angry edge. She was angry because something she valued had been snatched away. Her blissful relationship with Cookie had been snatched away. Ben was the thief, but Cookie was a traitor. She tried to modify her tone to show understanding even though she didn't feel it.

"I understand that you are . . . becoming a woman and . . . "

Cookie saw immediately where her mother was heading. She saw, but couldn't believe it. She was aghast.

"Mother! There is nothing like you're thinking going on between Ben and me. Why he doesn't even know I'm a girl. I'm just Eddie's little sister. He has said nothing or done nothing to me."

She had been near shouting. She got her voice under control. "We are just friends—good friends. I like him."

Mrs. White was very embarrassed. Cookie's tone and manner rang true. She'd made a terrible mistake. She had been the one to disturb the happy harmony. Was it possible to repair?

Cookie helped her out. "Look Mom, I can imagine what it's like to have a daughter my age. In part you want her to develop normally and sex is a part of that. At the same time you'd know there are hazards and you'd be watchful, want her to delay any involvement with sex. I think I'd want my daughter to wait until she was twenty-five." She laughed. "I hope that doesn't happen to me, but I assure you it's not on my agenda right now. She put her hands on her mother's shoulders. "Not for a few weeks, at least."

They both laughed and hugged.

In the barber chairs sat two of the town's leading citizens, Mr. Ashborn, who owned the Oldsmobile dealership and Mr. Rice, the President of the Hendersonville State Bank. Ben sat waiting his turn, looking through a copy of the *Asheville Citizen* where he'd read a repeat of the morning news about the invasion with the addition, as Eddie had mentioned, of the four thousand ships taking part. The two men in the chairs were having a conversation in voices loud enough to interrupt Ben's reading. He started to pay attention, being curious to know what important men talk about. Fred, the barber and owner, like an admiring Greek chorus, added a comment here and there, making it difficult to put together what the men were saying. But what made it worse is that they spoke in half-sentences the way people do when talking about family business while not wanting strangers to understand. In spite of this, he picked up that they were talking about a meeting of something called the "Rotary." He guessed it was some kind of club and wondered if it was like the Lions Club that his father belonged to, because the owner of the Lodge believed it would be good for business. Ben was annoyed by their semi-private conversation. If what they had to say was so private, why not wait until they were alone? Then he began to get it—they were letting people like him know they belonged to something he was excluded from.

Their topic changed. "Chief Housman told me they haven't made any progress finding out what happened to that high school teacher," said Rice.

Ashborn nodded and then in aloud voice said in a "from-the-horses-mouth" manner, "She had a date Thursday night and never came back. The police are looking for the guy."

Well, here was something Ben understood, only the guy had the day wrong and Ben had the urge to correct him.

Ashborn quipped, "Henry, you sure you didn't take that little lady out for a midnight swim?"

Henry shined shoes at the barbershop. Ben figured he was older than either of the men in the chairs. Every time Ben had been in the shop Henry had either been snapping that shining cloth or sitting quietly reading the paper. He was nearing the end of a shine now, snapping the cloth with a mounting rhythm.

"No suh!" he said laughing.

Rice took it up. "Being night, It'd be hard for you to tell a Mexican from one of your girlfriends."

Henry chuckled. "No suh. Ain't got no girlfriends."

"What? Good looking guy like you." Ashborn threw in.

The customer in the shine chair got up and gave Henry a dime. "Now don't spend that all in one place."

Ben heard these exchanges with an evolving understanding. When the bank president and the dealership owner had begun to talk he had been ready to attribute to them a wisdom and status that went with material success. Friends had pointed out both men, speaking in awed respect. Gradually, since he couldn't put meaning to their half-utterances, he began to focus on and discern the manner in which they spoke and recognized the same boastful intent he could easily identify in his peers and himself. He had put these men above that. At first he heard the kidding of Henry as being the same sort of humor his friends and he engaged in—the constant joking put-down. Then he became aware of the demeaning intent. It had been his mother's pointing out the injustice of "Jim Crow " in all its guises that now allowed him to hear the meanness in their remarks.

"Anyway, now you won't be able to spend that money on that Mexican honey," Rice said.

Henry smiled and picked up a magazine. The others had tired of the subject.

A few minutes earlier it had begun to rain and now large drops were drumming the shop's window onto Main Street. The door opened and Walter Abbott quickly entered and closed the door behind him. He took off his tattered Panama hat and shook the rain off.

"You ducked in just in time, Walter. You like'ta got soaked. Where you headed?" the barber said.

"Good afternoon, Gentlemen. I was on my way to the hotel to make my report to the President."

"You're late today. You usually call him in the morning don't ya? Why're you making him wait all day to hear from you?"

"I knew he would be very busy with the invasion."

"Of course, of course."

The Carolina Hotel was directly across the street from the barbershop. The hotel had a switchboard that still operated the phones in the rooms and also the lobby phone booth. The daily procedure had Walter telling the receptionist he was there to place his call and then he 'd go to the phone booth. She would alert another clerk that Walter had arrived. A ritual followed that was repeated almost daily during the summer months when Walter resided in the city. The receptionist would "connect" Walter to the "White House."

"Hello, this is the White House."

"This is Walter Abbott. I wish to speak to President Roosevelt."

"Just a moment, sir, while I connect you with his secretary." She'd then continue, "Mr. Walter Abbott to speak to the President."

"Good Afternoon, Mr. Abbott," the receptionist then would say in her presidential secretary voice. "The President is very busy and can't talk today, but he would like you to leave your message with me."

This part of the ritual was not varied. Walter's message would be appropriate to the occasion, at least the occasion as experienced by Walter.

Yesterday, Walter had spoken intimately and seriously. "I know you are very busy, so I won't take too much of your time, Mr. President. From my experience, men always work better when they feel clean. We had better be sure plenty of soap and hot water are available. Goodbye, sir and thank you."

The rain continued to pour. After looking outside and judging he would have to wait until it slacked before venturing to cross the street, Walter walked over to the shoeshine chair.

"Could you fit me into your schedule, Henry?"

Mr. Rice clapped his hand over his mouth to stifle a guffaw.

"Certainly Mr. Abbott," Henry said. "I always have time for you."

Ben had laid the newspaper he'd been reading down on the chair next to him, so Henry came to get it, looking to Ben, who motioned that he'd finished with it.

After giving Walter time to glance over the front page of the paper, Ashborn asked, "Is the invasion proceeding according to your plans, Walter?"

"I beg your pardon, sir, but I'm not allowed to discuss military affairs with the public. I hope you understand."

On one level, this statement was in keeping with Walter's grand delusion, but on another it effectively told Ashborn to shut up and mind his own business. Silence fell on the group.

Dave, the second barber, removed the sheet covering Ashborn with a flourish and he got out of the chair, while hair snippets were whisked from his jacket shoulders. Ben watched Ashborn take two quarters from his pocket and put them in the barber's hand, the price of a haircut and a dime tip. Not a big tipper, thought Ben, but then the guy wasn't selling any Oldsmobiles either. Dave motioned for Ben to climb into the chair.

As the barber spread the sheet over Ben and fastened a paper collar around his neck, Ben studied the pin-up on the calendar facing him—a brunette ballerina with a pink and black tutu. Not the sexiest the artist, Vargas, had achieved, but OK. He diverted his eyes before the barber became aware of his interest. He didn't want to encourage the guy's quip.

This was a big moment, a brush-cut for the summer and for several minutes all Ben was aware of was the alarming sensation of great gobs of hair falling from his head. Then his attention shifted to the closing drama of the shoeshine with its loud snapping of the polishing cloth. Henry tapped the sole of Walter Abbott's shoe and the performance was at an end.

Walter stood and looked down at the newly shining surface of his badly worn shoes.

"Excellent, Henry."

But Walter Abbott was not supposed to have any money; at least that's what Ben's friends had said. He felt embarrassed for the man.

Abbott reached into the inside jacket pocket of his baggy linen suit and came out with a paper matchbook, which he put in Henry's hand.

"Thank you, Henry."

"Thank you, Mr. Abbott. Always a pleasure."

Half an hour later and feeling very much lighter and self-conscious owing to the brush-cut, Ben took a place in one of Schauger's booths across from Bill Lawson, who'd just finished the day at his father's clothing store. Brother Packard, who had been behind the soda fountain, now drifted over to the booth to stand and talk, a damp cloth in his hand to give the appearance of working.

"How's business?" Ben asked Lawson.

"Slow."

"Slow here today," said Brother.

"That's one thing about the mowing business, grass keeps on growing every day."

"Except in winter," Lawson corrected.

"You could become a migrant mower - move with the season," said Brother.

"Good idea." Ben pretended to write it down.

"Maybe I can sell my mother that idea. She wants me to be a doctor, but I hate hospitals," said Brother.

Hank Edney walked through the door and seeing his friends he came to stand beside Brother, who began giving the table a half-hearted swipe with the cloth.

"Saved any lives today, Hank?" asked Lawson. "Have a seat."

"I'm here to pick up a prescription for my Mom. I didn't save any lives but I did give a swimming lesson to a very good looking girl who's staying at the Inn."

"Ah, yes the swimming lesson game," said Ben. "I picture you with your arm round her waist holding her up while she kicks her pretty little feet."

"Right on," agreed Hank.

"I'll bet she's a slow learner," said Lawson.

"How did you know? I don't think we'll ever get past this first part."

"I'll also bet the talk at the lake is about Miss Martinez's body being found there," said Brother, glancing back toward the pharmacy window to see if Dr. Schauger was looking out.

"And how. And to think while I was working those first days she was there in the water - since Thursday night the cops think."

"No, that's wrong," said Ben. "It was Friday night."

"Where did you get that?"

"Miss Martinez rented a room from a woman who works for my Dad. She said it was Friday night Miss Martinez went out on that date."

"Really? People at the lake are talking about Thursday and I'm pretty sure the newspaper said Thursday, in fact, I know it did. I remember reading: 'Anyone who saw this woman Thursday afternoon or evening. Please call the Hendersonville Police.' It also said she was wearing an orange dress," Hank insisted.

"What newspaper article?"

"It was on the front page. Monday. It was Monday, because there was nothing about the invasion yet," said Hank.

"I think he's right," agreed Lawson.

Ben was confused. If what Hank said was true it meant the body was in the lake the same night he was swimming with Valery. Monday's paper was likely to still be around the house. He'd look when he got home.

"I had a pleasant surprise today," Ben's mother said when he came into the house. "I had a visit from Eddie White's sister, Constance."

"Constance? . . . Oh, you mean Cookie. Nobody calls her Constance."

"So *she's* Cookie. I had the impression from the times you've mentioned her that she was much younger—a child really."

"What was she doing here?"

"I think she wanted to meet me. She said so, at least, and she brought me a jar of blueberry jam she'd made. She said she'd picked the berries on a trip to Pisgah Mountain. "

"Really?" Ben mumbled, even more puzzled.

"We had a pleasant chat. She's quite a gardener. Very knowledgeable. She said you'd told her about my rose garden and she wanted to see it."

Ben couldn't remember telling Cookie about his mother's rose garden - but maybe. He had noticed her in the White's garden from time to time, but had never associated the word "knowledgeable" with what she'd been doing. Also he was perplexed by his mother's glow as she described the visit.

"She suggested I would have less of a problem with fungus infections like black spot if I placed the plants farther apart. She said roses need good air circulation."

"Really?" Ben was having a surreal experience as if his mother were describing a visit by Alice's White Rabbit.

"Also it is important to keep the soil free from dead leaves." His mother was smiling as if she indeed had had a visit from the White Rabbit.

Again all he could say was, "Really." And then he asked, "When was she here?"

"Oh about an hour ago."

Curiouser and curioser, he thought. "When's dinner?"

Both men were thinking of how this could be explained if they were caught.

"Shit'ud hit the fan big time," Clint whispered.

"We're not going to get caught. Nobody's around. We'd have to set off fireworks to get anybody's attention in this town."

They'd picked eleven o'clock as a good time to break into Hunter Sinclair's house in Saluda. All the stores were closed, so foot traffic was eliminated, but there were still enough cars around so a single parked car wouldn't attract attention. They parked off Main Street on Church and walked up the hill to Seminary Street where the house stood. The street was deserted and only a single light shone from the window of a house one hundred yards farther along Seminary. They had taken the precaution of dressing in dark clothes, so they faded into the night as they left the sidewalk and crept quietly to the back door.

"We did good. Didn't rouse no dogs—so far," Clint whispered.

Kyle tried the door handle. Locked as expected. He circled the lens of his flashlight with his hand to restrict the beam and studied the lock.

"Yale and new." he said.

"Then it's the only thing new about this place. This window next to the door is the best one to break—kitchen window I expect," Clint said and reached into the bag of tools they'd brought to find the roll of masking tape.

The plan was to crisscross the glass with tape to dampen the sound when it was broken. Waiting as Clint searched for the tape, Kyle idly gave the window frame an upward push.

"Son-of-a-bitch. The thing's unlocked."

It took some jiggling, but little by little they were able to open the window enough for Clint, who was the thinner to climb through and unlock the door. They stood then in what had been the kitchen at one time and that time was long ago judging from the wood-burning stove against one wall. The only other furnishing was a refrigerator that held more than a dozen bottles of Schlitz beer and two trays of ice in the freezer compartment.

"Drink here, eat elsewhere," Kyle said.

What had been a living room or parlor at one time now contained only three cardboard boxes stacked in one corner. Dark blinds covered the windows that faced the road. Kyle unfolded the flaps on the top box and shined the restricted beam of his light into it.

"Looks like old business papers; invoices, receipts."

The only doorway in the room other than the one they'd used, was into a hallway at the end of which was a window with another drawn blind. A few yards along it was the door to a bathroom. It had no window, so as they entered they closed the door behind them and flipped on a light switch next to the door. They stood in a depressing cubicle with flaking green paint and a linoleum floor.

"Been spruced up a bit," commented Clint.

"You mean the new toilet seat?"

"That and the cabinet light." Clint pointed to the electric wire running across the ceiling from the ceiling light fixture and down the wall to the medicine cabinet.

"Obviously, Hunter didn't think he'd need a bath here." Kyle was looking at the chipped and rusted tub.

He turned and tried the faucets on the sink. Nothing flowed from the one with the large "H" on the handle, but cold water ran from the "C" tap. He opened the cabinet door.

"What have we here?" Kyle said.

"Ah yes, a bachelor's defence against overpopulation. Trojans. Let's see, one. two . . . . six. Enough for a week-end," Clint counted.

"In your dreams."

"Asprin and what's this?" Kyle turned around an amber bottle to read the label. "Elixir of Nembutal. What do you suppose he uses this for?"

"It's a sleeping drug I think. It's got the Abbott company trade mark."

"I know it's a sleeping drug. I mean why would a healthy young buck need help sleeping?"

"You're wondering if they are knockout drops?"

"I wonder."

They left the bathroom and opened the next door along the hall. The room was a bedroom now entirely empty. Across the hall Kyle pushed open the remaining door. The flashlight revealed a furnished room. The windows were covered with heavy drapes, so he turned on the light switch. No light came on. He aimed the flashlight at the ceiling and saw there wasn't a bulb in the fixture.

"I saw a floor lamp," Clint said and advanced into the room and switched it on.

"Yes, much more romantic."

The room contained a double bed, sofa, coffee table and a glass-doored cabinet. A large rag rug covered the floor between the sofa and the bed.

"Cozy," Clint said and then went to the cabinet and opened its door. "Evan Williams Bourbon. Three bottles and a stack of paper cups. Care for a drink?"

"Not during working hours."

"I hope to God these aren't our new working hours."

Kyle turned his attention to the bed. A chenille spread loosely covered it as if thrown in place with a quick toss—rumpled but clean. He pulled the spread back to reveal a single sheet covering the mattress. No tell-tale signs of Martinez's occupancy.

Clint, standing beside him said, "No maid service."

Kyle kneeled and looked under the bed, seeing nothing except a heavy accumulation of dust.

"I think you're right about the maid. She'd probably run a mop under the bed once in a while. The rest of the floor gets some attention."

Clint opened the closet door, looked inside and said over his shoulder. "Now here's something."

The first thing Kyle saw when he looked inside was a mop leaning in one corner and next to it a pair of sneakers.

"On the shelf," Clint said.

A bra strap dangled over the shelf edge. Clint pulled it down. Racing through both their minds was the possibility and hope it could be identified as belonging to Blanca Martinez.

"Man, I think we've found -"

"No," Kyle sighed. "No, afraid not. To start with Martinez was wearing a bra when we pulled her from the lake. In the second place, this is way too big—must be an "F" cup if there is such a size."

"Really? Shit."

"Won't fit Marie Boyes either," added Kyle.

"Yeah and that's good isn't it? If she'd been here and then he'd fired her, she'd be plenty motivated to stick it to him."

Kyle nodded.

"Hunter should really make an effort to return this bra. The woman obviously needs it. Maybe we should leave him a note," Clint quipped.

The closet held nothing else. They stood for a long moment contemplating what use their search of the house had served.

"We didn't accomplish diddly-squat," concluded Clint. "You're sure you don't want that drink?"

"I just went off duty."

Thursday, June 8th.

"Bacon and Eggs?"

"Yeah, Mom. Great."

Ben's father had already eaten and left for work. The Asheville paper lay to the side of his place at the table. Ben picked it up and looked at the front page.

"It says Bayeux has been captured and the road to Caen was cut."

"I know, your father read that. Bayeux is the name of a tapestry. I remember seeing a picture of it in history class. It's a picture of the Normans invading England. I don't know if it's in Bayeux or not. Probably in a museum in Paris."

Ben didn't reply to his mother's non sequitur.

"Thirty-one thousand sorties flown so far. Wow! A German counter attack failed," He continued.

"Yes, your father read that too. Anything else?"

Ben turned the page. "You can send a fruitcake to a service man for $1.85 from Belk's Department Store. Or buy a pinafore, whatever that is, for $3.98 from Bon Marche."

"That's my kind of news. I wish that's all there was."

Ben wasn't interested in continuing this conversation with his mother. Plaguing him since he'd returned home yesterday and confirmed by the newspaper article, was the fact that Miss Martinez had been missing since Thursday night, not Friday as he'd originally thought, which meant her body may have been in the lake when Valery and he were swimming. Ben tended to fall asleep immediately upon getting into bed, but last night his sleep was troubled.

This morning he met Eddie at Mrs. Blake's. This was a job apart from the mowing deal with Moses. Mrs. Blake was an elderly widow who lived in the same house she'd shared with Mr. Blake for forty-five of their sixty-year marriage. Although the garden yielded much more than she herself could use, its continued existence was an important part of maintaining her sense of self-worth. The vegetables she was able to give to friends and neighbors meant a link with the community. The man who had been doing the grunt work in the garden for the last decade had moved to Raleigh to be closer to his daughter. Hence Ben and Eddie.

On this first day she began orientation with a lecture on the genealogy and special needs of each plant species. The lecture was interesting . . . up to a point. They had been hired to weed, so their main interest was what to pull out and what to leave alone. Weeding was a mindless activity like mowing, leaving the mind free to range wherever it might. But, whereas their physical separation while mowing made conversation impossible, weeding allowed it. Eddie wanted to talk about Honey Huddlesford.

"Honey Huddlesford?" Ben repeated. "Is that a real name?"

"Yeah, Honey Huddlesford," Eddie said in a liltingly languid voice. "Flows right outa the mouth like honey from a jar. It's her real name. She's from Atlanta. She's staying for two weeks with her aunt and uncle, who live across the street."

"She must be a honey to look at or you wouldn't be telling me about her."

"Honey blond hair, the bluest eyes and lips begging to be kissed— and kissed."

"Looks to be the best two weeks of her life."

"I'll do my best. She's going to the matinee on Saturday with me."

"Interesting. I think I'll come and sit behind you—learn something."

The thought of Ben sitting behind him was not a good thought.

"You're not ready for that lesson, son. Don't forget I had to tell you what to do next with the Sinclair broad. How's that comin' along by the way?"

"Coming along just fine."

The reference to Valery brought with it the uneasiness he was feeling about the night at the lake. There was that guy in the boat, of course, but he was swimming. He couldn't have had anything more to do with Miss Martinez being in the lake than he and Valery had. What was it that continued to nag him? Some vague impression from that night that kept trying to get his attention like a knocking at the door when you're almost asleep.

Eddie continued pulling weeds and talking while Ben responded with muted grunts, occupied as he was trying to clear his mind. And then there it was, the end of the thread, which when pulled brought the image of a white shirt into view. The white shirt!

"Shit!," he barked.

Eddie, holding a weed in his hand looked at Ben with mock indignation and came out with another of his stock sayings, "Please define your terms, sir."

With a covering laugh, Ben said, "Nothing, nothing. Something I forgot to do at home."

Here was an opportunity to bring Eddie into the picture, but he hesitated. This was something he needed to talk over with Valery—plumb her recollection of the guy in the boat.

The Blake job finished, they each went to their homes for lunch, where Ben immediately dialed Valery's number.

"Sinclair residence," answered the now familiar voice of the cook whose name he now remembered, Mrs. Holden - Ulla.

"Hello. This is Ben Roberts, Ma'am. I'd like to speak to Valery."

"She's not here, son. She's very busy."

"I see . . . uh, please tell her I called and would like her to call me when she can."

"I'll surely give her the message."

Did he hear a note of understanding sympathy for his disappointment?

This time it wasn't just disappointment, he felt desperate. He needed to talk to her. He needed to talk to someone, bat the issue around, understand what had happened that night. If he couldn't use her input was there someone else? Talk to his father? No, he'd concentrate on his trespassing on the Inn's property. His mother? No, she'd tell his father, because she'd think she'd have to. Mrs. Ransom? She'd listen without criticism, but he'd have to include the nude swim to make her understand the situation. Who else was there? The German major? A surprising idea, but yes, he was someone who'd understand. Yes, Major von Kleist.

His selection of von Kleist as a confidant rested on several facts: Ben found him easy to talk to, he was from outside Ben's community, not a member of the group upon whose good opinion he depended and finally he was smart and inspired confidence.

Ben was meeting Eddie after lunch at the Henderson's. He called him at home and told him there was something he had to do that would take a couple of hours. "I'll do the edging and cleanup when I get back." Before Eddie could form a question, he hung up.

He rode his bike down the long drive into the Graham's farm, trying in his mind different approaches to the presentation of the story he planned to lay before the major. A new scene confronted him when he entered the open area in front of the barns. The prisoners were sitting in a long row on a bench made up of planks resting on milk cans.

They looked like they were waiting for a bus. Then he saw that each man was holding a paper plate on his knees. It was lunchtime. The man sitting next to the Major noticed Ben and nudged his neighbor.

"Ben," von Kleist called out, waving his fork.

This wasn't the setting Ben had been expecting. He'd pictured the major sitting in his chair at the side of the bean field. He couldn't say what he wanted to in front of these men,

"What brings you to the farm today?" asked von Kleist smiling and standing.

Ben pushed his bike to where the major stood.

"I have a problem I hope you can help me with."

Gerhard concluded it must be an unusual need that would cause the boy to ride his bike all the way to the farm to discuss it with an enemy prisoner.

"Yes, all right. I've just finished lunch."

Von Kleist left the bench and dropped the fork into a tub and the empty plate into a garbage can, He motioned to Ben to walk with him toward one of the barns, out of hearing of the others.

"Now that you are here I can tell you in person the message I asked your friend, Tim, to pass on to you. Tomorrow will be our last day here at this farm, and then we move to a farm near Arden. Do you know where that is?"

"Yes, near Asheville - little town."

"I gave the two books to Tim to return to you for Mrs. Ransom. Please thank her for her kindness. I enjoyed the Hemmingway book and I'll be sure to find another copy of the Fitzgerald novel when I have a chance."

He paused noticing Ben's reaction to this news. "I will miss our conversations, Ben. When the war is over and you are older you must travel to Germany and we can meet again. I'm pretty sure I'll be at the

University of Munich. You can send a letter there."

Ben didn't know what to say. He experienced a sense of unexpected loss. He had only just found an adult male in whom he thought he could confide and now he was saying goodbye.

Von Kleist sensed Ben's feelings. "But you rode out here with a problem you hoped I could help you with."

Ben hesitated. Had things changed between the major and him. It was a wide mental bridge to cross to conceive of a friendship separated by years and thousands of miles. The major had spoken like it was a sure thing. He decided to go ahead and lay his problem before him as best he could.

"Last Thursday night this girl and I went swimming nude in Lake Laurel." He glanced at von Kleist to see his reaction. Detecting no reaction except attention to the story, he continued. "We swam out to a raft that is anchored out from the beach as far . . . as that farthest barn. We had just got up on top of the raft when a car drove into the parking lot. A guy got out of the car and rowed the lifeguard's boat out toward the raft. So, we got under the raft to hide, since we were undressed. He rowed right by the raft and farther on out in the lake where he jumped into the water—I heard a big splash. He began swimming around. I couldn't see him, because I was behind the girl, so she described what the guy was doing. She saw him climb back into the boat and he rowed by us again going back to the beach. He got in his car and left."

Ben stopped, caught up in his own thoughts.

"Yes," urged Gerhard.

"Maybe you heard about the teacher who was killed and found later in Laurel Lake."

"Yes, I read about it in the newspaper."

"At first, I misunderstood something my father said and thought she had gone missing on Friday night. Then I learned it had been on

217

Thursday, the same night we were swimming in the lake.

"I thought at the time it was odd for a guy to row out into the lake to go swimming and not just swim from the beach, but I didn't think more about it, because I had other things on my mind at the time."

Von Kleist recognized Ben's anxiety. Why was he confiding in him, a relative stranger rather than his parents? Was it the sexual implications of the naked swim? He guessed Ben had made a connection between the man in the boat and the murdered woman.

"And so, when the day of the murder and the day her body was put in the lake was clarified, you began to wonder if the man in the boat was involved in the murder of the woman?"

Ben met the major's eyes and nodded.

"But you say he went swimming. Is it likely a murderer would go swimming?"

"Yeah, right. It's that kind of contradiction that's got my thinking tied in a knot."

"Then let's work on undoing the knot. You say you had the impression of oddness about the man swimming from the boat; was there anything else about him—anything?"

"Yeah. The moon was bright and as he rowed toward us the thing that stood out was the whiteness of his shirt. It looked to me like a dress shirt. He was also wearing it when he rowed back to the beach after swimming. Today, it came to me—jumped out at me—that it was his shirt that I thought was odd."

"Why was that odd?"

"It isn't the usual thing a person does. If you row out in the lake to jump in and swim you usually wear a bathing suit and maybe a T-shirt."

"Yes, and if you take off a dress shirt in order to swim, do you put it back on after you get out the water and are wet?" Gerhard added.

"Yeah."

"So usually if one sees a man rowing a boat wearing a dress shirt going and coming you'd conclude he hadn't been swimming."

Ben nodded.

"And yet, you heard a splash—a 'big splash'."

"That's right."

"You said the girl could see him and described what he was doing. Is that right? She said he jumped into the water"

"Yes. She could see between the barrels that the raft floats on, but I was behind - I couldn't see past her head."

Ben hadn't allowed himself to go that far for some reason, yet now that the major said it . . .

"So maybe he hadn't gone swimming like the girl said," Gerhard put forward.

Ben didn't answer.

"That would mean two things: the big splash was caused by something else, and . . ."

And Valery was lying to me, concluded Ben

"She lied," Ben said.

Gerhard saw this idea troubled Ben and he wondered about the relationship with the girl. Should he push the questioning further? Yet the boy had come for help—seemed desperate for help.

"You said you couldn't see what the man was doing because her head was in the way. Could she have purposely made it difficult for you to see?"

Immediately Ben remembered how he was moving into a position to see the guy as he rowed back past the raft when Valery grabbed his penis.

"Uh . . .maybe."

"She didn't want you to see the man clearly," nudged von Kleist.

He waited a few beats and asked, "Why would that be?"

That had been the logjam Ben now realized. He couldn't bring himself to think she had any agenda other than waiting until they could be alone together again.

Gerhard's next question broke through his reluctance like a battering ram.

"Could it be that she recognized the man?"

"You mean like she knew him?"

This progression of understanding had extended beyond what he could, or wanted to follow. It was like working out that you were indeed not you mother's favorite and then being told you were also adopted.

Von Kleist shrugged while raising his eyebrows. "You just suggested—didn't you—the possibility that the man in the boat dropped the body of the murdered woman in the lake—the splash you heard. Am I right? If she had seen this and knew the man's identity . . . then . "

"Jeez." Ben now remembered her abrupt change of attitude, from being sexually playful to the opposite—tense, preoccupied.

"She was different," he said. "I mean she acted differently from when we first arrived at the lake. After the guy left, she swam back to the beach and started getting dressed as if I weren't there."

Gerhard wondered if he'd helped to boy come to a conclusion that might be too much for him to handle. Where could the boy now take this revelation? And, he, Gerhard, wouldn't be here to help him with it. Ben's logic, however, took over and led to the next question.

"If she saw someone she knew dump Miss Martinez in the lake and if she'd kept it to herself, he must be someone she wanted to protect."

Von Kleist nodded. "That seems to follow."

Gerhard turned to begin slowly walking back across the parking area.

Ben's thinking was handicapped by his wish to retreat from his conclusions, to deny that Valery had lied to him as if he had not just followed a trail of logic that told him convincingly she had. Von Kleist guessed this was happening, because he knew he'd be experiencing the same kind of doubt if he were in Ben's place and the woman was Hilde.

"Do you know whom she might want to protect?"

Ben took a deep breath and let it out. "I don't know much about her really. I don't know who her friends are. I do know she has a brother."

"What about him? Have you seen him?"

"No, I haven't."

Ben could understand that she might lie to protect her brother.

The lunch gathering was breaking up. The men were cleaning up the area, throwing waste and paper plates in the garbage and lining up to walk back to the bean field. Tony, the guard, stood and looked over toward von Kleist waiting for him to break off his conversation with Ben.

Gerhard was deeply concerned about the position in which Ben was being left. It was good that the boy had been able to explore a very troubling event, but he needed more help and Gerhard was unable to supply it.

"Ben, I believe you need to be careful about what you say and to whom you speak about this. I strongly advise you to talk to your parents. Parents can understand more than we think at times. Above all it would be unwise to pursue this on your own—it could be dangerous. Your parents will want to go to the police. That would be the right thing to do."

He searched Ben"s face for evidence he understood. "Do you understand what I'm saying?"

Alarm that he hadn't felt before flooded, Ben. He hadn't for a moment thought his dawning awareness of the meaning of Valery's strange behavior at the lake might have dangerous consequences for him.

"Yeah, I see what you mean."

"Good, I have to go now. Don't forget that we are friends and I will look forward to seeing you in Munich" He clasped Ben's hand in both of his, giving it a firm squeeze and then turned to join his group.

On the ride back to Hendersonville, Ben reviewed every word spoken back at the farm. He, with the major's prodding, had arrived at the likelihood of Valery identifying the person who dumped Miss Martinez's body in Lake Laurel—someone she wanted to protect. What did her brother look like? The guy in the boat hadn't been unusually tall—or short, judged by the part of him visible above the sides of the boat. He'd looked sturdy, strong. Why that? He didn't know. The guy's hair was full and dark—not blond. These thoughts funneled down to his need to see Valery's brother.

At the Henderson's house, Eddie was still working, nearing the finish of the mowing. Ben would finish up, but first he'd decided to enlist Eddie's help.

He came up to him and said, "I need to tell you something."

Ben started at the beginning. When he got to Valery's suggestion of the swim, Eddie chuckled, "You bastard, keeping this to yourself." He listened then, punctuating the story with, "She did?" and "She said that?" Eddie savored the juicy details, while Ben tried to minimize them saying, "Look, I'm trying to tell you something important." Gradually Eddie understood the problem of the man in the boat, the man who might have killed Blanca Martinez.

"And, you wonder if he's her brother."

"I know she has an older brother. I don't know his age, but it figures he could be the age that guy seemed to be, like mid-twenties. The thing is I need to get a look at her brother."

"It was dark. Do you think you could recognize him?"

"The moon was bright. I got the general idea he was muscular, had a broad back. His hair was dark. I know that's not much to go on, but if her brother turned out to be skinny with blond hair, he could be ruled out. But I can't think of a way to go about seeing him—seeing him without his knowing ."

"Why do you care if he knows?"

The Major's warning was on his mind.

"I'd just rather he didn't know who I was."

"OK, what do you know about him?"

"His name is Hunter. He owns a tavern - the one Valery took me to. I don't know another thing about him, not even where he lives."

Eddie said, "We can't very well hang around outside the tavern, besides we wouldn't know him if he came out. Hell, I can't think of anyway to go about this either."

Eddie was now including himself in the project.

"Seems it should be a simple problem; how do you go about identifying someone you've never seen before without him knowing? Maybe if we don't think about it for a while an answer will come. Go ahead and take off and I'll finish up here."

A quarter of an hour later, as he pushed the mower up his driveway, Eddie spotted Cookie sitting on the front porch reading. He climbed the steps.

"Here's a problem for you: suppose you wanted to see what a particular person looks like, but you didn't want that person to know you were watching him. Can you think of a way to go about it?"

Cookie only half heard her brother. She looked up from the book.

223

"I beg your pardon."

He repeated the question adding that all you knew about the guy was his name and where he worked.

"Why do you want to know what he looks like?"

"That's not the point. Just how would you go about it?"

"A hypothetical question then."

"Yeah . . . I guess."

Cookie put down her book. She had become interested in the problem—not in her brother's affairs. Who knew what silly thing had grabbed his attention or why? A stream of possibilities flowed through her active mind meeting with logical obstructions and alternatives.

Finally she said, "You must get him to a place where there can be no question that he is the person you seek, only you won't be there when he comes. You will be hiding in a place where you can see him and he can't see you—or will ignore you."

She realized as she was saying this that it sounded like something out of a Victorian novel. "Get what I mean?"

Eddie thought about it. "No."

She passed her hand over her forehead. "Suppose someone wanted to identify you without your knowing it. He could call you and say he was the manager of the Carolina Theater and that your name had been selected at random from the telephone book to receive a year's pass to the theater. He'd tell you to come to the theater at one o'clock to pick up your prize and you should be carrying an object that would identify you, something unique . . . a telephone book. When you show up at the theater, the person who is wanting to identify you would be outside on the sidewalk pretending to adjust his bicycle seat. You'd disregard him. You'd be thinking only of the prize you were going to get inside the theater. You would pay no attention to him, while he'd be able to study you—a person entering the theater at one o'clock carrying a telephone book."

"Jeez," he sighed. "Yes. Yes, I get it."

"Good. I've solved your problem. Since you're not going to tell me the sordid circumstances, I'll leave the details of the method of contact, place of rendezvous and means of identification to you." With this she picked up her book.

Eddie looked out from the porch toward the street for a moment then sang out, "Yeah, OK," flew down from the porch and hopped on his bike.

Cookie watched wondering what that had all been about, then went back to reading.

"I've got an idea!" Eddie shouted as he rode up and skidded to a stop.

Ben was still raking up grass clippings. He stopped and looked up.

Eddie hurried over to him. "You know what we were talking about - finding a way to see -" He lowered his voice. "Hunter Sinclair."

Ben had been mulling over the problem as he'd worked until his brain was as depleted as a dead battery.

Eagerly Eddie began, "We call him up and say we know he was rowing a boat on Laurel Lake the night Miss Martinez was murdered. We say that for three hundred dollars the police don't have to know. He is to bring the money to a particular place at a particular time. We are hiding where he won't be able to see us, but we will be able to see him."

"Don't go so fast. Seems wild. How did you come up with this?"

"Something Cookie said."

"You told her?"

"No. Hell no. She thought I was talking about something else. The idea here is we get him to come to a place of our choosing where he'd be the only one to come there at a specific time we name."

"OK. I see. We could call him - No, he'd be able to tell how old we are and think it's a kids prank."

"He'd pay attention all right," countered Eddie. "When he heard the words, 'man rowing a boat on Laurel Lake,' he'd pay attention."

"OK, but why three hundred dollars?"

Eddie warmed to the question. The amount of money was the product of what he considered clever thinking. "Less money and he would think it was a kid's prank and more may cause him to take a chance it was only a prank. Three hundred seemed just right."

The plan was beginning to sound reasonable to Ben. "Where is this place we'd have him come to?"

Eddie shrugged impatiently. "I haven't thought of that yet."

"Oh great. That's half the problem."

"Keep your shirt on. We can work that out," he said, irritated he hadn't received the unqualified pat on the back he thought he deserved.

"OK, it has to be a place that doesn't have a lot of people coming to it, so when he comes at the time we pick we'll know he's our man."

"And where we can hide and not be seen."

"Right."

And not in a lonely spot in the woods where he can find us and kill us," Ben added jokingly.

"I'll buy that. You know you're not really helping."

"OK, but I can't think of anything."

"I did have this idea - the parking lot next to Barber's Bookstore. The bookstore closes at five. The doctor's office on the second floor above Barber's is open until seven tonight. My aunt, as you know, is the receptionist for Dr. Prevost. We tell Sinclair the meeting is in the parking lot at six o'clock. We would be in the waiting room that overlooks the lot. I'd tell my aunt we needed to kill some time until we met a couple of girls to catch the movie."

"OK, but why the girls?"

"You know how it is with mothers and aunts; tell them a story where their boys are interested in some girl and that's all they pay attention to. But it won't work. Sinclair might just stay in his car and wait and not get out where we can get a good look at him."

"Hmm. But it was a good idea. So, back to the drawing board. Come up with another like that, a building that overlooks a public place where only Hunter Sinclair would be going to."

They looked at each other in silence. They'd reached a dead end.

"I've gotta go," Eddie said. "Gotta go to the church and find the scarf my Mom left there after the prayer meeting last night."

"Keep thinking. See ya tomorrow at the Carpenter's."

Eddie turned to go and then froze.

"What's wrong?"

Eddie didn't answer immediately. He smiled. "It's perfect. The church."

Ben stared at him.

"Here's what we do; we call him and say he must bring three hundred dollars to the Gethsemane Garden behind the church at uh . . . six o'clock while it's still light out. Eli, the caretaker, goes home at five. We'll be hiding in the church before he locks up. We can look out the rear window that overlooks the Garden."

Ben laughed. "That's wild. But, what if he sees us looking out the window?"

"It'll be dark in the church. He wouldn't be able to see anything inside."

"The caretaker doesn't padlock the doors when he leaves?"

"No. You can leave by the side door out of the basement. People are always using that door after choir practice and the like. You just have to lock the door when you leave."

Ben reviewed the plan in his mind, looking for flaws. "Sounds good. When should we do it?"

"Nothing is going on at the church tonight—Thursday. It's choir practice tomorrow night. I don't know about Saturday. Tonight then?"

"Jesus!" The thought of acting so soon made the whole caper more dangerous.

"Call him at his tavern?" Eddie said.

"Yeah. That's the only place I know. We can get the operator to give us the number."

"There's a pay phone at JaxPax."

Ben sat on the bar of Eddie's bike and they rode the two blocks to the grocery store. The pay phone hung on a wall near the front. The only person in the store was Jack, the owner. He was stocking a shelf at the rear. Both boys knew him; Eddie's acquaintance dated back to the days of buying bubble gum, Ben's to two years of drinking Cokes outside on the bench. Eddie walked to the back and engaged Jack in conversation. From the information operator, Ben learned the number of the Elite Tavern in Saluda. He practiced saying Gethsemane a few times and dialed.

"I'd like to speak to Hunter Sinclair."

The guy who answered turned to someone and asked, "Is Hunter here?"

Ben couldn't hear the reply, but the guy said, "Who's calling?"

Ben wasn't prepared to answer that, but managed, "David" in a fairly even voice.

Ben was getting ready to be asked, "David who?", but instead the guy said, "Just a minute."

Ben's heart beat against his ribs.

"Hunter," said the voice in his ear.

Ben opened his dry mouth, not sure a sound would come out. He hoped his brain would take over on autopilot.

"I saw you rowing a boat on Laurel Lake Thursday night. Bring three hundred dollars to the Gethsemane Gardens behind the Oak Street Baptist Church at six tonight and the police don't need to know." He hung up, his heart beating max rate.

Eddie saw Ben standing as if in shock. He broke the conversation with the owner and walked to Ben.

"It's done, " Ben said.

"Good. Now we've got to get over to the church; it's twenty to five."

Eddie left his bike at Ben's house and they walked the three blocks. At the church's front door, Eddie said, "I know Eli's routine. He cleans the upstairs first and the basement last. I'll duck in and see where he is."

He was back immediately, waving Ben inside. "Follow me."

Eddie led the way down the center aisle of the sanctuary, touching the fourth pew from the front as he passed. He had sat there countless times mostly in a semiconscious daydream of what he was going to do when the service was over. To the right of a notice board that listed the hymns for last Sunday's service was the door to the vestry where they would hide. Eddie seemed to think nothing of violating the sanctity of the church. Ben, on the other hand, while he neither believed in nor acknowledged the church's authority, felt that he was committing some category of violation.

"We can hide in the closet if we hear Eli coming, but I'm sure he won't," Eddie said.

He noticed the uneasy look on Ben's face. "Still, why take a chance."

He pushed the hanging robes aside and they sat down on the closet floor. Seated with his knees pulled up under his chin, it occurred to Ben how strange it was to be sitting on the floor of a vestry in a

Baptist church. There was no way he could have predicted this morning he would be there. Pure chance. More and more he was faced with and impressed by the role chance played in one's life. You could put great time and effort into planning and then a chance encounter would dictate how things played out in the end. Afterward you tended to forget that it was chance that got you to where you were, choosing instead to remember your planning as more important than it had been.

They had only been sitting ten minutes when they heard a sound from the front of the church.

"I'll go check it out," Eddie whispered.

He came back speaking in a normal voice. "Gone for the day."

Ben took his first full deep breath since entering. He looked at the wall clock. "We've got an hour to wait."

"How about a game of Ping-Pong?"

The basement stairs ended in a long open space. At the end of which Ben saw a long table, a cooking range and a refrigerator.

"Would there be anything to eat in that fridge. I'm hungry."

"Could be."

The Kelvinator contained a pint bottle of cream, ten half-pints of chocolate milk and a plate-covered bowl of potato salad.

"The milk's for the Sunday school kids. This stuff in the bowl could be left from a picnic last summer."

Ben took a bottle of chocolate milk. Eddie did the same and noticed a paper sack on the table. "Donuts," he reported withdrawing a sugared one.

"If we get tired of Ping-Pong we can play horseshoes with these hard babies."

Ben had found a glass for the milk. He took a donut from the bag and dipped it. "Not bad at all."

After their make-do repast, they set up the folding Ping-Pong table, which in spite of their best efforts insisted in listing to one side. One paddle had lost the rubber cover on one of its sides. The other paddle had none at all. The only ball they could find appeared all right but made a strange sound when hit and wobbled in flight.

"Being accustomed to professional equipment as I am, I am at a disadvantage and should be given a handicap," Eddie said.

"Come over here and I'll give you a handicap."

Ben concentrated on getting the erratic ball over the net and towards the middle of the table. Eddie couldn't resist trying spins which mostly missed the table.

"Three games in a row," crowed Ben.

Eddie was tired of the crazy ball and the score. "Let's go upstairs."

After refolding the table and washing the glasses they'd used, they returned to the sanctuary where Eddie mounted the pulpit. He motioned to Ben to sit down in the first row.

"Take a seat sinner," he said. "Verily I say unto you that you are a sinner sorely in need of salvation. You have whispered Satan's message into the innocent ear of your righteous brother, Eddie, urging him to rob milk from the mouths of babes. You have stolen the holy donuts. Hell fire is too good for you. You have cheated at games, seeing to it that your righteous brother was given the crooked end of the table. Woe be unto you and all your issue world without end. There is but one way you can save your soul from roasting in hell for eternity plus one day. You must model your life after that of your sainted friend, Edward T. White. Follow in his footsteps in all things."

"Hell sounds better," came Ben's shout from the front row. "You know Reverend, it's about time for our visitor—if he comes."

"Right. Let's get up front."

The entrance cloak closet was wide enough for a person to enter it to hang up his or her coat, but the single window was too high for the boys to see out. Eddie ran down to the basement and returned with two folding chairs. When stood upon, the front walk of the church was in view. At five minutes to six their full attention focused on the sidewalk and Oak Street as it ran past the church.

A white pick-up drove slowly past along Oak Street. It came to a momentary stop and then drove on.

"I thought we had a bite there," Eddie said.

Light traffic continued on the street and no one walked by. The white truck then reappeared coming from the same direction as before moving very slowly.

"Look that's the same truck; it went around the block. It's turning into the church parking lot," Ben said tense with excitement.

A high forsythia hedge blocked their view of the parking area. Their eyes fixed on the sidewalk leading to the front door. They waited, tension mounted—no one came.

In that moment Ben experienced an avalanche of doubt. What supported the idea that Valery's brother had murdered Miss Martinez? All of the elaborate reasoning was pinned to the dubious assumption that a man after jumping in the lake and swimming wouldn't return to the boat and don his white dress shirt again,. Why the hell wouldn't he, his counter-reasoning shouted out. Odd behavior maybe, but not enough to condemn someone. He started to say something to the effect that this whole caper of theirs was a mistake, when Eddie gasped.

"Guy just walked down the side of the building. He must have cut through a small gap in the hedge—kids squeeze through it all the time. Quick, we gotta get back to the vestry!"

They nearly fell climbing down from the folding chairs in their panic. Sprinting as quietly as they could they raced the length of the church and carefully approached the window overlooking the Garden.

The man they saw standing at the Garden's entry, looking around, was in his mid-twenties, stocky and dark haired. Unlike the slicked-down Vitalis look that was popular, his hair was loose, looking very much like it had been deposited by pitchfork.

"What do you think?" whispered Eddie.

Ben's voice was firm and certain. "It's him."

Now another question was answered, a question that had not been clearly posed so it could be answered until now—a question of another impression Ben had subliminally registered as odd. The man's hair that night was full and dry as Hunter Sinclair's hair appeared now and it should have been wet and plastered to his head if he'd been swimming.

"You're sure?"

"Dead sure."

"Valery's brother?"

"I asked to speak to Hunter and the guy said, 'Hunter' when he came to the phone."

Hunter looked at his watch then took a packet of cigarettes out of his pocket and lit up.

"Move back a bit," Ben cautioned. "Be sure he can't see us if he looks up here."

Hunter walked to the back of the Garden where he sat down on a concrete bench. Ben's evaluation deepened in certainty. It was now twenty past six by the room's wall clock. With a sudden movement of anger, Hunter threw away the cigarette and started walking toward the door that opened from the vestry directly to the outside, the church's back door.

Both boys held their breath and riveted their eyes on the door. The knob turned and the door was given a shake. Eli had done his job.

Eddie left Ben without a word and sprinted to the basement stairs in the front of the building. He flew down three steps at a time and raced across the basement to the door to the outside stairwell. He saw that the locking button was in the vertical unlocked position. He turned it to the horizontal a moment before the knob was turned from the outside. He then ran back the length of the basement and up the stairs to the church's front door. The bolt was in place. He stared at the door as it too was shaken.

Ben noiselessly passed Eddie and mounted one of the folding chairs to see out the window."He's going—walking toward the lot."

"Shit, that was close!" exclaimed Eddie. "The goddamned side door was open."

"Do you think he saw us?"

Eddie thought about it. "No, I don't think he could. Too dark inside and if he'd seen us he'd have run to the back door not walked like he did. He was just wondering what that call of yours meant for him. Something we'd be wondering about too in his place."

"Yeah, he's gotta be a very worried guy, getting a call saying he was seen at the lake and the police might be told."

"We can't leave here for a while. We don't know if he has driven away or not."

"We do know where he is right now, over toward the parking lot. If we wait, he'll have time to get in a position to watch the whole church."

Eddie nodded.

"Isn't that the Pastor's house next door on the same side as the side door?"

"Yeah."

"Let's get out right now and cut through the Pastor's backyard."

"OK, let's go."

Twenty minutes later, after zigzagging through the neighborhood for several blocks, they were sitting on a bench in Ben's mother's rose garden.

"We gotta go to the police right now," Eddie stated flatly.

"That bothers me. I feel I should talk to Valery, give her a chance to explain. Sure she lied to me, but maybe she found out later that there was a simple, innocent reason for her brother doing what he did. Bringing the police might just cause him trouble."

"If that were true, would he agree to meet an unknown person who wanted three hundred not to go to the police?"

"Maybe he was just curious."

"Bullshit! If I got a call like that and I was innocent I'd go to the police so they could catch the blackmailer."

"Still, I need time to think about it."

"Damn!"

"Now what?"

"I forgot my Mom's scarf."

After dinner, when both parents were in the kitchen and wouldn't overhear a phone call, Ben called Valery. The same woman said she wasn't "available," but this time he didn't passively acquiesce, but added, "Please give her the message that it is important that she return my call, because we need to talk about a man in a row boat."

Ben thought he heard an amused tone when she said, "Yes, son, I'll surely see she gets *that* message."

Valery called back in five minutes.

"Hi, Ben, what's up?"

He was angry. Her sudden "availability" set him straight about being given the run around when he'd called before.

"We need to talk about the guy in the boat." he said barely above a whisper.

"What about the guy?" she said quickly.

"Not on the phone. We have a party line. We have to meet tomorrow."

After a pause she said, "All right, but Daddy and I are driving to Greenville in the morning. My mother's coming over from Clemson to my aunt's house for lunch. I won't be home until late afternoon."

"That will do. Where can we meet?"

"You could come here. We could have privacy."

"OK. When?"

"I'll call you when we get back from Greenville."

Friday, June 9th.

"You know I've been thinkin," Clint began as he sat on his desk stirring sugar into his first cup of the morning. "I got this strong notion - hell it's no notion, it's a sure thing. Hunter Sinclair is the perp. But we know what John Bell thinks of the only evidence we've got—that we only have the word of a 'floozie' that Martinez was in his truck and likely in a car with him on Thursday night. We gotta have more."

"I agree with you. We've got to interrogate him. Have him account in verifiable detail where he was last Thursday night."

"Shall we ask John Bell again for permission to question him?"

"I think not. If he says 'No' then we'll be going against orders to grill Sinclair. I say we just do it and if the shit hits the fan we claim ignorance of John Bell's wishes."

"I'm with you. An order to report to Police Headquarters shakes a person up. Melts their confidence."

"The problem with that, it gives Sinclair a heads-up. He can call his old man, who will then call the Chief."

Kyle, watching Clint sip his coffee couldn't resist any longer and got up to pay a visit to the coffee machine.

When he returned, Clint was waiting with the question, "Let's drive to the E-lite an' surprise him. Surprise has it's value too."

Kyle looked at his watch. "They say there's no time like the present."

"I'll drive," Clint said.

Kyle started to follow and then doubled back to pick up his copy of the *Asheville Citizen*.

Clint started the car and paused, "What's the paper say today?"

Kyle scanned the front page, "We're eleven miles from Cherbourg."

"Remind me where that is."

"The map shows it as a harbor on the Channel at the end of a peninsula. We landed farther down the peninsula and are working back toward the port. Here's a funny one; it says General Rommel claims the Bayeux defense is impregnable in spite of the fact we've already captured it."

Clint turned south onto the Spartanburg Highway.

"Is that the same Rommel who was in Africa, the 'Desert Fox?'"

"Same guy. It says the Germans are in full retreat in Italy. Our troops are having a hard time keeping up. Italians along the way are throwing flowers."

"It'ud be fun to be one of those guys right now."

"I'll second that," said Kyle as he turned the page. "It says here a general was demoted, because he blabbed at a cocktail party about the date of the invasion."

"I hope they bust the bastard down to buck private."

Kyle laughed. "It doesn't say here. Now here's a bit of news; it says an equal rights plank in the Democratic platform was rejected because of opposition from southern Democrats."

"Surprise, surpirse."

"Both of us could use this. 'Miss Ruby Wilburn of Route 1 Asheville says, "Vola-Vin is simply marvelous. I wouldn't want to be without this famous herbal compound."'"

"Will it grow hair?"

Kyle closed the paper and placed it on the seat between them.

It was ten when Clint entered the gravel parking lot of the Elite Tavern. Five cars and a pick-up were parked. The truck wasn't white and didn't have a spotlight of the roof.

Clint said, "I'll go in, since they know me and find out if he's here or when they expect him. If Hunter's here, I'll come out and wave."

"Got it."

Kyle waited, trying out in his mind, the first sentence with which to confront Sinclair. "We have a witness who saw you in a car with Blanca Martinez the night she was killed." Maybe not a good idea. Marie Boyes wasn't sure and if, in fact, he had not been with her, he'd have leverage to undermine the interrogation. As he began considering another opening salvo, he noticed Clint coming out of the tavern with a hangdog look."

Clint got in the car. "He's not comin' in today. I talked to Edard. I told him there was business I had with Sinclair. He said Hunter said he may not be in for several days—somthin' 'to attend to.'"

"Think he's on the run?"

"It'ud be great if he was. There'd be no more question of guilt."

It was already 7:30. Ben didn't know what to make of the fact that she hadn't called. Did she think she could just ignore what he'd said? He'd been pacing back and forth near the phone, ready to snatch it up. His mother had already looked at him quizzically, asking if anything was wrong.

At 7:35 it rang. "I'm sorry I'm late, but they just kept on talking. Can you come over now?"

He glanced out the window. It was still light. "Yeah, I'll be right over."

Ben was nervous. What he was going to say to Valery was explosive. He was going to say that she had lied to him, that her brother was the likely killer. He had no doubts he'd say these things. He only hoped it wouldn't mean the end of their relationship. He hoped she'd have an explanation. That would put them back on track, no further need for secrecy, nothing to stand between them.

He rode into the long driveway of the Sinclair estate. He wasn't filled with the wonder he'd had a week ago. She was standing at the end of the drive where it entered the parking area. He rode up to her and stopped, straddling the bike's top bar. Her beauty took him aback. Her expression was of appeal and vulnerability. His resolve toward straight forward confrontation wilted like a starched shirt in August.

"We can talk over here," she said pointing to a clearing among the laurel bushes.

Ben heard the crunch of gravel in the direction of the house and stopped.

"Don't mind him. That's only old Jim. He takes care of the grounds. He's worked for the family forever. He has a room at the back of the house."

She walked ahead of him and he followed pushing his bike. He noticed now she was wearing a kind of jump-suit he'd seen in pictures of women working in aircraft factories only the fabric was very soft and loose, shoulders padded, waist tight. Her hair bounced with every step.

She turned and faced him with a puzzled look."You said some-thing about a man in a boat?"

That irritated him. She damn well knew what he'd meant. He wasn't playing along with the puzzlement.

"Valery, it was your brother in the rowboat that night at the lake. I know it . . . and you know it."

She said nothing and he went on, "You lied to me about seeing him swimming. The loud splash we heard was caused by something he threw in the water."

She stared at him, speechless.

"I thought a lot about it. You may not have known what he threw in the water, but you must have thought it very strange for him to be out there and you were afraid that I'd find out he was in the boat. You heard about Miss Martinez being found in the lake and that she was likely put there Thursday night. I'm sure you more than wondered if it could have been her body he dumped in the lake."

There he'd said it all.

She looked down.

"You've been avoiding me, You must have hoped I'd forget about it."

"You're wrong," she said. "You say I know, but I don't. I can't believe Hunter would do that."

"Why were you avoiding me then?"

She heaved a heavy sigh and looked away. 'Because you had the days wrong. When I saw you on Saturday when you were here for lunch, you said the teacher went missing on Friday night. As long as you thought that you wouldn't associate her murder with the man we saw Thursday night. I thought that as long as we didn't see each other you might continue to be mistaken about the days."

She was right, he'd had the days mixed up until he was put right by Hank and the newspaper.

"Have you said anything about this to your brother?"

She shook her head.

They stood in silence that neither was comfortable breaking.

"I'll ask Hunter." But how can I ask, she thought, when asking would mean she thought he might be a murderer. And then there was his temper. He had always been angered by any criticism from her, however mild and would fly into a terrible rage.

"What would you ask him?"

She then thought of a way to avoid Hunter's anger. "I know what I can do. I'll tell him I was driving past the beach and saw his car in the beach parking lot. I'd say, 'That was your car wasn't it.' If he had another reason for being there at he lake, he'd say 'yes' and tell me what he was doing there."

Ben saw she wanted to believe that. He wanted to believe it too, because her fear that her brother was guilty was causing her to distance herself from him. He should agree with her suggestion that she talk to Hunter. He should raise no further objection, except he knew Hunter was guilty enough to meet a guy who was willing to take three hundred dollars not to go to the police. He didn't say that now, instead he said, "But Val, what good reason could there be? Why row out in a lake to dump something. That's a lot of work. Wouldn't it be easier to dump whatever in a vacant field?"

She looked desperate.

Ben felt an urge to comply with her denial, join her in a shared secret. On a deeper level he understood it might be the only way she could now have an ongoing relationship with him. He also sensed the slippery slope this would entail, how dishonesty would become a regular determiner of his thoughts and actions. He heard the major's voice, openly tracing the logical path of honest thinking. He pulled back from the conspiracy Valery offered—and the sweet rewards it promised.

"Val, a murder was committed—a very good person was killed. We have evidence. We saw a man row a boat across the lake on the night Miss Martinez was killed, the lake where her body was later found. We heard a loud splash that could have been a body entering the water. I know, and so do you that the man was your brother, Hunter. These are the facts the police should know about. The police then are the ones to determine what the facts add up to."

She looked frightened now.

"Look I can be the one going to the police. I can say I was swimming alone and saw this. This way your brother won't be angry with you."

She digested his offer in silence. "I want to go inside," she said.

She began walking toward the house; he followed pushing his bike.

Ben knew she must be feeling run over. He didn't know what to say except, "I'm sorry," to her back.

Then she turned back and faced him. "I know what I have to do. I've got to tell Daddy. I can't let this happen without his knowing. Yes, that's what I have to do. Please come with me. We'll tell him everything He always knows the best thing to do."

Ben hadn't expected this. If she was going to tell her father, he couldn't very well go the police before the congressman had heard the story . . . at least he didn't think so.

"You're going to tell him we were swimming . . ."

"Nude? Yes, so what? He'll have to accept it. It will not be a big deal, you'll see."

He didn't argue.

Valery led the way into the house. Ben dropped his bike on the gravel near the entrance and followed her inside.

"Daddy's in the den." She gestured toward a hallway leading off the foyer.

The foyer was as large as the living room at home. A large chandelier got his attention. He hadn't seen one this large outside the movies. This was a strange and impressive place. Valery waited for him down the hallway, her hand on the knob of a closed door. She met Ben's eye for a moment and then entered the room. Troy Sinclair sat in an overstuffed leather chair beneath a floor lamp, the room's only light. He was reading a magazine. Valery walked up to the chair and Ben slowly followed.

"Daddy, I need to talk to you." Her voice was barely above a whisper and conveyed desperation.

Sinclair looked up smiling. "Sure, Baby, what about?"

He closed the magazine, holding his place with a finger. He noted the urgency and dread in her voice. He hadn't seen that degree of disquiet in her since her childhood. More familiar and amusing to him was the practiced self-assurance she copied from her mother. He remembered the boy, the same one who came to his office seeking the phone number. He noted the boy's serious expression.

Valery sat down in a chair facing her father, while Ben remained standing.

Troy smiled his "this can't be so bad that Daddy can't make it all go away" smile.

"Tell me 'bout it, Sugar."

Valery had not given thought to how she would present the issue. As she began to speak she stuttered, the words jumbled.

"Slow and easy Baby. We got all the time in the world," Troy reassured her.

"Hunter," she said.

"Yes, Hunter what?" Troy nudged with a patient manner.

Valery spilled it all out. "Ben and I went swimming last Thursday night in Laurel Lake. We saw Hunter row out in the lake and then we heard a big splash and then we saw him row back to the beach and drive away. A teacher from Ben's school was murdered Thursday night and her body was dumped in the lake that night,"

Troy pondered what he'd just heard. He wanted to answer in a way to calm Valery's hysteria. "You said you were swimming at night?"

"Yes we were under the raft and the boat Hunter was rowing passed close by."

"Hiding under the raft," he thought to himself. He began to get the picture.

"You say you were swimming at night; how could you be sure it was Hunter you saw in the dark?"

"The moonlight was pretty bright."

He sighed and put the magazine he was holding on the coffee table.

"Did you speak to Hunter about this?"

"No. I was afraid to."

"Afraid of what exactly?"

Valery struggled with the answer. "Because I didn't want it to be true."

"Didn't want what to be true?"

"That he dumped a body in the lake."

"Wait, wait," said Troy holding his hands up in front of him as if to stop the flow of words. "Because of seeing someone you took to be your brother, in spite of it being dark, you concluded he was putting a body in the lake?"

His note of incredulity caused Valery and Ben to pull up short. Ben looked at Valery. She was the best visual witness.

Valery started to cry.

"There, there, sweetheart. I'm not accusing you of anything—anymore than jumping to a conclusion that is downright impossible as far as I can see." He leaned forward and squeezed her arm.

His tone became upbeat. 'Look we can resolve this by talking to Hunter. He can tell us what he was doing that evening. That was a week ago you say. I've talked to him a couple of times in the last week. One of his horses, Ike, has a limp that Hunter's worried about. He was his usual self. Certainly didn't sound like a guy who had killed someone." He laughed. "Nothing like that."

Valery's state of mind hit him. "Lord, this must have been one hellish week for you if you were thinking all this."

He looked at Ben with a frown as if he were wondering if he'd been responsible for fanning the flame of his daughter's imagination.

"Anyway not to worry. As I said we can talk to Hunter. I can't believe he was the person you saw, but if he was, I think I know what he may have been doing."

Troy looked at Ben for a moment and his mood became sober. "There is this, however. The two of you witnessed something that might relate to the young woman's death. It happened the same night so it's something the police need to know. It's your duty to report what you saw. Val you think you saw Hunter and you'll have to say so. Hunter will have to go through an interrogation." To himself he murmured, "Might do him some good."

"But, I think it would be fair to give him a chance to hear all this from us first and not from the police—give him a chance to account for what he was doing Thursday evening. After that the police must be told what you saw. I swear I think it unlikely you saw your brother, it must have been someone else.

"How does that sound to you two?" Troy finished.

Ben couldn't sort out the implications so quickly, but the congress-man's voice carried the sound of fairness.

Valery wiped her eyes with the back of her hand.

"When are you going to talk to him?" she asked.

"I'll do it tonight. Hunter told me he was going up to the hunting lodge today. He is taking a couple of days off to finish the outdoor grill he's building. He wants to take a group of friends up for a party next weekend. We can drive up there right now."

"Oh Daddy, I'm so afraid he'll be angry with me. I don't want to go,"

Troy Sinclair thought for a moment. "I'd really like to confront him with witnesses. It would be easier for me to judge if he's telling the truth. But I understand, Val. I know what you say is true, he gets very upset if criticized by his little sister."

He studied Ben. "Tell you what, Ben, if you'll come with me to the cabin, you can tell your story and we can hear what he has to say—half an hour there, half an hour to talk to Hunter and half an hour back. I'll have you back by ten o'clock. Then we'll call the police and tell them there are statements to be made. They'll probably want to talk to both of you tomorrow." He looked Ben in the eyes. "Can I count on you, Ben?"

The situation had unexpectedly changed from what he'd had in mind when he'd ridden his bike to the estate. Back then, if Valery had had no good explanation for what they'd seen, he'd intended to call the police. The situation had changed so seamlessly he was now off balance. Earlier, the last thing he would have considered doing was confronting her brother, and now here her father was saying he was counting on him to do just that. Troy Sinclair, both the person he was and the office he held, overwhelmed him. Just driving to their hunting lodge alone with him was heady. He was Valery's father. Having his approval was very important to Ben. The man had asked if he could be counted on. Since childhood he'd heard it was important to be a person who could be counted on.

"Yes sir. I'll go with you."

"Good man. Now do we need to call your parents, or can you handle this without their permission?"

"I don't need to call. Since school's over I can stay out until midnight."

Troy wondered if the two had told any friends about this. He knew it would be a great temptation for Ben to tell his buddies he'd been skinny dipping with the congressman's daughter.

"Have you two shared your thinking about Hunter with anyone else?"

Valery said, "No."

Ben lied, shaking his head. His denial was reflexive, a mandate of boyhood—never implicate a friend!

"You're sure? Because a rumor such as this put out in the community lives on even after it's proven to be untrue, and anything about our family makes juicy rumor material."

Troy smiled at Ben. "OK, let's saddle up. We men can put Valery's fears to rest." He embraced his daughter.

Valery's mind conjured up a possible scene at the lodge—Hunter confronted—Hunter flying into a rage. If caught in a lie, as sure as thunder follows lightning, he'd lash out. There were guns at the hunting lodge. Her fear for both her father and Ben ignited.

"Daddy. Is it a good idea if Ben goes with you? What if Hunter gets crazy angry like he can?"

"Don't you worry. I'll be there. I can handle your brother."

His assurance sounded confident and she wanted to believe him, but she knew her father didn't believe Hunter had been in the boat. "Down right impossible" he'd said. She knew differently and when Ben confronts him . . .

Ben read Valery's fear and began to feel it himself, when Troy, in a man-to-man tone put his hand on Ben's shoulder and said, "C'mon, Ben, let's find out what's what."

The Congressman's solid confidence in there being a simple, innocent explanation for Hunter's action even if he had been the man Valery and Ben had seen, along with his certainty of his confidence in being able to manage his son, swept away Ben's uneasiness.

Valery stood on the front entrance and watched them get into the Continental. The powered top began to close. She looked up at the sky where rolling clouds caught the last bit of daylight, their turbulence paralleling that within her. As the taillights disappeared around a bend in the driveway, she felt very alone and frightened. Panic set in.

248

At the corner of White Pines Drive, Sinclair turned west on Fifth Avenue. Standing on the corner was Walter Abbott, who waved at the car. Sinclair braked to a stop and yelled, "Storm's a comin', Walter. Better get inside." He accelerated again, laughing and saying, "Love that man, I truly do. This spring I had coupla' boys put a new roof on that shack he lives in. No electricity, but he'll be dry at least."

Troy worked hard to relieve the tension he recognized in Ben. He chatted on easily about everything from the coming football season to the history of the hunting lodge.

"At first it was a one room cabin that gave us some shelter when we'd come hunting—my brother and a few friends and I built it. Over the years we've added on until it's a very comfortable retreat now. Went from cabin to lodge. Up against the national forest—half a million acres. There's a nearby cliff connected to an Indian legend that people like to hike up to. Great view from there. It's only a ten minute walk from the lodge. Have Val take you there some time."

Ben wondered if this could be the same hike he'd read about on last Sunday's drive.

Lightning had been flashing to the southwest as they drove along the paved county road. Sinclair turned off onto a dirt road that soon forked. By the light from a lightning flash Ben saw and recognized the sign to the park where he and his parents had been. Sinclair guided the Continental along the other fork, the one blocked by the chain before.

"I know where we're at now," Ben said. "My parents and I went to that waterfall last Sunday. I wanted to hike up to the cliff, but my Mom wasn't up to it."

The lightning bolts were frequent now and overhead. The wind had picked up force whipping tree branches to and fro over the road, which climbed steadily at a steep grade. Between the sweeps of the wipers Ben saw a light ahead and then the headlights played across the stained logs of a large cabin.

Troy drove up close to the entrance and braked. "Quick," he shouted, "or we'll get drenched."

Ben yanked open the car door and followed in a lunge for the shelter of the cabin's porch. The rain pounded on the porch roof.

Troy shouted something, but the crash of thunder covered what he said. The cabin door opened and light poured onto the porch. Standing in the doorway was a man with a shotgun in his hands.

"Dad, what the hell? Who is this?"

"Everything' s fine son." Troy pushed through the door. "Let's go inside."

Troy waved Ben into the room. "Take a seat, Ben, while I talk to Hunter." He indicated a sofa facing the fireplace.

Ben walked around a box of firewood at the end of the sofa and sat.

"Sit down, son," Troy said pointing to an armchair. "I need to tell you something."

Still holding the shotgun, Hunter sat down. Troy moved to stand behind Ben.

"Ben came to me with a story we need to address. Here's the situation, Hunter. You were careless at Laurel Lake. Valery and this boy were swimming there Thursday night and they saw you. She had the Continental which should have been easy to spot if you'd been alert."

Ben couldn't comprehend what he'd just heard. It was as if Congressman Sinclair had had a stroke and couldn't say what he intended. And yet the words hadn't been jumbled—they were in logical order, but made no sense.

Hunter flew into a rage. "I wasn't alert? What the fuck do you mean. I didn't kill the bitch. So, who fucked up? Tell me that! Who fucked up?"

Troy realized his mistake. "OK, OK. The whole mess wasn't your fault. But I didn't mean to kill her either. I only wanted to get her to shut up."

There's something very wrong here, Ben thought and started to get up, when a hard blow with a piece of firewood on the back of his head sent him face forward onto the hearth rug.

"Jesus Christ!" Hunter gasped, looking down at the prostrate boy that his father had felled just like a calf at a slaughter house. He knelt and felt the carotid pulse and found it was strong.

"Calm down. Pull yourself together," said Troy. He watched his son take a deep breath and struggle to get control of his emotions.

"The kid identified you as the man they'd seen in the rowboat. He was going to the police, but I talked him into coming up here with me. Now we deal with him. I have a plan that came to me as we were driving up here.

"I was afraid of something like this. It's why I came to the cabin."

"What do you mean?"

"I got a call yesterday—must have been this kid—a guy with a young voice. He said I'd been seen in the rowboat and for three hundred dollars the police didn't need to be told." With an embarrassed, "I screwed up" expression, he said, "I went there to the place he said we were to meet. He didn't show up. He must have been hidden someplace where he could see me. He knew my name and then he knew the name went with the person he'd seen Thursday at the lake."

"I'll be damned," Troy said. Yes, he thought, it must have been this kid. But he hadn't told anyone else. "It's OK. That's all behind us now. I have an idea of how we can give Val an explanation of why you rowed out in the lake, and also how to deal with this kid. The first part I thought of while I was driving here. The second part came to me when the kid said he'd wanted to hike to Star Crossed Rock.

"Here are the two stories: We tell Val you admitted being the person in the boat. You went out into the lake to dump a case of whiskey. You'd got a tip the state police were going to raid the tavern. You and Barney emptied all the whiskey bottles at the tavern into the toilet. Edward took off in his car with the empty bottles. When you were driving home, you remembered you had put a case of whiskey in the trunk of your car to take here to the hunting lodge for a party you'd planned. You decided you needed to get rid of the whiskey immediately and dumping it in the lake seemed a good idea. We tell Val the kid here was satisfied with your explanation. This is the story we tell Val—she'll want to believe it.

"OK. Now here's the story we'll tell everybody—very sadly. I was driving up here with supplies for the weekend and invited the kid along. Valery seemed to have taken an interest in him, so it was an opportunity to get to know him better. On the way up he saw the sign to Star-Crossed Rock and said he'd learned about it only a few days ago and had wanted to hike there, but his mother didn't feel like it. When we got here to the cabin I told him a trail led from the cabin to the Rock and that he and Valery should take it sometime. He said he wanted to go and 'check it out' tonight. I said it was not a good time to do it, because it would be too dark to see the view and also the rain would have made the path slippery and dangerous. He wanted to go anyway, so thinking 'boys will be boys,' I gave him a flashlight. When he didn't come back right away, you and I went looking for him and saw the light from his flashlight at the bottom of the cliff. We raced to the nearest telephone and called for help."

Hunter was shocked. "You mean you're thinking of throwing him over the cliff?"

"Think a minute. If we let him live, he'll tell the story of you at Laurel Lake. You know what that means."

252

Hunter did think about it. Although his father had killed the woman, he was an accessory to murder.

"But what if he's already told someone else about the lake?"

"Good thinking. I thought of that too and checked it out subtly. I'm confident he didn't tell anyone."

Troy saw that Hunter had accepted the inevitable need to silence the kid.

"So here's what we do. We carry him up to Star-Crossed Rock, put his finger prints on a flashlight that we drop off the cliff and then send the boy after it . . . We need to do this now."

Hunter rolled Ben over. The blow with the firewood had split the scalp. Blood was on the hearth rug. Ben was breathing regularly, but was completely unconscious. Gripping both hands, he dragged Ben to the front door.

"You take him under the arms and I'll take his legs," Troy said.

Hunter opened the front door. The rain was steady.

Hunter had taken a flashlight from a drawer of a table near the door and clamped it in his armpit, when Troy said, "We need two lights, one to see the trail and one to throw down with the kid."

Hunter got another flashlight from the drawer and jammed it into one of his pockets. Together they picked up Ben and left the cabin.

Their progress was slow. The rain was so heavy they could barely see and the flashlight Hunter carried kept slipping to the ground.

"This is a bitch," Hunter yelled. "Help me lift him and I'll carry him on my shoulder." Hunter straightened up under the load. "It's OK. I can do it."

The trail led across a ridge to the base of the rock outcropping of the cliff, from which there was a sheer drop to the forest floor hundreds of feet below.

Troy walked immediately behind Hunter, directing the flashlight beam at Hunter's feet. This worked for one hundred yards and then they had to halt for Hunter to change shoulders. He stood again. Ben showed no sign of coming around."I hope I can make it. I may have to drag him."

"Don't do that. That may produce abrasions that aren't consistent with a fall."

Hunter didn't answer, but struggled ahead with Troy trailing with the light. The rain continued unabated. At last, a lightning flash lit up their goal, just ahead—Star-Crossed Rock.

"We're almost there," Troy shouted.

The solid rock outcropping rose several feet above the trail. Hunter sank to his knees. Exhausted he gasped, "I need help getting him up there."

"OK. Little by little," encouraged Troy.

They managed together to pull Ben up to the lip of the precipice.

Hunter took the second flashlight from his pocket, turned it on, pressed Ben's fingers around the barrel and dropped it over the edge. They followed the light to the bottom.

"Great! It stayed on," Troy said. "Now catch your breath and we'll roll him over."

"Stop! Don't move!" came a strident shout behind them.

The two men whirled around, stunned to be starring into a strong beam of a powerful light.

"Put your hands over your heads!" the voice commanded.

A hand came up into the light beam, pointing a revolver.

Saturday, June 10th.

An aching head led his emergence into the morning. Before he became fully aware of the room and the people in it, he remembered a series of agonizing awakenings—dragged up from a deep place again and again to be asked his name as if the disembodied voice couldn't remember it. His hand lightly explored the smarting in his scalp. Discovering an unaccountable bandage, he withdrew his hand, puzzled even more. Then he recalled his parents being by his bed and shook off his sleepiness to look for them. They were gone, but there sat Eddie and Cookie. They stared at him as if expecting something from him—like a welcome.

"Hi," he gargled.

Cookie left her chair and came to stand at the bedside - Eddie, behind her and to the side, concern on her face, an awkward grin on his.

"How do you feel?" she asked.

"I don't know. Headache. What happened to me?" His hand sought the bandage again.

Cookie gently moved his hand away. "You have a bandage you need to leave alone. You were hit on the head. You don't remember?"

"Hit on the head?" He looked from one to the other imploringly.

They exchanged a look that communicated their uncertainty about being the ones to answer that question.

Eddie moved forward and gripped the bed rail. "We don't know everything. We were waiting for you to wake up and tell *us*." He appraised Ben's puzzled face. "You really don't remember do you?

Well, this is going to surprise the hell outa ya . . . the police have arrested Congressman Sinclair for murdering Miss Martinez. And somehow you got a nasty bang on the head. You've been in the hospital all night, and you've taken your time waking up.""

"Ben frowned. "That's not right. You mean Hunter - Hunter was arrested."

Eddie said, "Yeah, well that too, but -"

"We were - the congressman and I - were driving to their hunting lodge to make Hunter explain what he was doing in the boat that night."

"What boat that night?" asked Cookie.

Ben pivoted back into his present world enough to know he didn't want to explain the naked swim to Cookie."

"He and Valery were swimming in Laurel Lake," Eddie said.

It took two seconds for Cookie to imagine the scene, not a scene she enjoyed.

"So you don't know what happened in the cabin once you got there?" Eddie said.

Ben strained to remember, but the memory cupboard was bare.

Cookie reached for his hand. "Don't worry; someone who knows the whole story will be here to make it clear. But do you know who we are?"

Ben chuckled. "How could I forget?"

"Names please."

He saw she was serious. "Cookie White and her good-for-nothing brother, Eddie."

"The year, please."

"1944 and Roosevelt is President."

Eddie said, "You know you owe me five dollars."

"Get out'ta here."

The nurse, who had bucked visiting hour rules to let them be there, spotted the doctor coming on morning rounds and said from the doorway, "You'll have to go now. Doctor McHenry is coming to check on your friend."

Eddie turned back to Ben, mimicked an authoritative voice. "OK son, take the weekend off, but we expect you back on the job Monday morning."

"Yes sir."

"Bye now," Cookie said.

Ben noticed now she was dressed as if going to church.

A minute later a man in a white coat swept into the room and up to the bed like a meter reader running late.

"Hi, I'm Dr. McHenry. You had a nasty bang on the head . . . follow my finger . . . x-ray shows no fracture . . . that's good . . . follow the finger . . . only concussion . . . you can go today.

He gave Ben a patronizing pat on the knee, turned on his heel and was out of there.

Ben couldn't make much of what he'd heard, but he didn't care. He dozed off. Then the nurse was awakening him, saying his name, apparently having learned it. She held a small paper cup and a glass of water.

"I have two aspirins for you. After head trauma, medication is withheld, because the doctor needs to monitor your consciousness level." She dumped the pills in his hand and gave him the glass.

"A detective from the Police Department is here to talk to you." she said taking the glass back.

Beyond her, Ben saw a young, heavy set man in a brown suit. With him was a woman and Ben's father.

"Hi Ben. I'm Detective Sexton." He turned toward the others. "And this is Mrs. Purvis, a court reporter, and I think you already know this fellow. I'm here to get a statement from you about what happened last night. Mrs. Purvis will write that all down, after which I'll ask you to read it over, and if you agree that it is what you said, sign the statement. Your father is here, because a parent has to be present when I interview you." He gave Ben a friendly smile and asked, "Understand all that?"

Ben nodded.

Kyle Sexton pulled a chair over to the bedside, made sure the secretary was ready and Mr. Roberts comfortable.

"Now Ben, I want you to tell me the whole story from the beginning just as if you were telling it to a friend so they would know everything. Don't forget you'll be asked to sign, swearing you've told the whole truth." He said the last bit with the same friendly smile while emphasizing "whole."

That word put this in a different light. No diplomatic censorship.

"A week ago Thursday," he began. And with only minimal editing, like not mentioning his dislike for Connie Walker, he described the evening. He deliberately avoided looking at his father as he related the skinny-dipping and merely said Valery had distracted his attention when Hunter rowed near the raft. Then he related his step-wise realization that Valery had lied to him and the help he had from Major von Kleist. He told this with a sheepish awareness his father might resent von Kleist's role of councilor. With relish he described the ruse they'd used to trick Hunter into showing his hand. Ben's description of Valery and him consulting Troy Sinclair revealed how impressed he'd been with the congressman's willingness to be open minded in questioning his son and his plan to bring what was learned to the police. It was obvious he'd been flattered—and still was—by Troy's believing him to be a person one could count on. He remembered it had been storming as they drove to the hunting lodge . . . and that was all. End of story.

"You don't remember getting to the lodge - not at all?'

"No."

Kyle turned to the court reporter. "That ends the interrogation. Please have it typed and ready to sign as soon as you can. Thanks for coming out this morning."

She put the notebook into a briefcase, stood and said, "I hope you're feeling better soon, Ben."

When she'd gone, Kyle went on, "The doctor calls the memory loss, 'retrograde amnesia.' He says it's common after a concussion. You may be able to remember more as time passes and if so, we'll take that down and add it to your statement. So, now I have things to tell you and your father that will surprise you. You did, in fact, reach the hunting lodge with the Congressman. At that same time, Valery, having come to a point of panic with her fear that her father and you were going to be in danger confronting her brother, drove to Police Headquarters to get help. Indeed, she was right, because when you got to the lodge the congressman proceeded to hit you over the head with a log and was planning to silence you for good by throwing you over the cliff known as Star-Crossed Rock.

My partner, Detective Edney and I were staying late at the office planning how to proceed with our investigation of Hunter Sinclair, because he was out prime suspect in the murder. When Valery got to the office, we couldn't understand what she was saying she was so panicked. When she finally made us understand she was afraid the man who was our prime suspect might harm two more people, we were into my car and on the road immediately. Even then, as it turned out, we barely arrived in time to save your life.

"I can see what I've just told you has only compounded your confusion. The rest, which came from Hunter Sinclair's confession, will clear it up. On the drive with Valery up to the hunting lodge, she told

259

us the story of seeing her brother at the lake in a boat. We were certain then he was the killer, so when we handcuffed Hunter we charged him with the first degree murder of Blanca Martinez. He cried out that he wasn't guilty, his father was the killer and he readily agreed to tell all.

"Troy Sinclair had been seeing the teacher. In order to get her to . . ." Remembering he was talking to a fifteen year old, Kyle searched for another way to say "have sex." He continued, "to get her to make love with him, he told her he would marry her and divorce his wife. When he didn't follow through, she began nagging him. A week ago, on the night you saw Hunter at the lake, Hunter had picked Miss Martinez up and dropped her off at the Sinclair house. She seemed to have finally concluded Sinclair was leading her on and began scream-ing at him. The congressman's story is that to keep her from alert-ing an old handyman man who lives at the house, he put his hand over her mouth and held her down until he became aware she was no longer breathing. He called Hunter at the tavern. Hunter said his father was always calling him to deal with problems he'd get into with women. However nothing like this! Hunter knew he had to get rid of the body. He took an old tool box he found in the garage and filled it with gravel from their driveway, tied it to the body and dumped it—as you figured out—in the lake.

"Is this clear so far," Kyle asked looking first at Ben and then his father.

"Yes Sir," Ben said.

Mr. Roberts nodded, but added, "Please tell us in detail what happened at the hunting lodge."

Kyle took a deep breath and let it out. "OK. Hunter says he was surprised when his father arrived there with you, Ben, not knowing who you were. His father began telling him that he had messed up dis-posing of the body, because you and Valery had seen him at the lake.

"This, of course, surprised you and you started to get up from the sofa where you'd been sitting. His father then hit you with a piece of firewood. His father said you would have to be silenced for good, or he would be arrested for killing the teacher and Hunter would be an accessory. Hunter agreed. It was a very bad decision. Up until then, he was an 'accessory after the fact' in what might have been charged as a second-degree murder. Here, he was becoming a partner in a clear first-degree murder. The story they'd tell would be that against advice you'd set out to see this popular tourist site. You slipped and fell - bad luck.

"When they started carrying you to the cliff, the rain was heavy. Because of that, and the fact their path faced them away from the parking area, they didn't notice our headlights when we arrived. I told Valery to stay in the car while my partner, Detective Edney, and I got out. In my peripheral vision I caught a small glint of light. It was from the flashlight they were carrying. We were undecided whether to follow the light or check out the interior of the building first. Clint started moving in the direction of the light and I followed. We caught up with the Sinclairs and watched to see what they were up to. You were never in real danger after that. Thank God we didn't search through the cabin first."

Kyle saw that Ben and his father were waiting for more.

"We handcuffed them. Clint marched them back to our car and I carried you. We used Hunter's truck, Clint rode in the back with the prisoners and Valery and you up front with me, Valery held you and cried all the way back."

Ben's thoughts were of Valery. What a step she'd taken to go to the police.

"She saved my life," Ben said. "She saved my life."

"That she did, that she did," agreed Kyle.

Ben badly wanted to see her.

Ben's father reached out and touched Kyle's arm. "I can't tell you how much we owe you: Ben, his mother and I."

"Thanks." Kyle laughed. "We all laugh when the cavalry arrives just in time—sometimes it really happens."

Sexton stood up. "As soon as the reporter returns with the statement, I'll be back for your signature. I'll need you, sir, to witness his signing, so please stick around. It shouldn't be more than half an hour. And, by the way, you mentioned Major von Kleist, the P.O.W. He happens to be a patient here, just down the hall. One of the other prisoners shot him."

"Shot him?" gasped Ben.

"Yeah, yesterday, but he's going to be OK. Excuse me, I have to make a couple of calls. I'll be back soon."

Ben's father leaned over the guard rail and took one of Ben's hands in his. "Someone was looking out for you, son."

"You're right. It was Valery."

Mr. Roberts blinked. Before he could add anything, the nurse was there again giving instructions.

"The doctor wants you to get up and walk around to make sure you're not dizzy and all right to go home."

She lowered one side rail of the bed and watched to see how well he negotiated getting out of bed. She held his arm for several steps and then let go when she saw his balance wasn't impaired.

"We'll walk to the end of the hall and back."

Once in the hallway, Ben said, "Nurse, there's a German prisoner of war here who's been wounded. I know him and I'd like to say hello to him if it's OK.

"You know him?"

"The prisoners have been working at the farm of a friend of mine.

I met him there and talked to him."

She thought about it. "If the guard permits it, I don't see any problem with that."

Von Kleist's room was the last along the hall. A soldier sat immediately inside the doorway, no rifle this time only a sidearm. The nurse spoke to him and he looked past her to take in Ben.

He was there to keep the Major from escaping, an event as likely as there being lobster at the evening's mess. He'd been given no instructions about visitors, so he was winging it. The scuttlebutt was that von Kleist was a decent guy, so what was the harm? He stood up and came to Ben.

"I'm Corporal Mancini." It was a foreign accent to Ben, like New York, Brooklyn, Boston, or somewhere like that. Mancini nodded toward the room. "You know this guy, huh?" This kid holding his hospital gown together behind him with one hand didn't appear to pose a significant threat. "It's OK with me if you talk to him - but only for a few minutes. He was a mighty lucky guy. Another two inches to the left and I'd be guarding a corpse."

Von Kleist overheard this and laughed. "My friend here has a very vivid imagination. You are dressed like a patient, Ben. Why is this?"

"It had to do with what I came and talked to you about—about the man in the rowboat. But, they say you were shot."

Ben now appraised his German friend. It was odd to see him in a hospital gown rather than a uniform tunic. Aside from that he looked the same except for taking shallow breaths.

"Yes, at the end of the work day, one of the men, Karl Hofmann, a man who was still fighting the war and very angry that we surrendered—he blamed me—grabbed the guard's rifle and attempted to shoot me. Luckily I only got a minor wound."

"Jeez," Mancini said from the doorway. "That's like saying the

263

Yankees won the series, because they won more games. You left out the real reason you're here with us today."

"Yes, my luck is many levels—many layered, I think you say. Apparently Hofmann thought Tony had the newer American rifle, the M1, which always has a bullet in the firing chamber. He grabbed the gun and aimed at my heart, but luckily for me the task of guarding prisoners who have nowhere to escape to only rated an older model gun."

"Springfield," Mancini said, who had walked up to stand next to Ben.

"Yes and to avoid accidents, Tony never kept a cartridge in the chamber."

"So," Mancini inserted, "It took Hofmann a moment to crank a bullet into the chamber once he'd realized his mistake."

"Right. In that time both Tony and I reacted. I twisted to the side and Tony hit Hofmann's arm. The result was the bullet only grazed me causing a gash in the flesh and a broken rib."

"What happened to him, Hofmann?" Ben said.

"The other men were on top of him immediately and Tony was yelling, 'Don't kill him! Don't kill him!' Yes, Ben, I was very lucky."

Mancini walked back to stand near the nurse at the door.

"But, you Ben, what happened to you?"

"Like we figured yesterday; the guy in the boat was Valery's brother"

He went on retelling the story.

Von Kleist listened stunned and astonished, murmuring "Mein Gott" to himself. Yet, as he visualized Ben ordeal he became more irritated that the boy hadn't followed his order—his advice—to talk to his parents. Then the reality of Ben standing there alive took over and he smiled and said, "But you are well and that's all that counts."

"Hey guys, I think we better wind up this gabfest," interrupted Mancini. "Since luck was mentioned, there's only so much flowing at a given time, so let's not push it."

"Ben, there's so much more you haven't had time to tell. They are transferring me to the Army hospital at Camp Butner near Durham today. Write to me there and tell me all the details. Keep me up to date."

"Yeah, OK. I can do that."

The nurse came and touched his arm. He followed her to the doorway and turned back.

The major said, "And don't forget you are coming to Germany to visit me when you can."

The idea of traveling to Germany, totally inconceivable until then floated for a moment in the realm of the possible and then landed on the solid ground of resolution. Yes, he would indeed go to Germany to visit Gerhard von Kleist. He made a gesture of "goodbye' and left.

Mancini said after him, "Take it easy kid."

It was past one o'clock before the discharge procedure was completed. Sexton had come with the statement for Ben and his father to sign and then he left for a meeting with the County Prosecutor.

During the wait for his discharge Ben's thoughts cycled between two needs: to bodily get out of the hospital and a desperate need to talk to Valery. He was also anxious to learn if the role he'd played in her father's arrest had affected her feelings for him.

His father didn't question him more on the way home and he was happy about that. He dropped Ben off at home and continued on to the Mountain Lodge. His mother, however, waited for him at the front door with an additional hug of joy for his survival, and said his lunch was ready.

"I'll wash my hands and make a phone call and I'll be right there," he said heading for the bathroom.

The phone rang five times before the same voice he'd heard on previous calls answered. "Sinclair residence."

Ben used her name. "Mrs. Holden, this is Ben Roberts. I'd like to speak to Valery, please."

The timbre of the voice changed. "She's not here, son. Her uncle came early this morning from South Carolina to fetch her."

This possibility hadn't occurred to him. "Ah . . . When will she be back?"

"Ben, she won't never come back. You see she only came here to see her daddy. Her home is in South Carolina."

Ulla Holden knew there was no reason now for Valery to come back, but she knew it would hurt Ben to hear that fact. The idea that Valery was permanently gone was several steps ahead of where he was emotionally.

"Did she leave a message for me?"

With a heavy heart Ulla said, "No she didn't, son."

The silence on the line was so palpable it could have been rolled into a ball.

"You no doubt know her telephone number in South Carolina," Ben ventured.

"Yes, I do, but I'm not supposed to give it out . . . but I would if I thought it was in your interest. You need to forget her now, son . . .You really do."

Ben couldn't continue the conversation. There was too much here to sort out and not make mistakes.

"Thank you, Mrs. Holden. I've got to go."

"Ben, I heard you were hurt. I'm so happy you're all right. Goodbye."

266

He replaced the receiver on the cradle reviewing what had been said.

"Ben," his mother called. "Your sandwich is ready."

He followed his feet to the kitchen and sat, but he was elsewhere, thinking that maybe Valery had been snatched away so quickly she hadn't had time to leave him a message.

Not wanting to take her son back over the trauma of the night, she searched for a subject while he ate the egg sandwich she'd made.

"I called Grandma and told her some of what happened. She, of course, was very upset. When I was able to convince her you were all right, she insisted we come north to visit. I know your father can't get away right now, but I thought you and I could go - just a short time, a week maybe."

Ben shook his head. "No. I can't do that, Mom. I'd be leaving Eddie in the lurch. I can't, but why don't you go. You can take the train."

She lit a cigarette, lost in thought. "Maybe."

Ben got up, thanked her for lunch and said that although the doctor's discharge order had been for him to take it easy the rest of the day, he was going to bike over to the Dickson's where Eddie was working. He took his bike out of the garage and wheeled it down the drive way to the street. Across the street was Abbie Ransom's house. Seeing it now, he was reminded that he should really stop by and bring her up to date. He owed it to their friendship. He walked the bike to the side gate and leaned it against the fence, then walked to the back door and knocked.

Abbie saw him through the screen and hurried to the door.

"Ben, my Lord! Oh, you have a bandage on your head!"

"Yeah, but I'm OK. They put in a couple of stitches and I've still got a headache, but I'm fine."

"I can't believe it. I just can't believe it. Troy Sinclair! I've heard bits and pieces from friends - mostly conflicting. I called your home as soon as I'd heard you'd been injured, but there was no answer. I reckoned your parents were at the hospital. I called there and made them connect me with the head nurse and all she'd tell me was that you were 'resting' and to think that Ollie and I paid for most of that building."

She put her hand to her forehead. "Just listen to me." She chuckled. "I'm sorry. I haven't given you a chance to say anything. Sit down and tell me everything - if you feel up to it."

Ben reviewed in his mind what she already knew. "Well, there was more to that evening I told you about than a ride in Valery's car."

"Aha," she thought to herself. "I thought there might be."

With the erotic bits left out as he'd done at the hospital, he related the whole story with Abbie emitted "my God" and "Oh no!"

When he'd finished, she appeared drained of energy. They sat in silence. Finally she said,"Ollie always said there is no such thing as evil—only ego. 'Above all me first.' I always knew Troy had a huge ego, I didn't know it was so warped."

She smiled at Ben. "But it didn't turn out the way Troy planned, did it? I'm amazed that Valery had the . . . guts . . . to go to the police. But, of course, she had no one else to turn to. That old handyman couldn't help her."

"Right," Ben murmured.

"Have you talked to her yet?"

"No. I called a little while ago but their cook told me her uncle came early this morning to take her to South Carolina ."

"I see. Took her back home in a hurry."

"She, the cook, Mrs. Holden, said she thought Valery would never come back to Hendersonville."

"Did she? Interesting."

268

"She said—I guess she was saying—I should forget about her for my own good."

"How did she say that? I mean what kind of voice?"

"Her tone wasn't the same as when I'd called before - more friendly, but serious."

"I know Ulla Holden. Back when I was a member of the school board, I worked with her to get more funding for the colored high school. She's a fine person. If she stepped outside her role in the Sinclair household to give you advice, it's worth listening to."

"Won't the Congressman be tried here in Hendersonville?"

"I'm not sure, His lawyer might claim he couldn't get a fair trial here, because so many people are furious with him. But, you're wondering if Valery would be coming back for the trial?"

"Yeah."

So, he's hoping Ulla's wasn't the last word on the matter. Abbie knew what Ulla was saying, She'd wondered along those lines when Ben had first told her of meeting Valery.

"I have to say that Ulla is sure she won't be back."

The full meaning of Valery's not having left a message finally began to penetrate. The possibility she'd been home those times he was told she wasn't there followed. Only weeks later would he come to see the evening at the lake as an impulsive act on her part. He would never know that she was well aware her father would be at home when she invited him for lunch. She only wanted to know if he had seen any connection between the man in the rowboat and the teacher's murder. She'd found out he hadn't, and that's all she'd wanted to know.

What could Abbie now say to her young friend to reassure him of his own worth after realizing the person he wanted most to love him, didn't? Telling someone a variation on "there are plenty more fish in the sea" never lessened the pain of loss. She remained silent.

Ben had an impulse to thank her for the lemonade, then realized he hadn't had any.

"Well, I'm going to ride to the Dickson's. Eddie is mowing their grass. I'm not supposed to work today—doctor's orders, but I can give him moral support."

"Something tells me you'll weaken and feel you should help him. Better do what the doctor ordered."

Ben laughed. "Maybe you're right."

Abbie followed him to the back door, said goodbye and sadly watched him walk to the side gate to retrieve his bike. She saw then a young girl waiting for him there. She had never seen Eddie White's younger sister. She wondered . . . Yes . . . Interesting.

"I was riding by and saw your bike," Cookie said as Ben came through the gate. She sat on her bicycle seat, one foot on a pedal, the other on the curb.

"Oh?"

"I thought we could ride to Schauger's and get a Coke."

Now here was a very novel idea - having a Coke with Cookie White. A novel idea and not a good idea - to be seen drinking a Coke with a thirteen-year-old girl - just the two of them.

Cookie guessed his thoughts.

"It won't be crowded at this time on Saturday. Everyone waits until later to go there."

That was true. It would be very unlikely for any of his gang to be there now. Ben shrugged and thought, Yeah, why not? He lifted his bike off the fence, stepped up on a pedal and threw his other leg over the seat.

"OK, Lead the way."

Smiling, she pushed off from the curb.

Acknowledgments

I want to thank Susan Ager, Jim Carpenter, Scott Craig, John Fitzpatrick, Mike Fleishman and Ellen Pisor for reading the original manuscript of this novel and giving me valuable feedback. A special thanks to Tom McConnell.